Jill Gascoine was born in south London. Educated at Tiffin Girls' School, she was taught acting, singing and dancing at Italia Conti's, and joined the theatrical profession at the age of fifteen. She is well known for the television series *The Gentle Touch* and also starred in *Cat's Eyes*. She has two sons from her first marriage, and now lives with her second husband, actor Alfred Molina, in Los Angeles. Her first novel, *Addicted*, is also published by Corgi.

Also by Jill Gascoine

ADDICTED

and published by Corgi Books

Lilian

Jill Gascoine

CORGI BOOKS

LILIAN
A CORGI BOOK : 0 552 14232 8

First publication in Great Britain

PRINTING HISTORY
Corgi edition published 1995

Set in 11/13pt Monotype Plantin by Kestrel Data, Exeter, Devon.

Corgi Books are published by Transworld Publishers Ltd,
61–63 Uxbridge Road, London W5 5SA,
in Australia by Transworld Publishers (Australia) Pty Ltd,
15–25 Helles Avenue, Moorebank, NSW 2170,
and in New Zealand by Transworld Publishers (NZ) Ltd,
3 William Pickering Drive, Albany, Auckland.

Reproduced, printed and bound in Great Britain by
Cox & Wyman Ltd, Reading, Berks.

For Sean and Adam,
sons to be proud of
and
Auntie Vi – because I'll miss her

Acknowledgements

Thanks to Jenny, who talked to me so freely. To all the other women who opened their hearts and secrets. To Judy Martin, my agent, who never fails to be supportive. To Fred for reading each page hot from the press and his constructive criticism. To Colette, my sweet friend, who always seems to understand what I'm writing. And, finally, to Diane Pearson, my editor, who works and encourages with such unstinting patience.

'The great woman does what she cannot do'

Thomas G. Waites
(Actor, writer, teacher, director)

Prologue

'Look at me, aren't I the clever one? Here I am, the beginning of a new decade of my life, one I once doubted I would ever get to, and a life full of everything I've ever wanted. I swear to God there are some days I feel so good about myself, the world and everything in it, I get up in the morning and have to fight the urge to adorn myself in one of those silly hats I swore I'd never wear. And me with still half a heart in the Home Counties of Southern England. Living in a city again after years of birdsong and little traffic has only half the charm it has in one's youth, but we all have to move on, either craving more space or less, depending on our needs. Selling the old house was the right thing to do at the time. There are no regrets. And these last years have turned out to be quite the most interesting time in my life. So much for the joys of youth. Don't have to spread myself so thin these days. All those people I cherished, loved, cared for, listened to, forgave. All grown and gone at long last. God only knows why it took so long to let them go. Others tend to them now. Other lives for them to fulfil. While I fulfil my own. Mine and yours. You're still here, my love. So much time at long last to focus on you. On me. And my gardening of course. Now even you have to admit to being surprised about all that. Going back to college as I did. Turning all that anger into a passion for making things grow. Designing beautiful spaces for people to sit in, to look at, to breathe fresh air and pray for rain in dry summers. Coming back at the end of a day with an aching back and hands and nails torn by thorns and still ingrained with the sweet smell of garden soil. No more manicures for me. Gone are the days of Beverly Hills' nail clinic. But how lovely it is to sleep the sleep of the genuinely weary. To wake in the morning and greet the day with anticipation. I can scarcely remember "the bad old days". Hiding myself from a world I really believed held nothing for me. But hey, I did it. Got through it all. I'm still here for God's sake! Bright eyed and bushytailed.

Thank goodness for you my darling. For never giving up on me. For always being there. Even when I didn't believe I wanted you. You knew me better. Unconditional love is the name of it. We seldom deserve it, but us lucky ones get it. And it's better than youth, better than passion, and if the truth is to be told, and if you can dodge all the clichés as they fall around us, it's even more satisfying than food.

So with a little money of my own in my pocket at long last, designing back yards is not that lucrative, I feel almost independent. Can take you out to dinner occasionally. Pretend we're young and slim again. Be glad we're not. I don't seem to look back that much anymore. Not that all the memories are painful. I have some beautiful ones. Ones I cannot even share with you. Not because you wouldn't try to understand, but because they only belong to me now. I've been left in charge of them, so to speak. And they are to be remembered and cherished. They changed my life. They changed me. I guess even the bad days were necessary. Like going through one's teens, or losing your first love. Painful, but necessary. Mum was right after all – the sickening way mothers usually are.

If I'd become a writer and not a gardener I could have written all this down. Given it to you like a love letter. Instead you got just me. No love letters. No words. Just the surety that I'm always here. Always will be. That it must show on my face when I greet you. Be in my touch when I lay my garden hands on you as gently as I can, knowing you won't complain if they are less than smooth or clean. It's enough. And that's the biggest prize of all that comes with age. Knowing you've got enough.

If someone had told me this ten years ago I would have laughed in their face. Or cried. But that was then. Just memories. Under the file, "Events in a Life." '

Nine years before . . .

Chapter One

The nightmare was the same. Intense. She waited for it to wash over her with the familiarity of an old enemy, and before the details faded, scurrying away into her subconscious, she forced the memory to join her for the beginning of her day, hoping, like Dracula, it would burn away in the weak spring light of an English dawn.

Her eyes remained closed. Outside, nature stirred, heralding the April morning. She knew without seeing that the mist would be drifting peacefully towards its daytime oblivion, swirling across the Sussex Downs.

It was hot for April. The house martins were busy under the eaves of the roof outside the bedroom window. She remembered once, when the boys were little more than babies and maternity was all her being, sending away the decorators until June so as not to disturb the feather fluttering and egg laying as their routine of mating and house hunting began.

Lying there, she heard the first cuckoo, desperation in its mating call as if rejection were already part of the seasonal ritual. It had always made her laugh, that irrationally frantic sound.

By her side Bill, her husband, stirred in his sleep, farted, then turned his back with a mutter. Her eyes flew open, wanting human contact, wanting the reality of her day to begin, despite the possibility of despondency. She saw the back of his neck that had once held the youthfulness of a small boy, and with light fingers so as not to wake him she reached to touch. She had always loved the vulnerability of young male necks, now lost to her as one by one her sons became men and grew past that once so touching and kissable part of their small, lithe bodies. No more those tiny, asexual, and hairless forms that had slipped so easily into a mother's possessive arms.

She heard the dog downstairs moving restlessly about the kitchen, and then the sound of the catflap banging. A weary feline back from her night-time prowling. She looked at the clock. Still so early. The day ahead loomed endlessly.

Each morning she longed to wake with the joy and expectancy that once came with every day, her ears buzzing with the morning squabbles issuing relentlessly from the boys' rooms down the hall. Schoolbags emptied of last night's unfinished homework: 'I forgot it, Miss – I did it – honest!' White lies falling easily from chocolate-smeared and smiling lips.

She lay listening to the silence in the old house, then, afraid to disturb the peace of the man by her side, she rose and went quietly into the second bathroom, lifted the sweat-damp cotton nightgown over her head, threw it on the floor beside the wicker linen hamper, and settled naked onto the wooden lavatory seat. Putting her head down onto her knees, by-passing the voluptuous spread of her once slender waist, she contemplated the chipped red nail varnish on her toenails.

Tears ran from her eyes, carelessly, without reason, filling her with quiet anger, morning secretions that formed her daily ritual. Outpourings from every orifice.

'Ask yourself,' her therapist had said at their last meeting, 'ask yourself, "Now, why am I crying? What do I have to be sad about?"' She had smiled, 'After all Jessica, most of your very best years are still ahead of you.'

The therapist's eyes were bright, her hair shiny with the gleam of youth. And Jessica wondered at the possibility of the help and understanding that could come from her twenty-eight-year-old, degree-laden mind. Young and confident, as yet unafraid of her own mortality.

She stood now to look into the mirror above the washbasin. 'Why are you crying?' the words came out loud to a reflection that showed nothing of the girl Jessica still was in her head.

'I'm in mourning for my life.' The quote came easily. She smiled at her cleverness.

Gazing still into the mirror, she frowned suddenly at the pleasantry on her usually grim countenance. 'Doesn't belong there.' And she erased it with the damp flannel she held in her hand.

Downstairs the dog barked just once, as if he knew it was still too early for his walk but had heard sounds of movement above him. 'Coming, Butch.' *Sotto voce*, more to herself than the dog, out of earshot as he was and too lazy to climb the stairs to see what was stirring. She hurried herself into the old towelling dressing gown that lived on the hook behind the door of the guest bathroom.

She padded in bare feet down the hallway. Past the boys' old bedrooms, still cluttered with annuals and tatty games of Monopoly and Scrabble. Rooms long since cleansed of school-boy smells. Sometimes a half deflated football or broken tennis racquet would emerge from her less than frequent urges to sort things out, but in her lethargy she would fail to rid herself of the memories and downstairs they would go to the cellar to share their recollections with other ancient memorabilia.

She longed for grandsons, blond and blue-eyed, heads falling asleep onto a shoulder already comfortable with the tears of their fathers before them. But the boys had still to marry. Their ambitious, ruthless-eyed and long-limbed girl-friends tossing heavy manes of hair back from blank and unlined faces, grimacing at the thought of being wives and mothers, as they sat round the large refectory table in the dining-room, now only used on Sundays.

The big old house these days smelled no longer of a family, not with just herself and Bill rattling around. The lingering of lemon-scented furniture spray was around for only a day after Ruth had been. 'She's only in on Mondays now,' Jessica had once said to Betty, her neighbour, who'd come upon her crying profusely over a pile of Bill's shirts she was attempting to iron with the same perfection as Ruth had always managed to achieve.

'With you in this state?' Betty had said briskly. 'Really Jessica, don't be crazy, Bill won't mind, get her in every day again. The place is a mess. Bill can afford her, and let's face it, *you* can't cope!' But Jessica, ashamed of herself, had not suggested such an idea to either Bill or Ruth. Other women managed. Other women of fifty-one.

Butch, their golden and forever moulting labrador, rushed with delighted fervour into the spring morning as soon as she opened the back door. Wild rabbits that grazed and copulated in the morning dew on the back lawn would scuttle in all directions at the first glimpse of his quivering and half-pink nose as he lurched round the side of the house, barking into the silence of the six o'clock countryside.

'He'll wake the neighbours.' She filled the electric kettle and put it on to boil. The sink was full of dirty dishes from last night's supper. Baked beans on toast had been the full stretch of her culinary imagination. Bill had eaten it without a murmur.

He would stare intensely at her face when he came home in the evening. 'Good day?' he'd say tentatively, his smile belying the look in his grey eyes.

'Fine.' Her back to him, or the side of an expressionless face outstretched for the ritual kiss, given from habit, without thought. Taken. Forgotten.

'And you?' she'd say at last, mustering from somewhere a grimace that she prayed would fool him into seeing a smile, forgetting his love for her, his knowledge of her every mood. She would turn away before she could hate herself even more when she saw the sadness in his eyes, make him tea. One round teabag in the last clean mug.

'Fine.'

When had they started to hide from one another?

'D'you want a sherry?' she'd ask, needing an excuse to join him in a drink.

'I'll change first.' Every night, Monday through Friday. Back from London, out of Austin Reed suit. Briefcase into study. Evening paper already read in the first-class compartment on the five-fifteen from Waterloo placed into waste basket, crossword half finished, not even bothering any more to ask these days, 'D'you want to see your horoscope?'

City bank closed until Monday. Weekend with wife to look forward to, or dread. Golf on Saturday, weather permitting. Sunday morning, drinks in local. Once a month, maybe, their adult off-spring with various and often different mates would be there for lunch. Round the familiar dining table, still echoing with squabbles over unfair portions of peas or ice cream.

'Three sons,' he would say proudly; her husband, her partner, her enemy, her love. 'Three sons. Good Lord, no, not married. Plenty of wild oats to sow yet. Chips off the old block, those three!' Chortle, chortle.

Had he really forgotten? All of Bill's oats had been sown in Jessica.

Twenty-eight, twenty-six, and twenty-four. All men now, their babies, all gone now, that particular sweetness in her life. Flown away. 'Depression mates well with melodrama,' she thought grimly, and then, out loud, to that other self she was learning to despise, 'For God's sake, pull yourself together, woman!'

But it was a morning beset with melancholy. The taste of youth clung around her, and the boys refused to fade from her thoughts. Weary, and the day still new, she did the thing her counsellor told her not to. Allowed the mind to wander. Hard to live in the moment when the moment is nothing, the past always waiting. She only had to turn the dial, find the frequency, and she was off on the journey that led nowhere.

She leaned against the Aga, pulling the warmth into her chilly heart, saw again in her imagination the schoolboy socks drying on the lids of the large hotplates, too damp to take for football that day. 'You can't wear them, you'll catch your death, I'll send a note.' Small life-easy faces raised towards hers, seeing only their reflections in her eyes. Trust written large into their innocence.

Need for the remembered dependence made the tears fall again from her scarcely dry eyes. The kettle boiled, and she made the tea – still crying. It was the way these days. She did the tasks she hadn't yet abandoned through a veil of tearfulness most days. Soon, even those would cease to matter. She wondered if she could just sit until the debris rose around her to keep her hidden forever from a world that seemed to hold no plans for her.

Life had sat so easily on her once. Now, she understood nothing, yet still she needed for nothing, but wanted only what was past. To relive it, hang on, resisting the present, let alone the future. Her uselessness, in a world where only the necessary or the decorative were given credence, faced her every day, and there seemed no way out. Ashamed, she wondered again at the depth of her self pity and her selfishness. It had settled on her with all the coarseness of a horse blanket, still smelling of the sweat from a race where she had come to believe that women come in last.

Unable to find the strainer, and with only loose tea leaves available in the jar marked coffee, she poured the tea from the old brown Betty pot into a mug still stained with last night's tannin. Leaves, wet and black, floated to the surface, standing out against milk just poured to reach the brim. So many dark strangers. Remember, remember, that game of her teens? She took a spoon and lifted the largest of the leaves onto the back of her hand and began to press it upwards with her other palm. Saturday, Sunday, Monday – on Monday she would meet him, or her, 'or even *them*', she thought when she stared closely at the surface of her drink. Her life seemed already full of strangers, where once they had all seemed friends.

She picked up the mug of tea, not holding the handle to carry it to the breakfast bar. It was hot, made her hand shake, so she steadied it with the other, enjoying the brief and scalding pain that had touched her fingers. Lifting herself onto the stool, she tipped the mug by accident. Hot leaf-speckled liquid covered her fingers and spread across the surface in front of her. She pressed the heat of the pain against her once full breast. Above her heart, where now there was nothing. No heart, no breast, no feeling. Just a flatness. Nothing since the operation.

'If it's really bad,' she'd said, drowsy and un-caring within the comfort of the pre-med, 'if it's better to remove the lot, don't wake me and ask. Just do it. Get it over with. I couldn't bear another decision.'

So that's what they'd done – 'Just to be on the safe side, my dear.' Scraped and emptied the cancerous cells, leaving a heart beating frantically with life against the emptiness.

She touched the scar. The place where once the children had fed, laid their heads, thumbs in mouths, fallen asleep in satisfaction, milk still smudged on puckered lips. She remembered the curious eroticism of those moments, and closed her eyes against the memory.

Bill's voice came from upstairs. 'Jessica? Are you all right?'

Quite suddenly, unable to bear the thought of being joined, she hurried into the hall, pushing the morning untidiness of her hair out of her eyes, smiling up at him with the deception of the lonely. 'I'm fine, darling. I spilled some tea. I'm sorry if I woke you. I didn't realize I'd been that vocal. Go back to bed. It's early. I couldn't sleep any longer. I've put the dog out. Don't worry.'

He hovered for a moment and stared down at her across the bannisters of the upstairs landing, unsure.

Fighting down irritation, she said again, 'Don't worry. I'm all right.'

His morning erection sat stiffly in the warm pit of his groin, standing out from the suburban prudery of his maroon-striped pyjamas. Jessica remembered a time she would have stretched out her hand and grasped that part of him with its separate existence, or knelt down and taken it in her mouth while he stood. Urged him to a satisfaction that needed no encouragement. And he would lift her and place her on the floor and enter her when he was ready again, bringing her to a wetness so quickly his eyes would fill with delight. He had never grown used to the rapidity or constancy of her arousal, so sensual, so erotic, so agreeable she once was to every suggestion of sexual intent that the then young man had thrown her way.

When they'd been new lovers, moons ago, they would get off buses only halfway to their destination and hurry back home, so eager were they to touch each other, fill their senses with tongues and fingers. Dinner with friends could wait, and often did. Parties would start without them; they often missed the first act of a play they'd planned to see, arriving tousled and replete, stuttering their excuses to acquaintances who smiled and found their passion for each other amusing. Seeing her dressed to go out, tailored and formal, gloss-filled lips parted over firm white teeth would leave Bill heady with desire. Sometimes she teased him, putting on suspenders and black stockings without panties and then whispering what she'd done as they sat down to dinner, sitting across the table from each other in restaurants, him trying to order in a grown-up fashion, fighting with the blush of youth, and the discomfort of his over-stimulated glands.

They were young. They believed they always would be, and that their rampant desire for each other would never end. Now it had been so long since they'd touched with any sort of intimacy.

She wanted none of it. The thought of all that life-giving fluid hurrying to its doom up her dead and barren tubes filled her with disgust, so she turned her back after only brief kisses of good-night. Knowing his disappointment, wondering at his fidelity. Who would blame him if he had been anything but faithful? And what was worse, she no longer cared.

She waved him back to the bedroom, then took her guilt and burnt hand back to the kitchen. The tears, for the moment anyway, were gone. Throwing the rest of the tea down the waste disposal, she filled the kettle again. Instant caffeinated coffee would have to do. If she made it strong enough maybe it would kick-start her into that tediously early spring morning.

Butch barked at the back door, abrupt and demanding, pretending that he didn't care that no rabbits had been caught again. He was growing too fat to run, and even a dog grows tired of chasing rainbows. Now was the time for his breakfast. 'Why can't you wait one second?' Jessica grumbled at him as he shot between her legs to peer into his still dirty last night's food dish, nearly knocking her off balance and treading all over her bare feet in the process.

'There.' She crumbled the last of the chocolate biscuits into his bowl and shuddered at the thought of them mingling with the remains of the canned dogfood he'd left in the corners of his dish where the long pink labrador tongue could never reach. He wagged his tail and buried his nose in the offering.

She knew the chocolate was bad for him but she'd run out of dog biscuits over a week ago. 'I'll have to shop,' she said to his still wagging tail. Butch didn't look up. He cleaned the bottom of his bowl to within an inch of removing the enamel.

She began to stack last night's plates into the dishwasher and realized it was still full of clean ones. That's why Bill had left the supper dishes in the sink after the baked beans. 'He's not the only one who hates unloading,' she muttered, and began the task with so much haste she dropped and smashed a plate. 'Oh, shit, shit, shit!'

Trembling, she made her cup of coffee before the water had decently boiled, and sat down again at the breakfast bar to survey the mess.

Bill, dressing gown over pyjamas, walked into the kitchen, banging his shin on the open door of the dishwasher. 'Christ, Jessica, can't you do *anything*?'

'No.' She watched him as he sighed, then got a dustpan and brush and began to pick up the pieces of broken white china. 'You're getting worse,' he muttered, head down towards the task in progress.

'What?'

He looked up. 'I said,' he was talking to a child, 'you are getting worse. What does that trick cyclist do, for God's sake?'

'She tells me I have the best years to look forward to.'

27

Jessica drank her lukewarm coffee, hating his harshness, understanding his exasperation. He spoke again, gently, seeing the moisture in her eyes, desperate for her in her unhappiness, feeling helpless even as he loved her, 'Why can't you believe that, darling?'

She shook her head, afraid to utter in case the wrong words came, wanting to smile at him, touch him, love him again. Wanted to want to.

He remained silent.

'What d'you possibly think she could mean?' she said eventually. 'She's twenty-eight, for God's sake!' Anger instead of love spilled from her careless lips.

He sighed again and went to empty the broken plate into the kitchen bin. The pieces clattered noisily against the plastic sides stained with weeks of neglect. 'There's no liner,' he said, his teeth clenched with all the patience he could muster. 'Where are the bin liners, for God's sake?'

'Still on the grocery shelves, I imagine. I haven't shopped.'

He threw the dustpan and brush into the broom cupboard and shut the door rapidly before the mess inside descended upon him. 'Jesus Christ!'

She giggled, alone with her mirth. And he bristled.

'It's not funny Jessica. The house is a mess. What the hell does Ruth do for her money these days?'

She shrugged and watched him while he walked

to the kettle and switched it on. 'She couldn't come last Monday. She'll be in after the week-end.'

'How can it get into such a state so quickly?' he asked.

She shrugged again. Mute. Her depression lay between them. Her ever increasing immobility was inexplicable to him, but a kind of sad comfort to herself.

'There are no teabags,' he said, exasperation blatantly obvious even from his back view.

'Try the coffee.'

He sighed, made his drink in silence, then came and sat opposite her across the breakfast bar. She could smell his familiar morning aroma and remembered how she had loved to wake and see him there beside her after years of fumbled sexual play in the back of cars and against the grubby walls of dark alleys.

Marriage had seemed so delightfully and legally wicked. 'Just think,' she'd say, climbing on his still sleepy form, selfish in her longing to feel his erection grow inside her, 'we can do this every single morning for the rest of our lives, and there'll be no-one to stop us!' But the babies did.

It had taken her by surprise; no-one had told her that having babies was a sexual experience, or how jealous a husband might get. And confused with the connotations of that emotion towards his first-born, Bill remained silent at that important time.

As soon as Stephen was weaned she wanted another. Making her happy made him happy, so they went on to have two more. Three sons. But then she'd wanted four, selfish as she was with her need for everlasting nesting. But it had stopped working. There seemed to be no reason.

'Fate,' he'd say, comforting her when the telltale signs of blood appeared like clockwork every twenty-eight days without fail. 'Maybe it's all for the best, Jessica.'

She'd pulled away, angry. 'You sound more and more like a shitty bank manager!' she'd yelled. Rationality had never been one of her strong points.

'Maybe that's because I am!' he'd yell back.

They still fought healthily, if fiercely, in those days. Fought and loved. Later, as they grew older, the comforting stopped, along with the fights, and she hid her painful disappointment every month. Bill put down her bad temper to pre-menstrual tension and she didn't enlighten him.

She had never suffered from that particular female affliction. As a teenager she had almost enjoyed the twenty-eight day ritual. It seemed in some way to confirm her overpowering and constant delight in being female.

Finally, in her early forties, desperate to give her biological urges one last spurt, crying out for the smell of baby breath against her neck, she went to see a highly recommended 'baby-doctor' in Harley Street. It was said of him 'the man makes miracles'. But not for Jessica. It seemed that miracles were shared out, and she'd already had more than her quota.

'I doubt you produce eggs any longer, my dear,' the specialist had said, in the cultured, patronizing tone of voice his sex and class adopts so easily. 'From what you tell me, your husband and yourself have been trying for some considerable time.' And then, casually, whilst washing those oh-so-genteel hands, as if it meant but a passing phase instead of a little death, 'It's without doubt an early menopause for you, nothing to get upset about, we'll prescribe some hormones when the time comes, and you'll be over this "empty nest syndrome" in no time.'

'Can't you do *anything*?' she'd said, her pride, along with her dignity, hiding in her french knickers on the chair by the side of the examination table, her legs open and raised in stirrups.

But his vaselined gloves were off, discarded into a small bin, by those doctor's busy asexual fingers.

'Now Mrs Wooldridge,' leaning over her while his nurse lowered her legs, 'you have three fine sons. Be content. At your age with an already satisfactory and extremely healthy family, I can see no reason for your husband to spend a great deal of money chasing what I'm a hundred per cent sure would be an impossible dream. Now's the time to start looking forward and planning a life for just the two of you. Go home and take care of *him*!'

Patronizing shit. But she had smiled, and cringed as if he'd patted her, and hated him thoroughly as she climbed into her knickers, trembling behind the screen, straining to hear the whispered conversation between him and the nurse, convinced they were talking about the silliness of women of that certain age.

So that had been that. Bill had commiserated and been secretly relieved. Jessica never mentioned babies again.

Oh, she stood on her shoulders secretly in the bathroom every time they made love after that. She no longer climbed on top of him, although she knew he liked that best, in case the sperm ran out as she rolled back onto her own side of the bed. And if Bill suspected what she was up to, he never said a word. But nothing worked. Gradually, their love-making lost all its old spontaneity. Bill concentrated more and more on his rapidly developing career at the bank. She brought the boys through the difficult teen years, then mourned with silent and inarticulate fury as one by one the men in her life drifted from her. She stood in the margins of their lives and felt her usefulness ebb away.

The specialist had been right. At forty-six her menopause was diagnosed and she was put onto hormone replacement therapy: 'To put back what nature so cruelly takes away.'

'Why does everyone have to be so damned coy about it all?' she'd thought. 'We can't reproduce any more, so the least they can invent is a tablet to keep us pleasant.'

A few months before her fiftieth birthday, cancer was diagnosed and she had a mastectomy. She'd been afraid to confront the obvious fact that her left breast had become misshapen, refused to see, not touching, it doesn't hurt, so it must be OK. Foolish, childish, close your eyes and the bogey man will disappear. It was Bill in the end, walking into the bathroom, catching her trying to cover herself with the flannel, so of course he was curious – she, of all people, being modest, when she would always walk unadorned from room to room, sending delivery boys diving into nearby shrubs, covering themselves with thorns and confusion.

The rapidity of the decision to operate saved her life. Biopsy, knife, counselling – all better now. 'Aren't they wonderful? In my day we would have been dead before they found it,' her elderly aunt had said, one visiting afternoon, flocking as they do to hospital bedsides when 'womanly problems' appear, lowering their voices when describing the disease, as if in itself it was to be ashamed of, something one brings on one's self. IT. 'Say it, damn you,' Jessica thought, 'say it. CANCER, CANCER, CANCER. There now.' A six-week battering with chemotherapy. Sickness, a greying of the skin colour. A small price to pay for the giving back of hope. Not certainty, mind you, but miracles occur. Regular check-ups. Caught in time. You'll live for years, Mrs Wooldridge.

Seething thoughts beneath her good woman's smile to the surgeon. Mustn't make him feel bad. After all, he'd done his best. 'Thank you, doctor. I'm so grateful.'

No more hormone replacement therapy. 'Not advisable, Mrs Wooldridge.'

It was all over. Bar the screaming, that was.

Bill took her hand in his, covering the back of it with small and well-intentioned kisses. It lay, unresponsive, in his, until he put it limply back on the breakfast bar and sighed, 'Jessica, Jessica, what are we going to do with you?'

'Is that the royal "we"?' she said, mustering a smile.

He took her chin in his hand and turned her face towards him. 'Tell me honestly, Jessie, am I wasting my money on that private – what d'you call her? – counsellor?'

It had been years since he'd called her 'Jessie'. Memories flooded her. She pulled away. He was incurably sad. And that was her fault, she knew it, and hated him for making her feel guilty.

'I thought it was *our* money,' she said, unnecessarily spiteful.

He rose to the bait. 'That was when you kept your side of the bargain!' He gesticulated round the mess in the once-gleaming kitchen.

She stared at him, confused with his uncharacteristic outburst, at his sudden anger and flushed morning face. And then she laughed, liking him better for his unexpected fury.

'You have developed a very strange sense of humour,' he muttered, and left the room, banging his leg once more on the still open dishwasher, to go upstairs and get dressed for his golf game.

He would have real coffee and most likely buttered croissants at the clubhouse, and enjoy the silent sympathy of Betty's husband, Peter, who would guess he'd gone once more without a proper breakfast.

She longed to find again the ability to talk to him, about real things, the way they once did. But this *thing* inside her, this 'clinical depressive illness' as their family doctor had called it, as he wrote the prescription for Prozac and slipped it into her handbag, this remained with her and blotted out all other emotions. Fermenting, growing, like some alien had taken residence in her once-strong body.

That's how she saw it, her sickness, her inertia, that came and lived with her six months after the operation. Not that it hadn't been waiting on the sidelines for quite a while. It seemed to have swallowed every real emotion and left her with just one supreme talent – the ability to cry at the drop of a hat.

The small sparks from the morning confrontation with Bill seemed to stir her into action and she began to unload the dishwasher, leaving the clean crockery on the breakfast bar and throwing the cutlery haphazardly into a drawer.

Then she went upstairs to stand before the open door of the closet where she kept her clothes. There to decide the momentous task of what to wear. She longed to stay in the old towelling dressing gown. Feel the softness of her belly move when she walked, unrestricted, without underwear. Let her bare feet collect the dirt hidden in long pile carpet and labrador hairs from the once always clean stone kitchen floor.

It took her an hour and a half, the choosing of the day's apparel. Trivial decisions were mountains to climb. 'Part of the illness,' the therapist had said. She patted the doctor's prescription, still lying grubbily at the bottom of her handbag after all these weeks. Still unfilled. Lying there, with the odd hairgrip and rubber band. Maybe this would be the day she'd go to the pharmacy. Maybe today she'd make the effort. Maybe today she'd decide to get better.

Bill left for golf. And breakfast. Jessica left for the supermarket. The long and empty Saturday had begun.

Chapter Two

Shopping passed in a blur, and making her way back to the car, Jessica congratulated herself on what had turned out to be her positive approach to the overcrowded supermarket. 'Try to achieve even just *one* thing a day.' The therapist's words, not hers. Maybe it was going to be a good day after all. The thought cheered her to the extent she felt able to face the crowd in the cafeteria, and decided to satisfy a sudden craving for a coffee and doughnut.

Families, husbands, wives, and children, jostled and pushed and chatted. 'This is good,' she thought, paying for her unseemly breakfast and pushing her way towards an empty table. 'This is very good therapy. I must remember to tell what's-her-name at my next counselling.' She would like Bill to have been there just at that moment. He would have been quite cheered at seeing her dealing with one of her better times.

No-one joined her at the table. She wondered if the unmade-up face with which she'd left home was more formidable than usual. She hadn't even bothered with pencilling in the eyebrows, she'd been in such a hurry to leave the house and get the trip over and done with. She'd plucked the damn things one evening about ten years previously with the vague desire to change the way she looked after watching one of those make-over programmes on Oprah Winfrey one idle afternoon. Boredom is dangerous at any age. Specially boredom with one's self. They'd never grown back, the eyebrows that is. 'Enough to frighten the horses,' Bill had muttered, which made her laugh, and then go out and invest in an eyebrow pencil.

Smells of fried chicken and hamburger all too suddenly flooded her senses. Sugar licked from a sugar-sticky mouth, taste of jam, fruit sauce unknown and indescribable, lingered on her taste buds, pieces of doughnut lodged behind the dental plate in her mouth. Nausea swept over her. The feast had turned to bile instead of pleasure and brought her rapidly to her feet, knocking reminiscences out of her mind.

She found the restroom and waited in line for a free cubicle, fighting down the increasing desire to vomit. The sweet and greasy lump of stodge came up easily, mingling with the coffee. She splashed her face with cold water after pushing her way to the basin and, ignoring the stares of small girls listening with open eyes to the fascinating sounds of grown up puking, emerged once more into the grocery store and found herself near the magazine section.

Shaky, eyes down towards feet determined to get to the car in case she disgraced herself again, she almost collided with Betty. Her neighbour's voice, loud in its cheerful greeting, brought her to a sudden halt before the quick getaway she'd hoped for. 'Hello Jessica,' Betty looked hard at her, a copy of *Country Homes* in her well-manicured hands, 'are you all right? You're a very strange colour!'

Jessica closed her eyes briefly, mustering strength to deal with the well-meant kindness. 'Hello Betty,' she smiled slowly, 'no, I'm fine. Something I ate, I'm afraid. Bad choice for breakfast. Silly of me. How nice to see you. Are you well? You're looking very well. I didn't expect to see you here on a Saturday.'

The magazine was placed back into the rack, and Betty took hold of her arm. 'Why on earth didn't you ring me?' she chided, 'I would have done your shopping for you. I've told you, just pick up the phone. That's what friends are for.'

They had been friends since the early days of living in the village, despite a lack of common interests, except golf-playing husbands and sherry parties at Christmas. Contact between them had been sparse in the last few months, but that was not Betty's fault. Jessica had become more and more ungracious since the operation. Depression was such a personal liability one felt one had to battle it out in private.

'Shall we have coffee?' Betty suggested.

'No thank you, Betty, I think I'd better go

home. I'm not sure what time the men will be back from golf.'

Her neighbour laughed, 'Good grief, dear girl, they'll be at the nineteenth hole for yonks! Tell you what,' she folded Jessica's arm purposefully in hers once again and pulling away was out of the question without turning obviously nasty. 'Go home, unpack your shopping, and then pop in to me about two-ish.' Then, leaning forward conspiratorially, she whispered, 'We'll toss down a few sherries to catch them up and I'll make you a sandwich.'

'God,' thought Jessica, 'how I hate that home counties attitude and manner. Why do these people always think they know better than you?'

'I can't drink,' she said, off the top of her head, and desperate to thwart her neighbour's plans, 'I'm on medication.'

Betty's eyebrows rose. 'Have they got you on it at long last?'

Jessica nodded, and the thought of the unfilled prescription at the bottom of her handbag came back to haunt her.

'Any help?' said Betty kindly.

'Oh, yes,' false and bright to match the lie, 'I feel *much* better. Soon be my old self again!'

'No sherry then,' Betty said, not to be deterred, 'but I'll expect you at two. I won't take no for an answer. It seems ages since we've had a good old chinwag and a moan about our far from better other halves!' And she laughed, too loudly, at her own cliché, kissed Jessica on both cheeks, and disappeared into the mass of seething shoppers without a qualm, clutching copies of *Country Life* and *Majesty*.

Jessica knew when she was licked. The neighbourly visit loomed ahead without even the comfort of the odd tipple. She went home, dumped the bags of shopping on the kitchen table, calmed down Butch who greeted her as if she'd been abroad for a month, and poured herself a gin and tonic. Too exhausted, or lazy, to bother with ice cubes she drank it at room temperature and waited for that special feeling as the alcohol hit her stomach.

'It's a depressant,' the therapist's voice sounded at the back of her head as she swallowed the lukewarm gin, 'I promise you, alcohol *is* a depressant, and it will only make you worse in the long run.'

So Jessica lied. Said she no longer drank. It was easier. Bill knew, of course, but he never said anything. Simply bought more gin and put it in the kitchen cabinet without a word.

'I guess he's frightened of me,' she said out loud to Butch who wagged his tail and pushed his wet nose into the hand that didn't hold the gin.

'*I'm* frightened of me.' And still shaky after the bout of sickness in the supermarket and cross with herself for letting Betty manipulate her, she poured herself another gin in defiance, took off her coat and began to put away the contents of the plastic bags.

The nausea had passed. She buttered two slices of bread and put between them peanut butter, whiskey-flavoured orange marmalade, a slice of processed cheese, and a chunk of liver sausage cut haphazardly from the piece she'd bought at the delicatessen counter that morning. She began to hum a little to herself and went across to put on the radio.

Depression at its worst had made not a dent in her appetite and she'd always loved strange fillings in sandwiches. Had never worried about putting on weight and, loving her food, she hated the thought of dieting. She'd enjoyed exercise, specially sports, when she was young. Relished hockey even on the coldest of winter mornings, and loved sweating over a tennis match in June. Not any more. On her really bad days, when the pain of being alive was at its worst, lying down or standing still were the only options. That way at least, was her reasoning, when the shit hit the fan, she was where she needed to be. In the line of fire. The more shit that covered her, the more justified were her bad moods. This she'd worked out for herself.

Vanity had never been part of her make-up. Aging was inevitable. The problem seemed to her to be with other people. No-one listened any more. Not to women. Not when they were no longer girls. So the screaming inside them turns to shrewishness. The nymph becomes the harpy. Or else cakes are baked in unnecessary abundance for Harvest Festivals that had been ignored for years. Church pews are full of old women. Maybe God is the only one left with open ears.

It had been the operation that made her face what had become the growing misery inside herself. The mutilation of her once-strong body seemed to be an unjust insult. Humour black with cynicism. Breast gone, cancer beaten; trouble was, the hole that was left was the perfect home for the voracious depression that had been waiting so patiently and homelessly in the margin of her life for longer than she had ever dared admit.

She saw the message light on the answer machine flashing and pressed the playback on her way between the kitchen table and the refrigerator. 'Hi Mum!' Her youngest son's voice sprung energetically into the space all round her and she smiled at the machine as if it were him, stopping in her tracks, a piece of cellophane-wrapped cheddar cheese in her hand.

'Hi Charlie,' she said back to him, as if he could hear, glad there were things in life that still filled her heart, moments of clarity in the foolishness of her despair.

'Just checking in, Mum. I'm away for the weekend so I won't see you till next Sunday. Hope you're feeling better. Everything's great with me. Love you lots.'

'And you too, my darling,' she said out loud, 'and you too.'

A click as his receiver went down. End of message. As if he'd slipped from her grasp. Her baby. The spoiled one. Or so Bill used to say. 'Even more than the others, you mean?' she'd joked with him. And Bill had laughed and shrugged. He never really questioned her about the way she reared the boys. That was her domain. Being a mother was where she excelled. If too much love could lead to spoiling, then the boys were spoilt. It was Bill's turn now. His time to be spoilt. But to his disappointment and her shame, it seemed she was all loved out.

Another message. Not immediately recognizable. A twang of mid-Atlantic extravagance on the English vowels.

'Jess, my darling? guess who? I'm ashamed it's been so long. It's Norma. It's sparrow fart here. Believe it or not, I'm on my way out to the gym. LA got to me at last. You've got the number, call me tonight, your time. I'm crazy with missing you, honey. What's happening in your life? Catch you later. God bless.'

Norma Matherson. The wonderful, 'they-broke-the-mould' Norma – 'this is Norma, Mum – my very best friend in all the world!' Jessica's nine-year-old voice rang in her memory and filled her heart with a warmth that threatened the solidarity of despair.

They had met at primary school, she and

Norma. Together, they'd passed their eleven-plus; gone by choice and endeavour to the same grammar school, there had fallen in love with the same prefects, and, as one, they had blushed whenever a certain athletic gym mistress had glanced their way and set those adolescent hearts all of a flutter; fought each other's battles when infatuated with the wrong kind of boy. Jessica eventually met and married Bill. The sexiest of them all and only Norma knew that because in those far-off days they had no secrets. She had been the chief bridesmaid at the wedding. She was the best lady, the very best of best friends. She caught the wedding bouquet when Jessica threw it deliberately in her direction, and together they giggled at the thought they would hopefully be 'Sadies, Sadies, married ladies' – as the song goes – together, happily ever after.

But it didn't happen the way they'd planned. When Jessica was first pregnant, Norma was still single. 'Practising, though,' she'd say, somewhat ruefully, 'I'm kissing a lot of toads!'

She was godmother to Stephen, their first-born, and then again to Charlie. 'Didn't Auntie Norma like me?' Sam had asked one birthday, with the curious lack of sentiment so often found in middle children. 'We've ruined his confidence,' Jessica had hissed to her bewildered husband, 'I knew we shouldn't have changed and asked your sister. Norma could easily have taken them *all* under her wing. My children are hers to share. All three of them!'

And, of course, baptism or not, official or otherwise, Norma was second mother to each of the boys. And Sam's confidence had remained intact, as Bill knew it would.

Jessica had watched her friend's often disastrous affairs, cried with her at Christmas when a married lover was 'incommunicado' while he was with his family, and finally seen her wed at thirty-five to a completely unsuitable younger man of twenty-three, and all but carried her through the divorce two years later.

'That's it,' Norma had said, 'no more. From now on I stick to being a mistress. Same old misery but at least there'll be no ironing or farting in bed! And no smelly socks. God preserve me from young men's socks!'

'It's the sneakers,' Jessica said knowingly, once Norma's tears had been dried by her sense of humour. 'That's what makes the socks smelly. Take it from one who is raising three sons!'

Norma had followed the advice, had stuck to the over forties. More than often married, 'But at least the farting in bed is kept for the wife. Me they have to impress!'

Then, at forty-five, she had met Chuck.

'Good grief! *Chuck?*' had been Jessica's first reaction. 'How d'you murmur that into his ear with passion?'

'It's easier than Fred. And I've had two Freds if you remember.'

46

Chuck Sarrison was ten years older than Norma when they met. He had seemed a nice man. Wealthy, in real estate, a Californian born and bred, but very much married, with two daughters who had grown and long since left home.

'Both Freds seemed sexier,' Jessica had said, hoping to deter her friend from making another painful mistake.

'But not as rich,' Norma had smiled. 'It's amazing how lusty you feel when you're screwing at Claridges.' It had been a new Norma. That all-out and obvious enjoyment of much and easy wealth. 'The pragmatism that comes with *years* of experience,' she'd explained.

'But when will you see him again?' Jessica asked when they were sharing confidences in the large Sussex kitchen before a Sunday lunch. Chuck had rather reluctantly returned to Los Angeles to placate a suspicious wife and several neglected businesses.

Norma had shrugged, resigned. 'Who knows? Twenty years ago, let's be honest, *ten* years ago, I'd be heartbroken. But no-one falls that much in love after forty. The heart doesn't blindly go on breaking for ever, you know. One learns to hold something back.'

'I suppose that's one of your usual sweeping generalizations,' Jessica had said, tasting a white sauce she was making for the broccoli.

'He was quite quite lovely, Jess, but I doubt if I'll ever see him again. I've heard all his dialogue

47

before. The words no longer have the power to deflate me, or even sap my strength.'

But it seemed that Chuck Sarrison had never met anyone quite like Norma. He'd been persistent, had called, written. And finally, irretrievably, told his wife. Norma was flown out, first class. 'Just for a vacation, you understand.' She had never come back. Except to sell her house, and say not too many reluctant 'goodbyes'.

'Except you, my darling Jess,' she'd wept. 'What will I do without you when it all goes wrong?'

But apparently it all went right. Chuck had got himself an expensive divorce from a wife who, according to Norma, didn't seem that upset: 'Maybe she knows something I don't.' Anyway, doubts aside, the best friend became Mrs Sarrison the third. (That *was* a surprise, but Norma swallowed determinedly, saying through smiling, clichéd lips, 'Third time lucky, Jess!')

Jessica and Bill had flown out for the wedding which had taken place in the Beverly Hills' home Chuck had bought for his new, but not untried (Norma's words, no-one else's) bride.

'Are you stinking rich?' Jessica had asked her friend over several glasses of Dom Perignon in the heat of that Californian summer day, their eyes half closed and squinting against the reflection of the swimming pool.

'Stinking,' Norma had replied. And sighed as deeply as only the truly contented can.

Jessica had seen around the interior-designed,

five-bedroomed, four-and-a-half-bathroomed, 'separate apartment for housekeeper', home, been introduced to all the new acquaintances and their various facelifts, then she and Bill had waved goodbye to the newlyweds, and hurtled back to West Sussex and their sons and their animals with a large amount of joy for Jessica, and not even a tear drop of envy for Norma.

When Jessica heard Norma's voice that Saturday on the machine she realized how much they'd drifted apart since her friend's marriage. It had been inevitable. Like any other woman, Norma's focus had changed as soon as a husband had appeared on the scene. It was the way of love, and the way of men. Then, from out of the blue, the phone call. Jessica couldn't help wondering if something was wrong. Maybe even Norma's little 'Eden' was developing a few weeds in spite of all that sunshine.

At fifteen minutes after two the telephone rang. She jumped violently and picked it up in haste. 'I'm just coming Betty,' she said quickly.

But it was Bill. 'It's me,' he said.

'Hello, me.'

There was a pause and then he spoke again. 'I won't be back until about four, Jessica. Are you all right?'

'If you mean, have I been drinking, the answer's yes.'

'Oh.'

'Don't worry, I'm not weepy.'

'I didn't suggest you were.'

'I'm going to Betty's,' she said after another pause.

'Good.'

'Norma phoned. She left a message on the machine.'

'Oh, that's nice.' His voice lifted. He'd always loved Norma. Jessica suspected once he'd rather fancied her, maybe even flirted with the idea of a threesome in the very early days of their relationship, before lust turned to love and marriage had quietened the imagination.

'I'll phone her tonight,' she said.

'Good.' The conversation ground to a halt. They said their goodbyes and she replaced the receiver, jumping violently for the second time when it rang again immediately.

'Jessica?' Betty sounded as if she hoped the anxious tone in her voice would hide the fact she was put out by tardiness.

'Sorry Betty. I got a phone call. Shall I still come? I don't want to ruin any other plans you might have.'

'Of course, dear, of course. I have Mrs Pritchard from the parish council coming at a quarter to four, but there's nothing that can't be discussed in front of you.'

'I'll be away by four,' Jessica promised herself. Mrs Pritchard was forever trying to inveigle every woman in the parish who didn't go out to work, into joining the wives' fellowship that belonged to the local village church. But St Peter's had never featured large in the Wooldridges' life. Except for Christmas, of course, all that 'holly and the ivy' stuff and midnight mass that drove most people to take their conscience and their children to church. And then there was Harvest Festival, all the delightful fecundity of it. She, Bill, and sometimes the boys if they were around, often went *en famille* to that. For some strange reason they all knew the words to 'We plough the fields and scatter'.

She knew Betty was brim full of good intentions, but doubted if her neighbour had ever had the passion to be despairingly unhappy in her life. But then again, how could one tell? British reticence and all that. Jessica knew she'd become overtly possessive of her own melancholy since the depression, and self-centred enough to dismiss anyone's attempt at understanding.

She brushed her teeth before going next door, even swirled cologne round the inside of her mouth, making herself gag in the process. If Betty smelled the gin when she opened the door she was polite enough not to mention it.

'Have you eaten?' she asked, bustling Jessica into the large pale living room where an unnecessary log fire was burning in the hearth.

'No, I haven't,' Jessica took off a hurriedly donned cardigan which she'd just noticed had a hole in the elbow. The heat in the room hit her a little too quickly. She was, quite suddenly, very hungry again, and so refrained from mentioning the sandwich she had just devoured, knowing by instinct Betty would probably have something equally delicious lying about in her refrigerator, even if it had been prepared in advance for Mrs Pritchard and would therefore be somewhat more conservative than her own culinary effort.

'I have some quiche in the refrigerator,' Betty said, as if reading her mind. 'It's not too early for a cup of tea, is it?' And pushing Jessica into the large, overstuffed sofa she disappeared in the direction of the kitchen, calling over her shoulder, 'Make yourself at home, dear, I'll only be a minute.'

Jessica regretted her fabricated story about being on medication. She would have liked another gin. Betty's husband, Peter, knocked them back enthusiastically all day and every day, so two-thirty on a Saturday afternoon would probably not have raised an eyebrow. Staring at the fire and mesmerized with the heat, she leaned back into the depths of the sofa with a sigh. Trapped by good intentions, she might as well lie back and enjoy it. The room was comfortable and decorated in intimidating good taste. Arranged bowls of flowers on the coffee table and sideboard echoed the same colours dominant in the wallpaper. It was impressive. Her own house had never been quite so *Homes and Gardens*, what with three sons, one dog, and a varying number of cats throughout the years.

Betty bustled back in only moments with a piece of quiche placed beautifully and precisely on a delicate china plate. Parsley and sliced tomato lay appetizingly beside it and, much too pretty to eat, two radishes shaped like flower buds. One well-ironed linen napkin was laid across Jessica's lap and a small polished table drawn from a nest placed to her right. 'There you are, my dear. Tea will be ready shortly. Now please dig in. You need your stamina.'

Jessica had begun to rather enjoy being treated like a child. It happened quite a lot those days. Maybe it was what her future held, sitting still and being nurtured. But then she'd have to learn to smile a lot, and be amazingly pleasant almost constantly. It would never work.

She ate the quiche and wished she'd remembered to bring her handbag so she could hide the radishes to show Bill later.

'I've made Earl Grey,' Betty said, coming back into the room with a tray. 'It gives one such a clear head.' So she *had* smelled the gin.

Jessica loathed Earl Grey tea. It had never captured her imagination let alone her tastebuds. She preferred her coffee caffeinated and her tea sweet and strong. Preferably with full cream milk, the kind that makes the fascists of the 'food police' break out in a cold sweat. 'Quite,' she said, smiling brightly and inanely at her hostess.

The pale liquid staggered from the covered teapot, a child embroidered teacosy with a hole left for the spout. The tea lay listlessly in the exquisite bone china cup. Betty hovered with a slice of lemon. Jessica began to feel like a Jane Austen heroine. 'Did you want milk?' Betty asked, the tone in her voice implying that only the uninformed would make such a request.

'Please.' And 'white sugar' Jessica yearned to call after her neighbour's disappointed back as she headed once more to the kitchen.

Over tea they talked. Or rather Betty chatted, and Jessica smiled and nodded and even laughed a little and actually felt that the afternoon was taking on quite a pleasant soporific shape.

Just as she was ready to nod off there was a loud knock at the back door. Betty's front hall was out of bounds to visitors in case mud was trodden into pale carpets that were as pristine as the day they were laid. There had never actually been a notice in the parish magazine relaying that fact, but somehow the entire village knew, as well as the outlying districts. Or so it seemed. Dirt from the path to the back door could be left on the easily washed kitchen floor and nowhere else. That meant clean soles by the time the sitting-room was reached, and then, when the visitor took his or her leave, the mud gathered on the path back could be deposited in one's own car. Simple really.

'Damn,' Betty said, 'she's early, and I really wanted to talk more about you. Have I been helpful at all?'

Jessica wanted to go home and sleep. Curl up on the doghair-covered sofa and put the television on quietly in the background. Her early rising was catching up with her. That, and the gin. She stood up as Mrs Pritchard came into the room. It helped her keep her eyes open. The room was unbearably hot and she had begun to feel sick again.

'Mrs Wooldridge,' tweed jacketed arms outstretched, energetic enthusiasm on her weather-roughened, elderly face, smiling under the old-fashioned felt hat. Mrs Pritchard, first warden of St Peter's, never had called her Jessica. She was waiting for 'that nice Mrs Wooldridge' to join the various parish activities. Even if she didn't bake or knit there *must* be something she could do that was useful. 'After all,' Mrs Pritchard had remarked to the minister at one parish meeting, 'she has brought up three fine young men. She obviously has talents we have yet to discover!'

Betty said she'd make more tea. Jessica put on her cardigan, keeping one hand over the torn elbow, and said she had to go. 'Walk the dog,' she lied. Bill would do that, Butch enjoyed it more with him; even the dog grew weary of her apathy these days. Anyway, sticks were thrown to greater distances by masculine arms, more walking mileage was covered, deeper excursions into really interesting parts of the woods where the deer dung lay resplendent, waiting to be rolled in by any passing dog confident of his station in life.

For Jessica, the sofa beckoned. She could count the hours to bedtime. Another day over.

As she walked home, Jessica thought sadly, 'I won't be content until I alienate everyone I love. Please God pull me together.' Not that she held out much hope He would be listening. She'd ignored Him for far too long. Even the Lord might shrivel from lack of attention. Butch's legs were crossed in desperation when she got home and, feeling guilty, she let him into the garden. 'You'll be walked soon,' she muttered. 'Believe me old boy, I'd be dreadful company.'

Leaving the back door open so he could just come back when he wanted, she headed for the living-room, the sofa, and the background sounds of the old black and white movie on Channel Four. She was asleep in moments. The dream, the crying, finally Bill, woke her, shaking her in panic as she struggled back into reality and sobbed against his chest, smelling his cologne, his warmth, glad he was there, unquestioning as he held her, let her sob, stroked her, waited for her to quieten, wiped the tears and let her blow her nose into his clean pink handkerchief that had once been white until she'd washed it with his red woollen sweater.

'Jessica, Jessica, talk to me darling – what was the dream? You're shaking. Tell me, my love, tell me.'

'I can't remember, don't ask me. I'm sorry Bill. I'm sorry.'

'Stay there, my darling. I'll make some tea.'

'Strong,' she said, 'with milk and sugar.'

'You've been to Betty's.' And for a moment they smiled together in mutual understanding.

She called Norma after supper. Bill had cooked lamb chops with oven chips and frozen peas while she bathed and washed her hair. The tub was very full, the water too hot and too much bath oil poured in with shaky hands from the purple jar that Stephen had given her last Christmas. The oil would eventually be used but her son's jar would be around forever. She was that way with every gift they had bought or made for her from the time they were tiny. Cardboard homemade jewellery boxes fashioned with grubby fingers still lurked at the back of lingerie drawers. Coloured childlike drawings once fresh from kindergarten had stayed on the door of the refrigerator until they yellowed.

She lay in purple water and sweated profusely. Bill had opened red wine and given her the first glass to sip as she bathed. Her full, soft belly floated comfortably beneath the surface of lilac scented foam.

It would be the way to kill yourself. A hot oily bath, sipping rather good claret, your husband cooking lamb chops downstairs; not too far away in case you changed your mind, wanted, needed to be saved at the last moment. Painless to cut your wrists in hot water. She'd read that somewhere. The red mingling with the purple bath water, claret spilling into a wet and slippery grave.

She began to feel better as she lingered there. It was the warmth and the wine, the thought she didn't have to cook dinner, and the slender communication that had sprung up between herself and Bill. She heard him singing as she dried herself, giddy from the too hot water, her body damp again as soon as she put down the towel. She put on a housecoat and brushed the wet hair back from her flushed and shiny face.

'Can I eat like this?' she asked when she got downstairs.

Bill had laid the table and put the rest of the wine into a decanter. Napkins in crystal glasses. Candles lit.

'There's posh,' she spoke quickly, without thinking, embarrassed at his attempt to make things easy between them.

She poured more wine. They ate supper. They made conversation. She told him about Betty's radishes, and they laughed together. It was almost right.

'Phone Norma,' Bill said, 'phone her now. I'll make coffee.'

'Put some brandy in it,' she said. 'I'll sleep better. Oh yes, and lots of cream.'

She called Los Angeles, and Norma answered.

'Jess, oh Jess, how wonderful to hear your voice. How are you?'

It was not the moment for pretence. 'I don't

know, Norma. I'm not well.' She was sitting in the hall, the desk phone in her hand, wondering if Bill could hear from the kitchen, wondering if he understood her ability to talk more easily to friend than to husband. She had longed for the easy companionship of Norma for so long, and only realized it when she heard her voice. It may just have been all the years of memory that rose up to support her at that moment. Memory completed by only the understanding of another woman. Whatever it was, and as inarticulate as she had become through those last few years, Jessica told her as best she could.

'You're in a state,' Norma said finally. The practicality in her understatement was cheering.

'You could say that,' Jessica laughed nervously.

'Why don't you come over.'

'Come over?'

'Yes. Come over and stay with me for a while.' She merely said it. Not as a question. Not even really an invitation. More like an order, a statement of what Jessica would be doing next. Norma hadn't changed over the years.

'Just like that?' Jessica said.

'Just like that.'

'There's Bill.'

'He won't mind. He'll probably be pleased to see the back of you.'

Jessica laughed. 'You don't change, Norma Sarrison.'

'Is one supposed to?'

'I'll ask Bill, about coming I mean.'

'Good. That's settled then.'

Jessica wanted time to think. She wasn't sure about hurtling off across the Atlantic, best friend or not. She didn't make decisions that quickly these days. She didn't make decisions.

'I need you,' Norma said. Plainly. Simply. And then, 'It's been too long.' They seemed to have discarded each other with much more ease than they had discarded their youth.

'Let me talk to Bill,' Jessica said. 'I'll talk to you again tomorrow.' There were times of trouble when friends needed to be face to face. Why had they been so foolish to let each other go and to fill their lives with men?

'D'you mind?' she asked Bill. 'What do you think? Should I go?'

'It'll do you good.'

'Thank you,' she said. Her smile was sweet. He smiled back and patted her outstretched hand, managing to be patronizing more than loving, which had not been his intention.

In bed that night his arms held her briefly, without passion, and there was always comfort in his familiar gentleness. But the back of his neck as he turned away, wanting nothing else from her these days, filled her with relief and made her sad at the same time. She wondered about desire and her lack of it. Then she lay awake for hours and stared at the ceiling, lit by a full moon through the undrawn curtains. Had she been manipulated into something she would be unable to handle? Was going away from everything that was familiar to her really the answer? She dreaded change. Longed only for what she had once been. And running away never helped anyone.

But she'd tried everything else. If there was anything to do in the rest of this leftover life of hers maybe away from all her loved ones would be the only way to find it.

Chapter Three

She left for Los Angeles three weeks later.

'Do you mind me going?' she asked Stephen, visiting with Charlie and Sam the day before she left. 'Will you all be all right?' One word, one shadow of hesitation across his face and the air tickets would have been in the bin. But he grinned, and hugged her, her gentle and loving first-born, growing more like his father as each year went by.

'Mum, don't worry about us. This is *your* treat. Time to enjoy. We'll all be fine.'

'Look after your dad.' She held on to him, hating to miss all the day-to-day details of his existence which, since he'd left home, she never could or would remember were his alone to make or ruin. Commonsense told her she couldn't take every sadness from her children, couldn't make all their days perfect, couldn't protect them from disillusion. It would be as selfish to withhold the pain of life as it would be to stop the joy.

'They have a right to their own mistakes,' Bill had once remarked quietly when she'd threatened to interfere in a romance that had gone wrong for the then teenage Stephen.

'But she's breaking his heart,' she'd cried, feeling her son's pain.

'It's *his* heart, Jessica.'

But she wanted them back as small children when 'mummy could kiss the place to make it better'. Los Angeles was thousands of miles away. Too far for even a mother's arms to reach.

'You have Auntie Norma's number,' she said, 'call me at any time. Promise me. Reverse the charges. She won't mind.' She kissed and hugged and cried them goodbye that Sunday evening as they piled into cars and disappeared back on to the A3. It had made them tease her until she felt quite stupid. And, that night, she was glad of Bill's arms. 'It's just a holiday, Jessica. Everyone takes a holiday sometimes. It's not the end of the world, people come home. Life carries on.'

He had booked her an open return ticket, first class. She hoped they could afford all the spoiling she was getting. Bill drove her to the airport. It was raining, which seemed right for Monday, an English springtime, and 'goodbye' smiles.

'It's warm here, Jess. Bring jeans and shirts. We can shop for anything else. Are you excited? I am. I'll see you at LA airport. Monday afternoon.'

'Thank you.' Somehow it was the only thing she could find to say to Bill as they stood awkwardly together, bereft of meaningful conversation, holding hands before she disappeared through passport control.

'What for, Jessie? Just come home feeling well.' He paused, desperate in his search for tact, finding it hard to edit his conversation to a partner of thirty years. 'I only want the old Jessica back. I'm lost without her.'

Me too, my darling. The endearment died before it reached her lips.

Then he was gone, with no words of love to speed him comfortably home, and she was alone on the other side of the barrier, panic nestling in her breast, in spite of the single valium she had succumbed to after much persuasion from the well-intentioned Betty, at the thought of the weeks ahead of her without Bill's strength.

Two glasses of champagne on top of the tranquillizer led her quickly and quietly into a dreamless sleep within the first forty-five minutes of the journey. She missed the lunch and woke after a surprising five hours, confused and extremely hungry. But at least her empty stomach was to be appeased. It was time to eat again. Tomato sandwiches and small scones with weak tea. Only flight hours from home and already the art of British teamaking was lost. In the suitcase, amongst the T-shirts and too many family photographs, was a large packet of extra strong teabags. 'For God's sake, bring them, Jessica, or you'll be on the first plane back!'

'Vacation or business trip?' The man with the west coast accent beside her opened the conversation with a smile that displayed the most beautiful set of teeth Jessica had seen in a long time.

'Vacation.' Her heart sank at the thought of small talk with a stranger. The confidence that radiated from so many Americans, often sorely envied by people like herself, led them easily into short-term acquaintances. She used to love them for it, years ago, when other people's lives were almost as fascinating to her as her own, and she enjoyed the abandoned exposure of a stranger's existence spilled without reserve into her ready ears. These days she wanted only good old-fashioned English reticence to confront her on her travels.

'Not the first time in the States surely?' He was still smiling. Amazing how her surly face in no way deterred him.

'No.' She wanted him to go away. Unreasonable of her, considering where they were. She would rather have liked to sit and be miserable on her own. The English understand so well the comfort of misery. They leave you to it. Avert their eyes from yours in an embarrassment hidden by arrogance. The relentless pursuit of happiness consumed every American Jessica had ever met. It seemed it was their right, their destiny, and if it vanished from their horizon for a second it was chased and reclaimed through any means available.

Maybe that was what Bill hoped for her. She gritted her teeth. Couldn't he tell that her depression was the only spark she had left? The only way she knew she still mattered? And as much as she would have liked to be 'the old Jessica' again, she suspected chaos was the one thing of which she could be certain.

Then, to her extreme embarrassment, the thought made her cry. She wanted to hide in her own bed, weep in her own garden, disappear beneath the willow tree, and drink un-iced gin standing over her own increasingly awful culinary efforts for a husband who didn't complain and had never demanded a smiling face at the end of his day.

'Are you OK, Ma'am?' Solicitous, the man behind the teeth at her side leaned towards her.

'Thank you, yes. I'm not a good traveller that's all. If you'll excuse me?' She stood up, the finished tea tray held high in her hands. Then the flight attendant was there to take it. 'I'm going to the lavatory,' Jessica said, and trembled all the way to the vacant toilet at the front of the first-class seats.

'Can I get you anything?' The girl who had taken the tea tray and witnessed the tears spoke as Jessica's hand reached out to open the door to the bathroom.

'Maybe a gin and tonic in about five minutes would be a good idea,' Jessica said. And closed the door on her smiling face. The light came on. She sunk onto the toilet seat. Alone at last. Except by this time she'd begun to see the funny side of it. Until somebody tried the locked door and she heard a woman's voice outside asking if she was all right. She splashed water onto her flushed face, making her skin feel tight, and then she was ready to face the remainder of the journey.

The man beside her smiled, but read a magazine and asked no questions. She clutched her gin and tonic, stared out of the window, and wondered what Stephen, Sam and Charlie were doing, and if they'd phoned their father yet.

Later, nursing a full stomach after devouring smoked salmon and stuffed chicken breast, a shared bottle of recommended Californian wine with the man by her side, and she was ready to enter into any sort of conversation, as long as it didn't involve personal disclosure. It could well have been the Chardonnay after the gin, but David (for that was his name) proved to be quite charming and shallow enough not to make her guilty if she never availed herself of the business card he pressed into her hand as the plane came in to land. It took Jessica by no surprise that he was a dentist. 'I could tell that by your beautiful teeth,' she said.

A seething mass of humanity swirled around her at LA airport, a melting pot of language and culture. Jessica's heart beat fast, the forgotten excitement of America settled on her as she faced the immigration officer with her usual trepidation.

Flushed with alcohol and jet-lag she forced her

lips into what she hoped was an ingratiating smile, and wished Bill was here with his frantic whisper at times like these, 'For God's sake, stop looking so guilty. They'll search the bags and find the cocaine!', which, of course, would throw her into hysterics in case anyone believed him.

'How long do you intend to stay in the United States, Ma'am?' Not a glimmer of friendliness lit up the face of the young man sitting at passport control. He looked up briefly, but confronting the woman that stood before him with that extra-ordinary smile on her face, weary, red-eyed, over fifty, invisible, he shifted his bored but suspicious gaze back to her spanking new maroon European passport.

'I'm just visiting a friend,' she mumbled.

'That's not what I asked you, Ma'am.'

She felt the sweat trickling down her underarms. His interest in her confusion was minimal. 'I have an open return,' she said, hoping her middle-class English accent would strike terror in his American heart. 'Is that not allowed?'

He shifted in his seat, sighed, pressed keys on a computer in front of him, threw an unintelligible remark over his shoulder to a passing companion and finally raised his eyes to have a good look at what she hoped was the friendly and innocent look on her face.

The thought of seeing Norma lay ahead of her. 'I'm staying with friends in Beverly Hills. The address is on the form. She's meeting me. My friend, that is. She's a resident. Married to an American. I expect to go home in about a month. I have a husband in Sussex. Children. A dog.'

The dog did it. She panted her way triumphantly to the luggage claim and put herself into the large, strong hands of the tallest and most handsome African-American porter she could find. The stirring in her loins brought a real smirk to her face, and he smiled back at her as he swung the battered old suitcases around with such ease she could have sworn her heart got almost fluttery. Quite sorry to lose him at the bottom of the ramp, and pleased as punch that for a brief moment his masculinity had made her feel alive again, she overtipped him. American men were amazingly sexy, she thought. She was either getting better quicker than even Bill had imagined, or else she was completely out of control.

Then, suddenly, Norma's face was there in the crowd, and Norma's hands waving frantically, hysterically, the way she'd done at school when cheering for Jessica at netball a hundred years ago, standing on the sidelines, yelling herself hoarse, glad she'd never made the team, hating sport as she did, but joyful for her lanky, redheaded friend as the ball fell into the net seemingly without effort.

The baggage trolley was heavy and unwieldy. Her cases packed with things she would never wear. Her friendly dentist had long since vanished into the waiting arms of his family, recognized by

Jessica immediately because they all had the same dazzling smiles.

'You're crying already,' Norma laughed as they hugged and clung together.

'The immigration terrorized me as always. They all give me the same feeling Miss Jones did in Geography. Remember? I was convinced he thought I'd come to murder the President. Is it the eyebrows, d'you think? They must make me look sinister. I'm so pleased to see you. Why on earth has it been so long?'

They stood back and stared at each other. Devoured familiar faces. 'You haven't changed a bit!' The practised lie fell from their lips simultaneously and they laughed ruefully. Holding onto each other's hands, eyes surrounded by more laughlines than either of them could have envisaged in never-to-be-forgotten schoolgirl springtimes, lips torn between words and smiles, they kissed and stammered inadequate 'greetings', until Norma turned and nodded to a uniformed man standing patiently behind her.

'José, can you get the car? If you take the luggage we'll wait by the pick-up point until you get back.' And then to Jessica, 'Darling, I'm sorry. This is José. He drives us.'

They held hands as they waited. Polite questions. 'How was the journey? Is Bill OK? What about the boys? So long since I've seen them. What a dreadful godmother I am. Are you very tired?'

Jessica could only say eventually, 'Norma Sarrison, you've got a chauffeur. How very clever of you.'

She was high with excitement and nervous exhaustion by the time they sat at last in 'we call this the library' at Norma's house. A housekeeper had greeted them – 'This is Maria' – José had disappeared with the suitcases up the wide staircase where apparently her travel-creased clothes would be unpacked for her in spite of her vague and not too passionate protestations. And Norma had opened a bottle of champagne that was waiting on ice as Jessica sank into the bottomless comfort of a Californian eight-foot sofa which didn't even look overpowering in the enormous pastel-coloured room.

'I could get used to this,' she sighed, enjoying the sensual tiredness that was creeping over her, and taking the glass from Norma's outstretched hand.

'I have.' The tone in Norma's voice jarred unexpectedly on Jessica's ears, but she pushed it away, hating to relinquish the comfort of the ambience that had so surprisingly found her. Maybe her imagination as well as the jet-lag were playing tricks.

They sat and looked at each other, faces wreathed in idiotic grins. 'Are you really here, Jess? I mean, *really* here, without the rest of your tribe. Who would have thought I could wrestle you free with such ease? Times *have* changed.'

'They couldn't wait to be rid of me if you insist on the truth.'

'Should you call Bill?' Norma said.

'It's the middle of the night there. He'll keep until tomorrow.' Jessica wanted no intrusion into the sight of Norma sitting there in front of her. She was afraid if she moved, brought England and family into this magical circle that engulfed them, then she might spoil those first hours of just being the two of them.

'Where's Chuck?' Jessica said at last.

A cloud crossed Norma's beautiful and expensively made-up face. There was no denying it. The smell of unhappiness, albeit faint and as yet unspoken, merged and competed with the aroma of rich perfume that rose from the human warmth that was Norma to invade that perfect and delectable dream of a Hollywood home.

'He's sorry he couldn't be here to greet you.' She stood to pour more champagne, her face turned away for only seconds. When she faced Jessica again, she was smiling. 'He'll be here tomorrow. You'll see him at breakfast. Are you hungry? Can I make you a sandwich?'

They went through to the kitchen, Jessica behind, wondering what pearl of contention was spoiling the oyster of such a seemingly delectable life, wondering suddenly who would be helping who over the weeks ahead. Her eyes on the chandeliers in the hall and dining-room as they passed into the kitchen began to feel 'a little spaced out', as her Charlie would say. Norma turned and squeezed her hand. Norma, who had grown rich, and probably spoiled, in the last six years.

'I sent Maria off tonight. I wanted you all to myself. I still can't quite believe a mess of boys and dogs won't spill through the door at any given moment!' She laughed, and opened the door of a fridge that looked as big as a cupboard. 'Unlike you, my darling, I can still cook.'

'You've been talking to Bill.' Jessica realized she'd probably known it all along. Norma's phone call out of the blue like that. Obvious really, that only Bill, sensible man that he was, would finally realize, and indeed hope, that Norma, and only Norma, could probably be all their salvations. 'What did he tell you?'

'Now don't be cross, Jess. He's worried sick and he loves you very much.'

'I'm not, and I know.' And she wasn't. She was glad. Clever old Bill, sending her to the one person who wouldn't let her wallow in comfortable misery.

'Do you still eat those dreadful sandwiches?' Norma said, searching and then finding a packet of thinly sliced bread.

'Oh, yes, what do you have?' They stood together and looked into the enormous fridge. 'Good God, Norma, every single thing in this fridge is fat free, sugar free, and salt free. Don't you have anything that resembles real food?'

Norma threw back her head and laughed, the way she'd always done as a girl, vulgar, with genuine mirth, a sound that made a stranger think she couldn't possibly be a 'lady'. It filled Jessica with joy.

'You seem just the same to me,' Norma said eventually. 'Are you really suffering from depression?'

'If being unable and unwilling to move forward in any sort of emotional direction, and crying over baby photos of the boys, of not being any sort of wife to Bill, to feel as if the best part of my life is over, to drink too much, and basically be a pain in the neck to everyone that crosses my path; if all that spells severe depression, then yes, I am. There are times it feels like madness.'

Norma handed her the sandwich of fat free cream cheese, low salt peanut butter, and sugarless strawberry jam. 'Bill also warned me you'd become inarticulate,' she said with a straight face.

Jessica laughed loudly and took a bite of the food in her hand. 'This food has no taste,' she grimaced. 'Haven't you got any pickle?'

Jet-lag eventually won out and Norma took her upstairs to the large guest room, and turned down the bed as Jessica got undressed in a soporific haze, content with only a perfunctory cleansing of the face. 'The boys will be getting up now,' she said, as her head met the pillow that looked as big as a mattress. And she muttered, 'America's so enormous,' as her friend left the room. There was no reply, and anyway, she could not have explained why she'd said it. But the thought pleased her, and she smiled her way into her dreams that night, enjoying the feeling of being uncrowded.

Sometime during the night, or even the polluted Hollywood dawn, sun gulping for breath, Jessica seemed to hear voices raised in anger, or perhaps it was a dream. Somehow Norma's tones, vibrant with hysteria, struggled through her consciousness. Or was it herself, crying out for something? Then a man's voice, reasoning, patience turning rapidly to irritability, becoming an exasperated Bill as she fell again into a deeper sleep, the dreams following, changing story lines, but travelling the same path. The road was familiar, mapped out by her own footsteps. Charlie, Sam, Stephen, tumbling in with demands she couldn't meet. Then Bill again. And then his usually gentle smile turning inwards with impatience. Then it was gone. Reality waited to impose itself.

Morning, midday, life waiting tenaciously for her to wake and cope. Her mother, long dead now, slaughtered by a cancer she'd passed unknowingly to a now cured daughter, pushed her away and into the American morning. Afraid, eyes closed, thinking like a child – 'If I can't see them, they can't see me' – she saw her mother's face. Sad, smiling, resigned to the inevitability of her short and tragic forty-six-year-old life. Tears, hot and real, forced Jessica's eyes open, finding her mother's tragedy superior to hers, leaving her with only shame at her own malaise.

'Mummy.' Whispered aloud, a child's word from the breathlessness of a woman too old for that kind of plea, and at her moment of waking Jessica was angry again with herself for the travesty she was making of her own life, a life her mother had earned and never had.

The sun was hot at the window, dancing brazenly through the slats of the vertical blinds. Anger became confusion. Strange furniture all around. A chandelier, brash and dust-free crystal, hanging above the bed, shadows and sunlight competing on every glass pendant. Silk embossed curtains not fully closed, allowing the smiling Californian day to challenge the hangover of a bad dream. Last night's clothes heaped, abandoned as if in haste to accommodate a new lover. No Bill at her side. Unbroken pillow smelled only of unfamiliar perfume, more reminiscent of Norma and comfortable wealth than her bed at home, with its faint aroma of labrador and Old Spice.

Depression easily finds the path to the soul those first moments when the dream fades. Mornings are bad for the disillusioned, waking as one does with too much apathy to fight the blues. They get in quickly while you're still thinking of something else, and then they're not easy to shake. But that first morning, what with the sunshine, and the strange surroundings, they found Jessica difficult to locate. Then, before she could gather the strength to open herself to the first exquisite moments of misery, there was Norma's voice in her ear, Norma's smell, and smile, and touch, leaning over, pulling her up, stroking her face with delight. 'You are awake, aren't you, darling? Do you want juice? Tea? Did I wake you?'

Jessica let herself be pulled upright. And for one glorious moment she greeted the day like a girl again. 'Don't you dare give me juice,' she muttered, pretending to be cross, still sleepy. 'You know it makes my stomach curl at this hour. I have some decent tea in my bag. Can you find it? Along with my dressing gown?'

'You can borrow one of mine. Try the hook behind the bathroom door, and Jessica Byfleet, I intend to make you healthy while you're here. I realize the thought is abhorrent to you, but you'll have to suffer it. This is California. Healthy body, healthy mind. It's easier to believe that than fight it.' And before Jessica could even inject a groan she went on, 'I'll get Maria to squeeze some oranges and I'll stand over you while you drink it. Your vitamins will be by the glass. See you downstairs.'

She'd gone before there was time to retort. But Jessica was smiling at the familiar and comfortable bossiness that came so easily to Norma.

*   *   *

'You called me Jessica Byfleet.' Dressed and showered, towel wrapping shampooed hair, she was smiling as she stood in the bright, large kitchen and drank the bittersweet juice that the housekeeper had prepared.

'Isn't that your name?' Norma put tea in front of her, 'Or have you so easily discarded your own identity?'

'I've felt like that nice Mrs Wooldridge for longer than I care to mention. Even Mrs *William* Wooldridge actually. Not very liberated of me, is it?'

Norma smiled. 'You never were liberated, Jess. You merely wanted to be. We all did. Maybe that's what's gone wrong. *Has* it all gone wrong? Or is is just the aftermath of cancer?'

Through the window, geraniums and impatiens were growing with ridiculous strength and abundance, and Jessica, taking in the colours, was silent for a moment, not wanting to think about the bad things, not ready yet for an opening of the heart. Too early in the morning, and the good feeling of the day was too vulnerable.

She said finally, 'D'you know, you're the only one to say the word cancer to me? Isn't that unbelievable?' She turned back to watch her friend making toast, filling the air with the smell of family breakfasts through the years. A nursery comfort, almost alien, mixed with the high glamour of that Beverly Hills house. 'No-one else seems able to utter the word. Not Bill, not the boys. Not even the bloody doctor, for God's sake. Can you believe the whole damn lot of them are that coy?'

Norma put the finished toast on the table between them. From another room the sound of vacuuming began. 'Why are you so surprised, Jess? You're afraid and unhappy. They love you. In their misguided wisdom they truly think that's the best way to handle you.'

'If *I* can say it, and cope with it in the only way I know how, why the hell can't my nearest and dearest understand? Anyway,' Jessica turned again to the window. Two gardeners were mowing the lawn and dodging sprinklers that watered the beds, 'anyway, it's not just the cancer. At least, I don't think so. All that did was knock in the final nail and induce anger in the one breast I have left.' She laughed ruefully at the imagery, 'It's stupid, but my life burst into one big cliché as soon as I hit the change. I found it hard to believe I could be so *average*. Ludicrous.' She looked at her friend then. Norma's morning face looked weary. Jessica remembered the dream.

'Is Chuck here?' she said.

'Been and gone, darling. Sorry about that. He's burning the candle these days, what with the slump in realty and everything.'

'Is it serious? The slump, I mean. Is it as bad as England? Could it be? It seems to have killed the spirit back home.'

Norma pulled a face and busied herself un-necessarily at the clean tiled surface beside the microwave. 'He says nothing, but I think we're probably all right. Chuck's money is very much family based, *old* money, so to speak. Hard for us working-class girls to comprehend. Just making less profit from the business has thrown him, I suspect. The richer one gets, the more riches one wants. We don't discuss it.'

'What about you,' Jessica said, 'are you still happy, in love, whatever?'

Norma smiled, reached across and took her friend's hand, stopping her in the middle of cramming her mouth with hot buttered toast. 'What a surprise,' she replied, 'you're still a romantic.'

'Ballocks.'

'See what I mean?'

Easy rapport as if they'd never been apart. Jessica said, 'Don't make me smile too much, Norma Matherson, I might have to start enjoying life again, and I'm afraid I may have lost the knack. I've got the hang of misery. Even begun to enjoy it. Gives me something to think about. It's not as exhausting as happiness somehow. And people avoid you. I like that these days.'

'Happiness is an illusion, Jess, you have to lie to yourself to survive.'

Jessica said nothing. Norma's statement seemed to be wiser than any conclusions they'd come to in their youth. 'Are you still hungry?' Norma removed the empty toast plate.

'Of course. Some things never change. I drink

a lot as well.' Jessica looked up at her, 'or did my better half inform you of that as well?'

'Only a hint. Or rather, not in so many words. Good old loyal Bill. He doesn't change either, does he?'

'Maybe he should.'

Norma raised her eyebrows.

Jessica shifted in her seat, aware of the scrutiny, wondering just how much of herself she would be able to reveal to even a best and dearest friend. It wasn't as if she actually *knew* what went on inside her own head at all these days. Here she was in this strange and perfect house, aware of it trying so hard to be a home, clean and neat, and empty, flowers in every alcove, struggling in their Californian loveliness to perfume the loneliness that all at once was so apparent.

'Your home is beautiful Norma.'

'Isn't it just? Designed by committee and scrubbed by others. Belonging to everyone but me. Who would've thought it?'

Emotions of their other lives hung tentatively between them. Smiling again, they acknowledged it with a silence born of trust. 'What plans do you have,' Jessica said. 'To do with me today, I mean?'

'Are you jet-lagged?'

'I don't know, I always feel like this.'

Norma drove them a mere two short blocks in her Mercedes sports to sit amongst tubs of flowers in bright sunshine and drink coffee from white mugs and watch Jessica devour blueberry scones and too much butter. 'You'll be enormous when you go home,' she said, always amazed at the size of Jessica's appetite.

'When did I care about such trivia?'

'I wonder if you'd change if you actually lived here?' Norma mused. 'Probably not. Although fat is a dirty word in Hollywood. Look around you. What d'you see? Did you think all these people were running for buses? Not a bit of it. They *exercise*. Then they eat. Then they go to the gym.' She leaned forward, 'Let me explain something to a visiting alien.'

'Is that you or me?'

'You, you fool.'

'Are you a citizen these days?'

'No. Never will be. I want to die in England. Have my ashes scattered under a gnarled apple tree somewhere.'

'Are there no apple trees in California?'

'Not one that's been allowed to gnarl. They'd be sent to therapy if there were as much as a bent twig.'

'Poor apple trees.'

It was not the lack of freedom for nature they mourned. Jessica wondered if the edge in Norma's voice, the bitterness in the irony, would loosen her tongue right there and then. She hated the sadness on her friend's face, and with selfishness born of pain, she found herself wanting only her own problems to be the centre of any depression that was making the rounds. Eventually she said, 'What were you saying?'

'Oh yes,' Norma continued, 'American fast food and how you will love it. Fatty hamburgers in sweet white buns—'

'Yummy.'

'What you do is work out at the gym for an hour or two, specially if you're an actor, and remember, most people in this monstrous town are connected in some way with the movies; anyway if you exercise that much it gives you a golden, if insubstantial, reason to stuff your face in between times. They work it off, you see. At least, that's what's supposed to happen.' She patted her stomach, 'I'm old-fashioned. I believe you must starve to stay thin. It's deathly dull but my vanity still thrives as much as it ever did, I'm afraid, only not enough for me to work up a sweat more than once or twice a week. I prefer hunger to hot armpits. On the other hand, *you* were never vain.'

There was a timbre in her voice that fell uneasily on sensitive ears. Jessica had begun to realize that Norma's dreams of the perfect existence, so long awaited, might well have gone awry. A waiter refilled their coffee cups. And eventually the small talk ran out, and they sat there, staring out into the hot and noisy street. A stunning quiet fell like a sheet of glass between them, and neither of them could find a way to break it. Arriving late in the day, misery came like indigestion to Jessica, and settled relentlessly at the top of her chest. She was afraid she'd come all these miles to find a solace that was no longer available. Eventually, she put out a hand to touch her friend. Moisture, the beginning of an embarrassment of tears, glistened at the corners of Norma's kohl made-up eyes as she said, 'How I hate the powerlessness of middle-age.'

'Don't.' Jessica's hand stretched across the table, 'Don't, Norma.'

'I'm sorry, Jessica.' Her friend's voice was softer, braver, kinder. 'I didn't sleep.'

Jessica was moved to shame with her own inadequacy.

'What's wrong?'

'Nothing. Silliness. Forget it.' Norma laughed then. 'Would you believe I still get pre-menstrual?'

And without waiting for Jessica's reply, she stood up. 'Come on,' both hands outstretched, pulling her companion to her feet, shaking them both from their lethargy, their self-absorption, 'Let's go and dig Chuck from his office and make him take us to lunch.'

Chapter Four

The thing about Hollywood, as far as Jessica was concerned that first bright morning, full of sunshine, was that it didn't let her down. It was everything that every movie had ever told her it would be. She obviously had not appreciated it in the short time she'd been here for the wedding. Maybe she hadn't wanted it then. Now she did, and it was all there before her eyes. Long avenues lined with manicured palm trees, saving their burst of greenery until the very top of their tall pineapple growth; oversized limousines hiding the wealthy and famous ('and some hope-to-be's' according to Norma) behind opaque windows; jacaranda trees weeping their large purple, scentfree blossoms; Disneyland; beggars on street corners wishing you 'a nice day', the extremes of the wealthy with their facelifts and body tucks, ('penis extensions as well these days,' Norma said); and then, of course, the possibility every day at the very least of an earth tremor. 'As if even the Lord himself had yet to get this spot of paradise right,' Jessica said. 'Still, the big one must have been terrifying. Were you here?'

'No, thank God. We'd gone to New York.

Chuck on business, me to shop. That's the only place to be in January. For the sales, I mean.'

'Did you get much damage?'

'We lost a chimney. And I wanted to be back in Surrey. The after-shocks were almost as horrific. I kept thinking it was going to happen again.'

'How d'you live with that?'

'Part of the deal if you live here, I guess. And everyone gets on with the business of living again with great pragmatism. I believe the earthquake ride at Universal was opened almost immediately.'

Jessica laughed.

'Bad taste trails a mere breath behind the vulgarity of extreme wealth,' Norma went on. 'It's all so seductive, it fills you with an envy that you didn't know you were capable of. Frightful. But I'm as affected as the rest, I'm afraid. A relentless pursuit of money or immortal youth and beauty. You either love or loathe it.'

'Looking at it now, it fascinates me. It didn't before, when we came for the wedding. But then all I could think about then was you living thousands of miles away and there was no-one left in my life with whom I could have our sort of conversations. I thought then I'd hate to live here. I was angry at you for leaving. I wondered how long you'd last.'

Norma didn't answer, and Jessica turned to gaze out of the window again. Los Angeles shrieked at her like the dark side of fairyland. A place where old goblins came in search of their youth, a place to reinvent themselves as Oberons or Titanias. She laughed softly at her own thoughts, and Norma said, smiling, 'What's funny?'

'I don't know. This place, I suppose. I feel quite at home. So many crazies.'

'All in cars, you've noticed.' She leaned heavily on her hooter as a young man shot out in front of them in a well dented yellow convertible without any sort of signal. 'Jesus Christ!' Norma yelled through the open window as the offender raised one hand as if to thank her, music from his stereo blasting into his soon-to-be-deaf ears and across the four lanes of traffic.

Jessica laughed once more with the sheer delight of it all. Sussex would never be the same again.

Norma had never been one of the world's great drivers. Living as she did now, in Hollywood, was obviously life's way of paying her back for all those years in rural England when she had driven too fast and carelessly down narrow country lanes, sending unsuspecting horses rearing in panic as she came upon them too hastily round blind, hawthorn-hedged corners.

'I thought American motorists were the best in the world. You always said that,' Jessica teased.

'That was before I came to LA. They all drive like me. Serves me right, I guess.'

What with the sunshine, and the overpowering noise of car hooters and sirens, there seemed no silence left in her head for Jessica to dwell on depression. She'd swung almost too quickly into a good mood. 'I'm almost delighted to be alive. That's an extremely alien emotion these days. Dangerously seductive, I imagine.'

They pulled into the underground parking lot at Chuck's office and Norma said, 'So you're glad you came?'

'I think I must be. It's all so wonderfully foreign. I'd hate to miss anything, so with any luck there'll be no time to be my usual miserable self.'

'You always used to have such a genius for living. What happens to us?'

Jessica shook her head. 'God knows. He's just not telling.'

They left the car to be valet-parked and went to the elevator. 'Is Chuck all right about me being here?' Jessica asked as they were carried silently and rapidly to the penthouse.

Norma stared straight ahead and spoke without turning, 'My husband is delighted with anything or anybody that keeps me occupied.'

It was hard to imagine a more unsatisfactory reply.

The doors opened and they stepped out into a cold, air-conditioned, luxurious suite of offices. Putting a hand up to her heart, Jessica felt the familiar growth of palpitations that coincided with panic. All because of Norma's remark in the elevator. She guessed she'd walked into a situation with her friend's marriage she might find difficult to comprehend. Disenchantment loomed even with the lunchtime ahead, ruining what had promised to be a delightful day. Other people's troubles. She didn't want to care. Doubted she had the energy. Norma should have warned her before she'd ever stepped on that plane, damn it. Despite the air-conditioning, she could feel the perspiration running down the inside of her too warm English shirt, unidentified smells and strange murmurs filled the atmosphere around her, invading her space. Her heart cried out for a place where the birdsong was gentle, not drowned by traffic, a country where misery was embraced, not denied. A place where she could avoid confrontation, even of herself. She wanted home. 'Will Chuck mind if we just turn up unannounced?' she said at last.

Norma tapped her long red nails on the reception desk, shook her head, and spoke to a tall, long-haired girl. 'Would you tell Mr Sarrison his wife is here with Mrs Wooldridge.'

'Certainly Mrs Sarrison.'

Jessica watched the red tapping nails of her friend and tried to remember when she'd last had a manicure. Maybe before one of the bank's Christmas dances when so much autumn gardening had left her hands in a bad enough condition that even Bill would comment. She pushed her hands into her trouser pockets and, in need of something, anything, to cover her discomfort, she buried her nose into the arrangement of flowers that stood majestically in front of her and breathed deeply. They were artificial.

'Good God!'

Norma burst into laughter. 'You're such a fool Jess, and you will never know how much I've missed you.'

'Is *anything* real?' Jessica whispered.

'Just the hysteria.'

They were shown into Chuck's office. 'Mr Sarrison's in a meeting.' The secretary offered coffee and magazines. 'He'll be with you directly. Can I bring you anything else?'

'Mineral water?' suggested Norma, and arranged herself, somewhat dramatically, on a chaise longue behind a marble coffee table.

The girl left the room before Jessica could find the courage to request a gin and tonic. 'Very few Californians drink at lunch.' Norma had read the expression. 'If you do it often enough some well-meaning acquaintance will drop you a list of addresses for AA meetings. People do business deals there, I'm told.'

'Good grief.'

'Exactly.'

Trouble was, Jessica longed for a drink. It was past her usual tipple time, and she needed that fuzziness to soften the edges of the weeks ahead, let alone the lunch with Chuck, and the unknown territory of his and Norma's marriage. She walked to the window and looked out across Sunset Boulevard. Norma flipped through the pages of *Esquire*. Another long-limbed girl came in flashing yet another Californian smile and carrying two glasses of ice and a bottle of Evian on a tray. Piped music trickled into the room through the open door, and then left them again in silence when the secretary went, hair bouncing with all the zest of a commercial as she closed the door behind her.

Norma tipped the contents of both glasses into the waste bin. 'I'm sure your taste doesn't lend itself to all this ice,' she said, and poured water into both glasses. 'The Yanks love it, God bless them. Not that it cools them down any.'

Jessica looked at her carefully. The light from the tinted window played cruelly on what was so obviously a deeply unhappy face. All the make-up in the world would not erase that downward sweep. 'Was this a bad time for me to have come, Norma?' she said, and made her way across the room to join her friend.

Hands reached out to touch one another. Briefly. As if afraid of compassion, and too old for that fear. 'No, Jess. It could never be a bad time for us. Forgive me. I've grown selfish in my middle years.'

'Haven't we all? It's the only thing left when no-one pays attention.'

'I find that hard to believe about Bill.'

'You're right, of course. I've just grown appallingly mean-spirited. It seems to come with the territory. I hate me, so it stands to reason that everyone else should. Take no notice when I say things like that. Ignore me. I'm loved as much as always. It's just that I feel I no longer deserve it, so I do my level best to drive them all away so I can say, "I told you so". There's no solution and no pleasing me. I want to change but I can't, or won't, or I'm too shit scared. Is it the same for you?'

'Same, but different. Except I'm just as scared. To move on, I mean. I always believed that when I eventually "grew up", so to speak, I'd be settled for life and things would remain the same and that's the way I'd want it. Forever and ever, Amen.'

Then the door opened and Chuck came in, both arms outstretched to them, and Jessica stood up to offer her face to be kissed, responding immediately to his warmth that she now remembered. What could be wrong with Norma?

'Jessica, Jessica, this is great. It's been so long. Welcome, welcome to LA. Sorry we missed each other last night. I know Norma will be taking good care of you.'

Not this lovely man, it couldn't be him that was making her friend so unhappy surely. Maybe it was Norma. Maybe she'd fallen in love with someone else. Age didn't always bring wisdom.

'You look so well, Chuck,' Jessica turned to bring Norma into the conversation, 'You both do. Thank you so much for letting me come.'

'It's nothing but a pleasure,' he smiled.

'And keeps me off the streets,' said Norma.

A glance between them, too quick, too furtive

to be interpreted by Jessica's out-of-practice instinct.

'Exactly,' Chuck quipped, an arm around each of their waists, 'Now then, where can I take two such beautiful ladies to lunch? I'm all yours for the next two hours.'

Jessica lay on the Californian king-sized bed later that afternoon and tried to doze away the remains of the jet-lag. West Sussex, Bill, almost everything seemed to have faded so quickly into the jumble inside her head. She'd called home after lunch and had the usual stilted conversation about the food on the plane, and confusion over the time difference, and lots of 'I feel better already' type chat; the kind one has at hospital bedsides when the bell for the end of visiting time is long in coming. Whether it was the jet-lag, or the catapulting of a person who hated change into a strange land, she felt almost as if she were in limbo, looking down on herself from above, wondering who or what that other person was doing in her old body. It seemed that life was going on regardless. Perhaps she was, after all, going mad. Solve a lot of problems. She'd long since begun to envy the certified confused of this world. What a blessed relief, just to opt out and into one's own little impenetrable existence.

'I feel rather peculiar,' Jessica had said in the car after lunch when Norma began driving perilously towards Beverly Hills again. They had toyed with the idea of a drive around to view all the flamboyant homes in the area, but after only two glasses of Chardonnay Jessica apparently looked as strange as she felt, and Norma decided to head straight home.

'You need rest,' she'd said firmly and bundled her friend upstairs to the solitude of the guest room.

Jessica had muttered various things like, 'God, you're so bloody bossy,' and 'I can always sleep tonight,' but she'd not put up much of a fight.

'I'll bring you tea later. You're still disorientated, and the alcohol didn't help. We're dining out tonight, so get yourself some peace and quiet before tackling any of Chuck's friends.'

The tiredness took over, taking Jessica with soporific and pleasant surprise, and the smell of Norma's perfume stayed around her even through her drowsiness. She wanted to say, 'Not your friends, too? Do you and your husband have separate friends, then? Is that how it's done these days?' But there wasn't the time. Norma had already left the room while she was still forming the words.

Deep sleep eluded her. She was aware of drifting in and out of daydreams and daymares, and a confusion of incomprehensible questions and dysfunctional answers concerning her hosts chased themselves round and round in her thoughts. Later, when Norma knocked at the door, the room was dark. The light filtering through half-drawn silk blinds had a sort of polluted gloomy look about it. She sat up too quickly and peered at her friend through the gloom, wondering what strange place they had both found themselves in, or was this still part of the dream? Norma put a hand out and twisted the switch on the bedside table, smiled, sat on the bed, and took Jessica's hand. 'Are you feeling better?' she asked. 'More on this planet, so to speak?'

'I think so. What time is it?'

'Six-thirty.'

'Good grief, in the morning?'

Norma threw her head back and laughed. There were no lines on her neck. Not a blemish. Had she succumbed to the supposedly Hollywood inevitable and had things 'lifted', so to speak? Jessica could hardly wait to ask.

'Don't panic, Jess, it's still Tuesday.'

'Tuesday? The way I feel even that's news to me.'

Norma laughed again. 'We need to leave in about an hour,' she said. 'Are you up to a fun-packed Beverly Hills dinner party?'

'How can I tell? Is it my style? If you can recall what that was, please tell me, because I have very little memory of a single social occasion that was fun-packed.'

'You used to say that all parties were a waste of time once you were spoken for. Don't you remember? "Parties are just for getting laid." Your very words. How could I forget? You were always so adamant.'

'I use them solely to get drunk these days. Not so much fun, but you only feel ill in the morning, instead of embarrassed.' Jessica flung the sheet back and sat on the side of the bed to drink the weak tea Norma had brought. She said, 'What shall I wear? We don't go out much at home any more.'

'It's cocktails, then dinner. Any little dress will do. Nothing is ever that formal here.'

A picture of her black linen dress that had been hung in the wardrobe the previous night, after it had experienced the eleven-hour flight in a badly packed suitcase sprung quickly to mind. 'I'll need an iron,' she said as she threw back the quilt.

'Maria will do it.'

The dress was found and handed over.

'You'll never know how wonderful it is to have you here, Jess.'

Jessica said, 'There's so much to say. I don't know where to start. Or even how to.'

'There'll be another time.' She pulled away and headed for the door. 'Shall I send Maria with a glass of wine for you while you're dressing? You always loved that. Is it still on your agenda?'

'Even more so! I'll never face a whole room full of strange people without a little help.'

She left the room, calling over her shoulder, 'Chuck will meet us there. OK?' And she was gone. Down the wide staircase to call for wine from a housekeeper, who would no doubt bring it on a silver tray, pale and well chilled, in a crystal glass, asking if there was 'anything else I could do for you, Madam', and 'Here is your dress, Mrs Wooldridge, do you have everything you need for your bath?'

Norma's world, on the surface, seemed to be paradise. So why the restlessness? Why the disillusion in the eyes? Wouldn't it be terrible if, when girlhood dreams came true, they all turned out to be nightmares?

The seduction of wealth was everywhere. Hot bath towels like sheets to wrap around a damp body when stepping from a shower that to Jessica's eyes looked and felt as big as a room, an array of perfumes and body oils laid out in well-ordered colours to match the decor, even the towelling gown placed on the bed matched the pink in the wallpaper. 'It's like a photo session for *Hello* magazine,' she muttered gleefully to herself, determined to remember every detail to carry home with her, and wondering if Bill, or indeed herself, could ever live in what seemed such a contrived environment.

The glass of wine was waiting. Quietly brought by Maria, along with the black linen, better pressed than it deserved. Churlish to find such perfection irritating, even for a brief moment. She found her far from clean make-up bag that held her collection of ancient tubes and packages of out-of-date Max Factor. Make-up had never been an interest of hers, not even as a teenager. Norma had always been the one with the very latest mascara or lipstick. She'd been crazy about false eyelashes when they'd been all the rage in the Sixties, insisted on experimenting with them on any volunteer. At one stage, she even managed to glue the damn things onto Jessica's eyelids upside down, leaving her poor friend to spend the entire Boys' Brigade Christmas dance leering at her very-hard-come-by date through what must have looked like, and indeed felt like, nylon spiders' legs. The memory made her smile, and she began to stroke mascara onto her lashes. So out of practice was she, it was all she could do to avoid sticking it in her eye.

She had thanked Maria profusely on the return of the black linen. 'It looks almost new again,' she'd enthused, which was so patently untrue the housekeeper scuttled away with embarrassment as if she'd been given a tip. She smiled to herself, wondered as she'd often done if the English were sometimes a disappointment to the untravelled American. Norma believed they expected the Brits to behave as they did in a Merchant-Ivory film. Romantic and gentle. Speaking with restraint and perfect grammar. Confusing when faced with the reality of a culture and society long gone. Jessica rubbed a tissue over her old pair of black patent shoes. No wonder Bill was always saying, 'Go out and get some new clothes. We can afford it for God's sake.' But she loathed clothes shopping.

Even in her good days she preferred grocery shopping to the patronizing veneer of the department store. Every article of clothing she possessed had been good and fashionable some years ago. But then, they no longer went anywhere that called for anything more than the occasional new anorak.

Ready at last, she made her way down the staircase and stood feeling lost in the marble hall.

'Norma?'

'I'm in here, on the telephone, come and help yourself to more wine.'

It was the room she'd called the study. The bottle of Chardonnay stood elegantly in a crystal bowl full of ice. Norma motioned her to help herself, and having forgotten to bring the used glass from upstairs, she half-filled another that was standing ready.

'How do I look?' Jessica said tentatively when her friend had put the phone down, 'Will I do?'

Without answering Norma came across and hugged her.

'What's that for?' Jessica sounded surprised. 'And watch the linen. You know how it creases!'

'Just that all at once I saw the young girl again in your face. You were always convinced you were wearing the wrong clothes wherever we went. Remember? It took me back, back to the days when everything was possible, and we never knew the next adventure until it happened.'

'You look beautiful,' Jessica smiled, and because she was filling up nicely thank-you with that style of aggressive confidence that alcohol can give you, went on, 'Have you had your face lifted?'

'Isn't it great?' Norma moved her face from side to side, encouraged by the interested curiosity.

'Did it hurt?' Jessica touched her friend's face very gently. It was the first 'lift' she'd come across, and she found herself intrigued.

'Like hell.'

'God, you're braver than me.' And she shuddered.

'No, darling. Just more desperately vain.'

Jessica peered intently into all the shadows of that so familiar face. 'Did it change anything?' she said, 'I mean in your life or anything?'

'Not a thing. Silly, isn't it? What can I say?' She laughed. Brittle. Frightened.

'What about Chuck?' Jessica was curious, 'Didn't he mind? I believe Bill would divorce me.'

Norma turned away and put her empty glass behind her onto the bar. 'Aah, but Bill is Bill, bless him. I don't think I told Chuck.'

'You don't *think*!'

'He was away on business or something, and when he came home I don't believe he noticed. Telling him seemed irrelevant.' She turned back, smiling brightly, falsely, desperately, 'That's men for you.'

Jessica frowned briefly, then touched Norma's arm, 'Well, I think you look stunning. Not that I could ever be tempted. There's no-one's desires

I want to fuel these days, not even my own. Passion hasn't been on my list for longer than I care to remember.'

'I would never have believed I'd ever hear you say that. My God, you were the most rampant of us all.'

Jessica looked down at the glass in her hand. The words were whispered. 'It was all for babies. All for sons. Except I never knew that until after Stephen was born. No-one told me in my teens how all-consuming being a mother would be. No-one warned me it was all I'd ever want.'

Then she looked up, smiled grimly, ashamed of her silliness when she had so much. 'Listen to me,' she said. 'It's the wine. Damn my emotions. I shouldn't drink. I've been told and told. That's half the reason I do it. I loathe the way everyone believes they know how to help depression when it's so obvious they don't. *I* don't for God's sake, and it's *my* depression.'

'Is there a lot of "pull yourself together"?' Norma's voice was gentle, her hands soft on her friend's arm. The hands of a lady, Jessica's mother would say, a lady that does no chores.

'They've stopped saying that. Most people have given up.'

'You as well?'

'Good God, yes. Giving up came easy. Travelling through the days is the hard bit.'

Norma said, 'D'you want more wine? Or daren't you risk it?'

'Do you really want me drunk when I meet your friends?'

'It never shows with you, Jess. Never used to anyway. Used to make me frightfully envious, watching you drink. I believed you must have hollow legs. That, and being lovely and tall.'

'I get nasty with it these days. So Bill tells me. It's my belief I always was. Nasty that is. I just sat on it to get what I wanted.'

Norma laughed. 'I don't believe a word of it! You've had a lot to be depressed about. What with the operation. You just need something different in your life. Make you believe there's more to you than just babies and youth.'

'Now there's a thought. A reinvention you mean? Like the movies?'

Norma laughed again, 'Don't knock it till you've tried it, girl. Now, drink up and we'll go. José will drive us. We'll be able to get pissed as hell and swim naked in the pool. Nobody would bat an eyelid. They'll put it down to European decadence. They expect it of us. Gives them a chance to feel superior.'

'I like Americans. I thought you did. Why have you gone off them?'

'I haven't really. Their lack of cynicism gets me down sometimes. And I realize that's not in the least fair as it was exactly that very characteristic that made me so disgruntled with the English. Cynicism, I mean. I hate it so, and the Brits are superb at it. Still, the Americans are better mannered than we are. At least they seem to be. And at least they're positive. Ignore me. I'll be fine when I get there. A credit to any party, and a wonderful ambassador for tired old Britain.'

'Does Chuck know how lucky he is?'

'You'd better believe it!' And she laughed in a way that chilled the heart, took her friend's hand and led her out into the front drive, stopping only to pick up and throw round her shoulders a very expensive-looking fur coat.

'Mink?' Jessica said. 'In this weather?'

'Yes. It makes me feel like an expensive hooker. I suspect that's why my loving husband bought it for me. Don't look like that, as if you don't approve.'

'I don't disapprove of the *fur*. It's my kids who have insisted I can't even wear my old fox cape any more. It seems quite ridiculous when the silly thing has been dead for years as it is. We all eat meat so I'm not sure we're politically correct anyway.'

'Politically correct. Well, well – I must remember all this when I next visit. I don't want them hating their favourite aunt, even if she has become stinking rich.'

Chapter Five

At her first Beverly Hills party Jessica had rather been looking forward to tasting a 'perfect manhattan', or something at least as American. But it was champagne they were offered. Never one of her favourite drinks. 'Lot of fuss about nothing really,' she'd once remarked to Bill. 'Gives me a headache and makes me sick in the morning.'

But she took the drink from an outstretched tray and was pulled into a group of people by Norma to be introduced. The black linen was horribly creased after the car ride and she could feel the static of her underslip pulling it against her thighs. The room was noisy and their hosts had been over-zealous with the air-conditioning. Norma whispered, 'Come through to the other room, I believe there's a fire.'

Jessica raised her eyebrows. 'A *fire*? It's eighty degrees outside. No wonder they need cold air. Are they mad?'

Her friend pushed her gently in the back. 'You're in Hollywood. When you like log fires you light one.'

'They are mad.' A glass of champagne later and she felt brave enough to wander round the room by herself. She studied the paintings on the walls for want of something better to do, and because it prevented her from a face-to-face with too many strangers. She was very hungry, and wondered when dinner was being served. The doors to the large terrace were open and she could see the trees and bushes in the garden lit up with white lights. 'And it's not even Christmas,' she muttered to herself.

Everyone around her was confident and bright, or so it seemed. So much to say to each other, so many positive attitudes filled the atmosphere she found it quite daunting. Passing Norma as she made her way to the buffet table on the terrace she murmured, 'Not a bit like Betty's on Boxing day is it?'

But people smiled at her, drew her in, and she couldn't help but warm to them. She found a waiter eventually who had a tray of canapés in his hand, and she took three, which was all she could hold in her one free hand, and one of the eggs looked suspiciously like it was stuffed with genuine caviar. Then she stood alone for a while and surveyed the scene. What felt like excitement was stirring inside her. As if something was about to happen, she thought. And then, 'I like being away from home,' she remarked to Norma as her friend grabbed her arm and led her to the long buffet where everyone else was beginning to fill their plates.

'They all have perfectly wonderful bodies,' she

said suddenly, and much later, when everyone was drinking coffee, and she was trying to find the courage to ask one of the waiters to bring her another plate of food. She hadn't seen one person ask for 'seconds', and she was beginning to wonder if it was the done thing.

'Who has?' Norma looked around her. 'D'you mean all these too thin and too rich Hollywood ladies?'

'I'm talking about the waiters, for God's sake.'

'You're not that ill then.'

'I was merely remarking. Believe me, I never feel like doing anything about it any longer. Sex stays where it starts as far as I'm concerned. In the imagination. I'm far too exhausted for activity of any kind.'

Norma said nothing.

'Mind you,' Jessica went on, 'I've been trying to catch the eye of the blond one over there for the last five minutes, but only to get me more food. Why does no-one pay any attention to the middle-aged?'

'You wouldn't get that much attention from him if you were a blond twenty-two-year old with the biggest breasts in the room, darling. He's gay.'

'Oh.'

Chuck arrived as she started on her second plate of food. He came and greeted them both. Norma offered him her cheek. 'Enjoying yourself, Jessica?' Chuck kept his hand on her shoulder as he smiled down at her.

'I think so,' she said. 'We're not used to all this glitter in West Sussex.'

He nodded vaguely, the way people do when they're less than fascinated with the company involved. His eyes roamed the room. 'Excuse me Jessica, I'll be back.'

'He never listens. It's not you, I assure you.' Norma watched her husband as he propelled himself into a group of friends with obvious enthusiasm.

Bill always listened, Jessica thought. She just wasn't certain if he always heard. All at once she missed him. She stared at her watch. The one he'd painstakingly chosen for her fiftieth birthday, forgetting the others he'd bought when she'd reached twenty, thirty and forty. Watches she had an abundance of, sitting unused and unwound in the old jewellery box on the kidney-shaped dressing table she had inherited from her mother, and which now inhabited the smallest spare room at the end of the corridor in the Sussex house. It sat in front of the window, and in the few weeks that made up an English summer, the sun would touch it, pushing triumphantly through the net curtains and onto the aging mahogany, rickety drawers creaking open to show the odd lurking mothball, and still the faintest hint of Coty L'Aimant. Her mother's favourite perfume. After all those years, nostalgia-inducing fantasies. 'More of a scent than a perfume.' Her mother's voice, sarcasm mismatching that sweetest of smiles.

She worked out what time it was at home. Bill would be asleep. She wondered if he'd moved to her side of the bed, feeling as deprived of her physical presence as he'd been over the loss of the spiritual one. Maybe he was too warm under the duvet without her, missing the permanent chill of her feet whatever the season. Even though he had loathed, from the first winter they'd been married, the love she had for electric blankets, he had bought her a single one, hoping no doubt that her lower extremities would be warmed before she draped herself all over him. Sometimes, in the very depths of an English winter, his feet would sneak their way towards her side and the patch of electric warmth, and she would laugh, tell him jokingly to buy the double blanket and confess the loss of his British belief that a cold bedroom was character building, or keep to his own side. Then she would fling herself on top of him and warm him in the best of all ways. But those were the old days. Lately, he hadn't even attempted to creep to her side of the bed, even on the very coldest of nights, especially when her heart was as chilly as the snowiest of winters. But maybe even her un- welcoming back when she was asleep, or feigning it, had been better than the empty space he had now. Amazing in his fortitude was Bill. Enduring.

Norma moved away, leaving her food un- touched, and began talking to a group of people at the other side of the flower-filled terrace. Jessica watched Chuck as he came to stand behind her and saw him place one hand on his wife's neck. Even from that distance she could see how Norma stiffened, and how his hand fell back to his side as he sensed her detachment. Body language of the cruellest kind. The deterioration of a failing love. Disintegration of affection seemed heavy in the air, but then it could have been the melancholy that dropped at times like a shroud on Jessica. Dropped without rhyme or reason, try as she might to pin it down and face it enough to understand it. Early Sinatra, his voice, sexy with youth, caressed her senses, almost as vividly as the day she'd first heard that special sound that only Frank could make, the one that convinced you it was you, and you alone, he sang for. It was the wine, makes you maudlin if you have things to sadden you, and, if you're fifteen, even when you don't. The combination of alcohol and Sinatra. Remembered teenage parties, long and gawky as she was, blushing too often and too easily, un-awakened, chosen to put the records on because of her single status, hiding her acne in the darkened room, listening to the sounds of secret petting, falling in love with a voice on a plastic disc, going home alone, pretending she didn't care.

She moved now through the french windows and into the living-room, draining her glass. Only despondency lay grittily on the bottom. Large coffee pots sat on the buffet. She filled a cup and pulled a face at the first sip.

Lilian Peterson had watched Jessica's progress through the party with interest, from the moment she'd seen Chuck's wife introduce her to the hosts, to the disappointed look on her face when she took the champagne, the rapidity with which she drank it, looking round for the waiter before it was even finished, her tall strong body as she endeavoured to control the static of her underslip, her obvious enjoyment of the food, and the fearful look on her face when a person spoke to her. Nothing about her was American. Obviously a friend of Norma's from the UK. Lilian had gone on watching, up till the moment Jessica came in from the terrace and took the coffee, brushing the unruly grey-red hair from a face almost devoid of what had once been the wrong shade of make-up. A face so full of what was going on in her life at that moment, talk would almost be an afterthought. Tired of Hollywood parties, weary of constant movie talk, bored with the swapping of hairdressers and facialists, Lilian moved across to finally introduce herself to Jessica as she grimaced at the first sip of coffee.

'It's raspberry and french vanilla flavour.' The small, thin, dark woman stood at the other side of the buffet. She held a cup of coffee in her hand and was balancing a too large piece of cake in the saucer with such deftness it could only mean a woman in total control of herself.

Jessica frowned. 'It looks like chocolate,' she said, nodding in the direction of the confection as

Lilian bit into it, and crumbs fell heedlessly around her. She didn't even glance down. On her head was one of the silliest hats Jessica had ever seen, which made her wonder if the woman had as much as glanced into a mirror before leaving home for the evening. Surely not. Eventually Lilian looked down at the mess she was making and rubbed at it with one of her black lacy boots.

'Good for the carpet,' she smiled.

'I think that's cigarette ash.'

Under the hat, the woman had a face that held secrets, but Jessica couldn't have explained why that thought entered her mind with such celerity.

'And,' Lilian went on, 'I meant the coffee. I'm afraid to say that's what's raspberry and vanilla.'

'How extraordinary.' Jessica looked down at the cup in her hand, 'It looks just like coffee.'

'What did you expect, something pink and white? This is Hollywood. No point in reality, we might as well be in Baltimore.' She moved towards the table and put her cup down. Her eyes seemed to be mocking and friendly as they scrutinized Jessica, which made her feel rather uncomfortable. No-one looked that closely at her these days.

'Shall I cut you a piece of this great cake?' Lilian had the knife poised. 'No-one else will eat it I assure you.'

Jessica took the piece of cake, balancing it in her other hand.

'My name is Lilian,' the woman said, still smiling. Neither of them had a free hand to shake.

'I'm Jessica.'

'You're British.'

'Yes.' Jessica's heart had predictably started to beat rapidly with panic at the thought of having to make pleasant conversation with this bright and confident American. She felt suddenly rather tired and uninspired. Everyone she'd met so far seemed so full of energy. Everyone smiles all the time, she thought to herself, maybe they really are all on Prozac, as Norma said.

'What part of Britain?' Lilian had finished her cake and drunk her coffee.

'We live in West Sussex.' There goes that 'we' again, she could hear Norma saying. But after so many years it was difficult to speak of herself in the singular. She never felt like an 'I'.

'Chichester?'

'Quite *near* Chichester,' Jessica said, surprised at the woman's accuracy with such a wild guess. Or maybe the home counties stuck out all over her. Must be the black linen, she thought, and then, 'Do you know that part of England?'

'I've been to the Festival Theatre there,' she said. 'And you? Do you go much? I miss the theatre, living in LA. There's very little here, and what there is, is hardly taken seriously.'

'We're lazy, I'm afraid, what with the children and everything.'

Jessica wondered if she'd looked as embarrassed as she felt, calling those three grown men

112

'children'. She could hear Charlie's voice – '*Mu-u-um!*'

'How old?' Her new friend was relentless in her curiosity.

'Me?'

Lilian laughed loudly and grabbed two glasses of red wine from the tray of a passing waiter, putting one in Jessica's hand, not asking, sure of her complicity. It seemed churlish to point out she'd been drinking white. Anyway, out of nowhere she suddenly seemed to be enjoying herself.

'Why do you laugh?' Jessica said, smiling, wondering if one or both of them was very drunk.

'It's you, assuming I was asking *your* age. It was the children. I have very little idea of the age of even my closest friends. No-one asks such questions in Hollywood.'

'It's the English, I'm afraid. We seem to be obsessed with age.'

'And homosexuality, I believe?'

'I don't know about that. Not where we live.'

Lilian started to laugh again, louder than ever. A few people looked and smiled across at them. Jessica felt foolish, and wasn't quite sure why. A country bumpkin. An old fool. An old fool who still blushed. Lilian stopped laughing suddenly and put one hand up to touch the heat on the face in front of her. And to Jessica's embarrassment the blush deepened, and she wanted desperately to be anywhere but within the gaze of this extraordinary woman, who seemed to be touching her hot cheek with the intimacy of a lover.

'They're not really children any more,' she said, pulling the conversation back to the mundane, hoping maybe she would bore the stranger and therefore be left alone to wallow in her foolishness. 'Not any more. More like men. They're all grown and gone. Silly of me. Still kids to me, I'm afraid.'

Lilian's hand dropped to her side. The cheek felt cold at the loss of her touch. They drank their wine. 'Did you want red?' Lilian said suddenly.

'It's fine. I've had too much anyway. I believe I'm still jet-lagged. I only arrived last night. I'm not the best of travellers.'

The words were falling out of her without much thought behind them, wishing Lilian would go away, stay, stop staring, anything that would make Jessica more comfortable. She longed to sit down. Her knees had locked and were starting to shake with tiredness. The long sofa nearby looked completely uninviting. Everything was so white and clean, well-puffed cushions that matched in symmetrical rows, indented at the top, the way they were done in Norma's house, defying one to sit or languish anywhere near the upholstery, housekeeper hovering to plump up as soon as one stood again. All this unmolested perfection behind a glass coffee table that looked as if it had never experienced the grubby chocolate fingers of a passing child who believed soap and water was the ultimate in parent-inflicted torture, and indeed, never been licked to within an inch of its life by a labrador's pink tongue in search of the odd forgotten and often-dropped cake crumb.

'Come and sit outside,' Lilian tipped her head towards the terrace. 'You can't sit in here. The maid will tidy the pillows as you make the move to get up.' Jessica laughed, and allowed herself to be led outside. 'What d'you do?' Lilian asked when they'd found a seat between two flowering shrubs of bougainvillaea covered in lights. The evening had grown chilly and tall-standing gas fires were lit around them. The swimming pool glistened at the other side of the terrace, remote in its stillness and unbroken surface. Jessica remembered Norma's suggestion of a naked swim. It would have been a shame to destroy the serenity of the water.

'Do?' she said.

'Yes. Or are you here on vacation?'

'That's right. I'm with Norma and Chuck Sarrison. D'you know them?'

'Chuck sold me the house I'm in now. A friend of mine once worked with him.' She waved at a waiter for more wine, then turned once again to look at Jessica. 'You are Norma's friend I would say, more than Chuck's I mean.'

Her head fell to one side as she smiled again. Secrets once more in her eyes, on her face, hidden in her smile.

'Norma is my best friend,' Jessica said, 'has been since childhood. I see very little of her these days.

Since she married Chuck, that is. We've grown apart. I've missed her. I miss the comfort of women.' The words spilled. Jessica wondered what had suddenly possessed her. Her tongue was unused to meandering in the company of strangers. The party was thinning out. She looked at her watch. It was ten-thirty.

'And you? What d'you do?' She needed to put Lilian in the question box for a change.

'I'm what is called an independent TV producer. Movies for television, that is. I also write.' She'd leaned forward and helped herself to more wine from the bottle that had been placed on the table by her side. Jessica found that tiredness was beginning to overtake her. She wanted now to be alone in the centre of that enormous bed in Norma's guest room.

'You didn't tell me about yourself,' Lilian said, 'not what you do. Except your relationship with Norma. What else? Who are you?'

'I'm married,' Jessica said, as if that explained everything, her life, her existence, her reason. 'To a bank manager. Have been for a long time. Thirty years. He's not with me here. Not on vacation with me, I mean. He's still in Sussex.'

'Do you always take separate holidays?'

'No. First time.'

'So you're the wife of an English bank manager and the mother of adult children.' She'd made it sound over-important and Jessica bristled. 'But what d'you actually *do*?' Lilian had the persistence of a terrier with a bone. And the smile of an angel, thought Jessica from out of the blue.

'Nothing.'

Lilian raised her eyebrows. 'Nothing?'

'I'm a housewife.' Her own overstatement made Jessica smile.

'What's funny?' Lilian leaned forward and touched her arm. Her hand was warm against the coolness of Jessica's skin. Heat on chill. Sweet on sour. She shivered in the evening air.

'You have a great face,' Lilian said, 'specially when you're amused. As if the emotion takes you by surprise.'

Jessica stared at the composed face of the woman at her side, wondering how anyone could tune in so quickly to a total stranger. 'I'm a very *bad* housewife,' she said, answering Lilian's previous question.

'Me too.' Lilian's hand remained on her arm. It felt like trespassing, and Jessica didn't want strangers inside that barrier she'd built. When she shivered again it was not just the cold.

'I must find Norma,' she said at last. 'We're probably going home. I've been ill, you see.'

They both stood and Lilian put out her hand.

'Maybe we'll meet again Jessica.'

'Yes.'

'I hope you'll be better soon.'

'Oh, yes.'

'Norma has my number. If you want lunch one day, call me.'

Jessica smiled, turned away, left Lilian standing there. Norma and Chuck were ready to leave. The maid brought Norma's mink and they said their goodbyes. Standing at the front door, slow in their leaving as one often is at parties, not wanting to be the ones who break up the evening, Jessica looked again in the direction of the bougainvillaea, at the hundreds of white lights that danced over the pale, naked face of her new friend as she talked to someone else. Their eyes met. And with a smile, Lilian raised one hand in her direction, the one that held the full glass of wine. Jessica smiled back. Looked away. Wanted the solitude of her empty bed. The party had drained her.

But at least no-one had asked her to put the records on.

Chapter Six

The birds woke her the following morning. Californian birds. Hollywood chicks. Not exactly the delicate twittering that began a Sussex morning. The dawn chorus outside the window was more Ethel Merman than Julie Andrews. Wake up, wake up, the sun's shining as always, the day is yours, grab it before someone else does. The house was silent. She lay still beneath the lightweight comforter. Go gently into the day. There's nothing to do but what you want. No-one to please but yourself. No reproaches or looks of disappointment from a husband desperate for the return of a wife he could recognize. Something remained in her head from the night's reveries. What was her name? Lilian. That was it. What about her she couldn't remember. There was no residue of sadness within her, so it had probably been a good dream. She would ask Norma about the small, dark woman with the silly hat. They'd been too tired for much conversation when they'd reached home the previous night. Chuck had poured all of them a nightcap, but Jessica had fallen asleep with the glass still full, and had been packed off to bed. All she could remember was Norma's promise that, 'Tomorrow we'll spend the day by the pool, catch up on everything, I'll wake you when I get back from the gym.' She was sure Norma had actually said that because it made her laugh, thinking of her old schoolfriend doing any sort of exercise. These days apparently she even played tennis.

She sat up, awake suddenly, amazingly bright considering the alcohol she'd drunk the previous night. She would go to the kitchen and find the teabags before Maria brought her orange.

But Jessica was too late. Norma was up, sitting at the breakfast bar, dressed in shorts, long hair tied back, her face naked of make-up made her look younger than all the glamour of the night before.

'Goodness Jess, you're up so early.' She pulled a stool forward with her foot and motioned her to sit down.

'It was the birds, I think. I feel just fine.'

'Raucous, aren't they? The birds I mean.'

'Somewhat.'

'Do you want coffee?'

'Can I make my own tea?' Jessica stood up and went across to the kettle. Through the window she saw Chuck in the garden, dressed in sweats. 'Are you both going to the gym?' she asked, surprise in her voice. Chuck's portly outline had given her the distinct impression a stairmaster was the last thing on his list of priorities. Norma laughed.

'Well, he makes the journey,' she said, 'but the

hour is spent in the sauna. I suspect he talks shares, investments, that sort of thing?'

'God, I hate saunas. They make me panic. All those humans with so much damp, loose flesh. It reminds me of a butcher's shop.'

Norma stood up and tapped on the window and mouthed 'I'm going' in Chuck's direction. She put an arm round Jessica and kissed her on the cheek. 'Will you be OK? I won't be long. Maria starts at eight. Help yourself if you want breakfast straight away. Anyway, you don't have to wash up.'

'Nothing was further from my mind, I assure you.'

'Good.' She banged again on the window. 'Christ, that man is slow in the morning. If they had mixed saunas he'd be up at dawn.'

Jessica stared at her, forming a question in her mind, but Norma's head was down, rummaging for car keys in her tote bag. 'Found them!' She moved to the door, 'Tell him I'll wait in the car, or else he can wait for José.'

Alone, Jessica took the mug of tea back upstairs. She would shower and dress before she tackled Maria's strong Spanish accent. Putting on her swimsuit, she stood and looked at herself in the long mirror and realized just how much weight she'd put on in the last year. She seemed to have developed two sets of hips, one nestling under the other, at the top of her long thighs. It made her laugh.

Maria put out six packets of cereal, which added a deal of confusion to the morning. Jessica was particularly bad at making decisions before noon. So she read the back of all the packets, plunged her hand unhygienically into all of them in case there were any free gifts, and remembered with almost tearful nostalgia the boys' breakfast time squabbles over one small plastic car or plane oh so many years ago. It was nearly always Charlie who won. She smiled at the memory of a son who believed the world was made for him and him alone. She wondered if there would ever come a time when she would be able to remember their childhood without longing for it back. It was the change in all their lives she hated. Feared. Couldn't embrace. How could she learn to overcome that?

Seeing her push the cereal aside, Maria made toasted bagels instead, and left the 'sad English lady' alone with her melancholy in the sunny breakfast room overlooking the pool.

The housekeeper wondered briefly if it was anything to do with being European, seeing as her employer and this friend of hers seemed to sometimes have the same look in their eyes. Perhaps they were homesick. Maria had been at first when she had come across the border all those years ago as a teenager with a mother who ran long and hard to escape the poverty and abuse she'd left behind with Maria's father. But not now. America was home. Here she had blossomed. Here her belly was always full, and she had a roof over her head without depending on any man. Here women could have their own lives.

In the kitchen, Jessica lingered, drank fresh coffee, and watched the sun start to play on the pool outside the window. The gardener was scooping leaves from the water, unhurried, pushing his baseball cap back to front on his head. The sprinklers in the flower beds sprung to life. Maria brought the *LA Times* for her to read, along with some magazines. The man on the terrace wheeled out two long loungers and placed them side by side at the pool. The breakfast table was cleared. Norma came home while Jessica was still reading the newspaper.

'Go outside,' she said, 'it's lovely and warm already. It's going to be in the eighties. I'll be out with the tanning lotion as soon as I have a word with Maria.' She threw in front of her a copy of the international *Daily Express*. 'Just in case you felt homesick.'

'Yuck. I don't read it at home, why should I start while I'm here?'

'I couldn't get the *Mail*.'

'How did you know I still read the *Mail*?'

'I bet you do.'

'I seem to be stuck like an old 78 record. My life does, I mean.'

Norma laughed.

They lay all morning on the loungers. Norma wanted to catch up on everything that had gone on in her friend's life since the operation. But it wasn't the old days. Words weren't as liquid in their mouths. They each had their own problems, and it was hard to know where to start and who should go first. Norma had changed. But then, Jessica realized they both had, they'd stopped liking themselves, and the reasons for their personal self-loathing quite obviously came from different bases. Trying to explain her depression was difficult enough for Jessica, specially in such surroundings. Lush greenery, the sound of water from the fountain in the pool, hot coffee brought to them so easily, anything they wanted. All that worried Jessica at that moment seemed to shrivel in its own trivia.

'I hate what I'm doing to Bill. And then I hate him for making me feel guilty. Silly, isn't it?'

Norma shrugged. 'But you're still OK? You and Bill, I mean?' There was a tone in her voice that was dreading Jessica's answer, as if she was thinking, 'Tell me you two are still OK, for God's sake.'

'We're fine. And they tell me the depression will pass. Apparently it's normal after the operation. Trouble is, I don't believe it's the op I'm depressed about. I'm just so angry about everything. As if someone else did all this to me.'

'Like what?'

'I don't know.'

Norma didn't answer. She seemed lost in her own thoughts, and Jessica could find no more words, not even the ones that would lead her to her friend's own problems.

They lay in silence until it was lunchtime when they moved to a table beneath an umbrella. Two friends with stories to tell that were, in all probability, no worse than millions of others, except they'd reached an age when they found it hard to get people's attention, so all they had left was the anger, and an inexplicable sadness that a time had gone for ever when as schoolgirls they could giggle their secrets to each other with impunity.

So all Jessica could say, falling back on small talk over a lunchtime salad, unsure whether she could find the courage to ask for a gin, was 'Who's Lilian?' It seemed safe enough. And the woman in her silliest of hats had stayed in her memory with a tenacity that was unusual.

'Lilian who? Peterson?'

'I was talking to her last night. We had coffee and cake together.'

'Lilian Peterson. Nice lady.'

'She was unusual. She said Chuck sold her her house.'

'That's right. I don't know her that well. She's OK. If you don't mind dykes.'

Jessica stared at her. 'Dykes?'

'That's what I said. Would you like a gin and tonic?' Norma waved to Maria through the window and mimed a drink. 'You know what a dyke is, Jessica, for God's sake. Remember

Gwenda Darwin in the sixth form?'

'Very clearly. She was caught in the stationery cupboard doing something unmentionable with that student PE teacher. The teacher lost her job, and probably her career.'

Norma started to laugh, 'And Gwenda Darwin was suspended during the inquiry where they decided she'd been led astray. You asked her for the details, I remember. All the things we all wanted to know but didn't dare voice.'

'God, yes. Like, "Do you strap anything on?" I had such audacity in those days. I'm surprised I survived.' They both laughed at the memory.

'Anyway, Lilian Peterson is one of *them*. Quite a few in this town,' Norma said, as she put a piece of lemon in her drink from the plate on the trolley. 'Didn't you guess?'

'Why should I? I don't ask people about their sex life when I first meet them.' Jessica was feeling quite relaxed by this time. She could feel her shoulders begin to descend from their usual position of round her ears. She went on about Lilian, 'She was rather intense, I thought, and I don't know, different. Silly hat. She actually listened to me. Seemed to be interested. Or am I being particularly naïve, as usual? I haven't been here enough to even smell bullshit.' Then she sat up, suddenly, horrified with a memory that had just sprung to mind. Something about the absence of homosexuals in West Sussex. No wonder Lilian had laughed.

'Oh, my God!'

'What? Don't tell me she hit on you?'

'Hit on me?'

'It's a rather unpleasant American expression for flirting.'

'I don't like the sound of that at all.' The second gin had made Jessica giggly.

'You drink too much.' Norma's voice was accusing.

'I know.'

'In plain English,' Norma said, 'maybe she fancies you.'

'Don't be ridiculous.'

For some reason, Jessica wasn't shocked, which took her by surprise. It simply made her giggle even more.

'I wish I'd known,' she stuttered with increasing mirth. '*She* might well have been able to answer the question that upset Gwenda so much.'

Then the telephone rang inside the house and when Norma got up to answer it, cursing herself for not having the cordless one by her side, Jessica remarked the gin had made her very hungry so could she find her some bread and cheese in that enormous fridge that was worth eating.

'Full fat,' Norma said when she returned and placed a plate of crackers and cheddar on the table. 'Just for you alone. Went to the store on my way back from the gym.'

'No wonder I have two pairs of hips.' Jessica said, and began to eat without another thought.

Norma sighed, 'It must be great not to bother.'

'It is. You should try it. Bill loves me whatever, so he keeps saying anyway. I sometimes wonder if it's more habit than feeling. You know, like the record's stuck or something. But if he had a good storyline of Julia Roberts going through his head if we did ever get it together, not that we do any more, mind you, well, as long as he had the manners not to insist on sharing his sexual fantasies with me, good luck to him.' She raised her glass, 'And all who sail with him!'

Norma was staring down at the empty glass in her hand, almost as if she hadn't been listening. Jessica leaned forward and touched her tentatively with cheese-sticky fingers, her voice suddenly soft, the memory of how to care flooded back, along with all the other memories of how often her shoulder had been there for her friend to cry and lean upon. 'What is it Norma? Something's terribly wrong, you're so brittle, so unhappy. Can you tell me?'

'I'm ashamed of myself. I promised Bill I'd be here for you.'

'You are. Just being away from home has made me leave some of the guilt behind. I needed a rest from all the patient understanding.' And taking both their empty glasses, she placed them on the table. 'If it makes it easier, have another drink. I'm aware it's not the perfect answer, but it's the only one I have in the short term.'

Norma shook her head. 'Nothing makes it

easier. I'm ashamed of my life. How I'm living it. My lack of courage, integrity, you name it.'

'For God's sake, tell me, Norma.' Jessica threw her arms apart, taking in the beauty that breathed so uneasily around them. 'Look at this. You seem to have everything. You wanted it. You'd reached the age, you said. Wouldn't have appreciated it when you were young, you said. Now what? Dearest friend, there's nothing you can't tell me. Don't you remember?'

'Yes. You never judge.'

'Are you in love with someone else?'

Norma stared for a moment, then threw her head back as she laughed. Tears ran down her cheeks. You could see the paths they made through the make-up she'd painted over that beautifully unadorned face she'd dared to show at dawn. She must have been afraid the rest of the world would see the woman's fear that Jessica had seen so clearly, not understanding the loveliness of it had been the bravery of the exposure. Tears and smiles. That was it, in the glorious middle years. Just tears and smiles as one rants towards old 'rage'.

Finally, when the tears and the laughter had gone, along with the last of the gin, Norma began to tell her what was wrong.

It was hard for her to begin, so Jessica tried to help, lead her into it. 'Is it Chuck? Is he having an affair, and you realize how much you love him, but he won't give her up?'

'I wish,' she said. 'There's not just a mistress. I would know where to start if there was something that tangible.' She stared out at the pool. Scarcely a ripple touched the surface. Jessica waited.

Norma said at last, 'He likes hookers. He goes to a certain kind of party, ones to which I'm not invited. Organized parties, sometimes he lays them on himself when there's business clients in town. I think it's known as "turning tricks". That's it. He supplies the "specials" who turn the tricks. Doesn't just supply them either. Turns a few himself.' She turned to look at Jessica. Her eyes were cold, lifeless. 'Do you have any idea what I'm saying? Is it all too Hollywood for you to comprehend?' She looked away again and said with some bitterness, 'You said yourself this town doesn't let you down, everything you've imagined and all that. Well, there you are. If it was happening to someone else I'd be laughing about it with you.'

Jessica could find no words.

'Say something,' Norma said at last. 'Or have you become too innocent in that middle-class village of yours?'

'I don't think I understand. What the hell do you say when your best friend tells you she's married to some sort of – I don't know. Is there a word for someone who does what he's doing?'

'Pimp. Except he gets the kind of sex he wants instead of money.' She held her hand across to touch her friend's arm. 'I think I'll change my mind about that drink now. Is there any left?'

Jessica shook her head.

Norma shrugged, dropped her hand down to her side and said without looking up, 'Aren't you disgusted?'

'I don't think so. I'm almost fascinated. Or I would be if it wasn't happening to you, as you've already said. How did you find out? How long has it been going on?'

'He told me. After a while – I don't know – we'd been married about a year, maybe less, I knew there was something. It was all right at first. The sex, I mean. There were times he had some difficulty, but then that can happen, specially at his age. It didn't seem important. I'd get a little dirty – you know, certain lines of chat and so forth. Then even that didn't help. I'd become too – what's the word? I don't know. He'd got too used to me. Too predictable. I believed it was me. Don't we always think that? He wanted, no – *suggested*, that I dress up, play games, that sort of thing. You know what I mean.'

Jessica put one hand over her mouth. She was beginning to be afraid she might find all this amusing.

Norma went on, 'All right, so you *don't* know. You and Bill have never got bored with the missionary position by the look on your face.'

Then Jessica did smile. 'I wouldn't exactly say that. I seem to remember some years ago he quite liked me spread on the bed wearing nothing but suspenders and black patent stilettos. He went on something chronic when pantyhose first came in. Hated the blasted things.'

'Well, there you are, darling. All the men I've met in my life have hated pantyhose without exception.' Norma pulled a face, 'I wish that was all it was. I mean, as far as my husband was concerned.'

'So Chuck likes hookers,' Jessica said. 'Is it really such a big deal? I mean – well, I don't know, dress up for him. Who's to know? I really can't see what was so terrible. If the pair of you get to play the monk and the shepherdess now and then maybe he'll knock the parties on the head.'

In the past, Norma had confessed straying into some strange situations in her love life, but as far as Jessica was concerned this seemed to be the most bizarre.

'Beats the WI,' she said.

Norma laughed shortly. 'The thing is, Jess, he can't actually do it unless it *is* a *hooker* these days. And he likes, needs, people to watch. Christ, he *told* me. He wanted to bring people in to watch *us*! He once even suggested handing me round to a few of his friends so *he* could watch. Jesus!'

Jessica said tentatively, 'Have you suggested therapy?'

'Yes.'

'Well?'

'He thought I meant myself.'

The giggling erupted at that. Norma stuttered, 'Oh dear, Jess, I might have realized you'd think it funny.' She looked sad even through the amusement, 'I just feel so old and unattractive. I can't find myself another man, too old to go through all that first-time nonsense, so I must grin and bear it. I wake up afraid some nights, knowing without a doubt that this is all there is, after all. The candy that he offered looked so sweet on the outside. No wonder his other wives left.'

'So could you. Come home. Back to England. Leave him alone to enjoy his silly parties. It's all so pathetic, poor little man. I feel quite sorry for him. It's laughable more than disgusting. For God's sake, leave him.'

'And lose all this?' She glanced around her.

Jessica leaned across and said firmly, 'Isn't there a property law in California? Even I've heard of that. You'd get half. Wouldn't even have to mention the parties, or even the hookers.'

There was a silence. 'Norma?'

After a moment, she said, 'I signed a pre-nuptial agreement.'

A pause, then Jessica said quite loudly, 'You did *what*?'

'You heard the first time.'

'Why?'

'He asked me. And it seemed fair. His other wives had been so ruthless. I wanted him to think I was different. Anyway, he seemed so in love with me, still is, according to him.'

'Just can't get it up, huh?' They had to hang on to the funny side.

'What there is of it,' hissed Norma, venom in her smile.

They both shook with mirth.

'Now let's review this,' Jessica said at last, pushing her hair back from her face, ashamed of the undeniable fact that she hadn't enjoyed a conversation so much for years, 'You, my dearest friend in all the world, are married to a billionaire with a very small dick who can only screw hookers, and then he needs an audience.' They stared at each other. 'Sounds like any good old-fashioned, middle-class family to me.'

'Jessica Byfleet, I expected more advice than this,' Norma shouted. 'And you're supposed to be depressed. You're hysterical, for Christ's sake.'

'How can I take it seriously? Or advise? You either stay and keep with the plastic surgery and retail therapy, or leave and hang on to your dignity and pride.'

'Oh thanks,' her voice sarcastic, 'you are a real help.'

Jessica could feel the beginning of a headache. Alcohol and hysteria. Maybe she should have taken Norma's problem more seriously, but it was easier to only see the funny side. It was the kind of thing that would have kept them amused for years in their youth. For a while they had both forgotten that the things you see as amusing or silly when you're young and therefore immortal are not so easily shrugged off in later years. Now Jessica felt she should have at least tried to be more helpful. All she'd done was make her friend believe for the moment that her relationship with Chuck was one big joke. But nothing that makes you settle for second best is funny. Not at any age.

Maria came and cleared the lunch things. Norma said, 'Maybe I'll get some sort of perspective on it now. It's nothing compared with what you've been through.'

'I just feel lost. Without a purpose. It's such a cliché. It's like standing in a hall with closed doors all round me and I don't know which one to open.'

'I don't know what to say to you. You're in there somewhere. The old you, I mean. It's just a matter of time.'

'Aah.'

'I know, I know. Time isn't endless as it used to be. Maybe the rest and the sunshine will help. Everyone these days says lack of sunshine makes some people deeply depressed. Maybe you're like that. And maybe you're more frightened of the cancer coming back than you care to admit. I would be.'

Jessica remained silent, one hand going subconsciously to the space by her heart. Maybe the luxury that surrounded her, and the sunshine, would fill the emptiness for a while. It was an adventure, a healing, a vacation from a life that had been slowly and surely driving her crazy.

She went upstairs to rest and shower away the suntan lotion which had done nothing to stop the usual lobster-like flush the sun always brought out on her oh-so-English skin. She would have to try very hard not to remember everything Norma had told her about Chuck when she faced him over the dinner table that night. It would be difficult to control the image of that elderly and apparently under-endowed man cavorting in a room full of hookers. Lying on the bed after her shower, she thought about all the growing up years and dreams they'd shared. No-one would have prepared Norma for what had become of her life. Nature had endowed her with so much; looks, personality, and after a few trials and tribulations, she'd met Chuck, and walked, yes – walked, not even run, for God's sake, into a world of satin sheets that she never had to wash herself, no fear even when bills shuddered monthly onto the mat, champagne to drink as a matter of course, and the total confidence to order dinner in a restaurant without glancing down the right-hand side of the menu. Then, whatever it was that formed our lives must have realized the roulette wheel had spun too far in Norma's favour, and, just for the hell of it, it seemed, thought, 'Well, here's a nice little bundle of trouble, let's see how clever clogs deals with this little bit of mischief.'

But it was worse. Norma was afraid to leave. Scared of being on her own. She would sell her pride for a house she didn't have to clean, turn her back on all those old dreams for the sake of a facelift that her husband didn't notice.

Later, at dinner, sitting opposite her host, the 'master' of the house, Jessica did her best to smile across that white-oaked dining table without giving away the grotesque images that whirled round and round in her imagination. She almost wished Norma had kept her mouth shut. She remembered once one of the girls in the sixth form in their last year at school had delighted them all by relating her first sexual experience in the back of her Jewish boyfriend's old Morris Minor. They had huddled round the classroom radiator in the morning recess ('Don't sit on that girls, you'll get chilblains!') and soaked up all the gory details. Arms folded across blossoming bosoms as if they lived in fear and hope they would be touched, or at least that, by listening to the experience, some of the tingling excitement would rub off and drive them into the frenzy they all imagined. It had been the first time a circumcised penis had been explained to any of them. Jessica was fascinated. She remembered Margie, the girl in question, had said, 'It looks just like a baby's arm holding an apple.'

Well, that did it. Everyone insisted on Margie drawing a picture, and Jessica kept the picture in her imagination, and there it stayed, only to emerge every time she was in the company of a Jewish man. For years, in fact, until she actually found herself in bed with her first Jewish lover, and she was able to inspect to her heart's content. The man in question was highly flattered at the time, believing he'd really landed on his feet and found a young woman who was sincerely fascinated by a penis.

So there she was, making small talk with her best friend's husband, and trying to stop her eyes wandering to his crotch.

Classical music soft on the stereo. Easy, accessible. Well known Beethoven, the kind you could sing along with. The tension in the room was thicker than the slices of skinless chicken breasts that Maria placed on the plates in front of them. Jessica almost asked for 'skin on the side please'.

'We're watching our weight,' said Chuck somewhat ruefully. 'Well, I should say, my *wife* is watching my weight. She's the boss.'

'I'm not,' Jessica said, trying to sound bright and funny, 'watching my weight, that is.'

Norma laughed, 'Maria, be a darling and bring my English friend the butter. It's most likely hidden at the back of the refrigerator.'

Maria muttered, 'If José hasn't eaten it all.'

'She loathes him,' whispered Norma as Maria hurried to find the butter. 'They enjoy hating each other. They seldom talk.'

'Ssh,' Chuck gestured at her as Maria came back. Every day seemed like an opera in their house. Lots of life in the conflict.

On the second glass of wine Jessica said, only half joking, 'I could always eat with Maria perhaps. I rather fancy the sound of refried beans. They sound to me just the sort of thing that would bypass every part of my digestive system and aim straight for both sets of hips. Cut out the agonizing, so to speak.'

Both her hosts laughed. Norma said, 'Chuck's been told to cut back.' Jessica caught Norma's eye. She turned and patted her husband on the cheek. 'Not getting any younger are you, my darling? Time to give up childish delights.' Her tone was enough to make one draw one's breath, as if you'd swallowed a lemon.

'Too many parties,' Jessica said blithely. She couldn't believe she'd said it. Her mouth had opened and the words simply fallen out and into the chill of the dining-room. It had come out without any hidden agenda. It arrived at the table drowning in innuendo. Norma's eyebrows disappeared into her hairline. Chuck ate the remains of his dinner and tried to look replete. Jessica felt quite sorry for him and found herself hoping he slunk out now and again for Kentucky Fried Chicken when he was out of the beady eyes of a wife who had nothing to do but make his life as uncomfortable as she dared without actually confronting the real problem.

The undercurrents whirled round them and Jessica found herself terrified of doing and saying the wrong thing. What d'you talk about if the food is dreary, the wine dangerous, and the subject of sex is to be avoided at any cost?

'I've caught the sun,' she said eventually. She was no good at all this. Her life, by comparison, was decently dull and ordinary. Just the occasional nervous breakdown. The loss of a breast that wasn't often used and the mislaying of one's sex drive were mere hitches in a family's suburban life compared to all this Hollywood carry-on. 'I'm all striped,' she went on. 'Didn't we go the same colour all over when we were girls?'

'Norma uses a tanning salon,' Chuck said. Then, 'Is there more chicken, darling?'

There was fruit and ice cream for dessert. 'You might even make the acquaintance of your hip-bones while you're here,' Norma hissed when Chuck took his coffee into his study with, 'I'll join you two girls for brandy.'

'Why does he do that?' said Norma.

'Do what?'

'Call us girls in that tone of voice. Doesn't he know he's driving me crazy?'

'Is it like this every night for dinner?' Jessica whispered, just in case her voice carried to where she could hear Chuck on the phone. 'I wish you'd never told me, Norma Sarrison. I can't stop the pictures in my head. I don't know what to say to him. He's taken on all the proportions of a clown.'

'What a farce,' Norma sighed. 'Thank God we don't eat in often. Unless we entertain. Then we put on a great act. One that no-one notices because the town's full of actors anyway.'

As Jessica was feeling far from girlish, and

Norma had drunk too much at dinner, they were both delighted Chuck remained in his study for what was left of the macabre evening. Jessica longed for bed and the end of another day. Nothing changes. Almost like the end of a day in Sussex. But not quite. The world was getting almost interesting.

Chapter Seven

Jessica slept restlessly that night. Not that her dreams were either nightmares or, for that matter, boring. The content of her semi-conscious mental wanderings owed more to the related antics of her best friend's husband than her usual melancholy. She even woke herself in the morning rather abruptly by laughing out loud. Not the worst way to start a day, specially when memories of the dream lingered long enough for contemplation. The previous day's revelations confused her somewhat in the clear light of a Californian morning. The lack of purpose and energy in her own life left her unsure, and selfishly unwilling to attempt to even try and advise her friend. If that's what Norma wanted, of course. Or was it just a sounding board that was called for? And did laughing about it help? Jessica doubted if either Norma or Chuck would make a move. In his way, he needed and wanted a wife, if only to cement his respectability. That, and the fact he obviously adored her. Just wanted his sex life kept separate. Oh well, stranger things have kept marriages together. And maybe in the long run that would be enough for Norma. Jessica tried hard to put herself in her friend's place. It was impossible. A similar predicament with Bill was unthinkable and unimaginable. She laughed out loud again.

'Shall we shop today?' Norma said when she brought coffee to the guest bedroom that morning. Jessica had already given up on the tea. It just didn't seem to taste the same.

'What kind of a shop?'

'Clothes. Bill said you'd lost all interest in your appearance and that I should take you shopping.'

'Some women would kill for a husband like that.'

'Exactly. So get ready. We'll have brunch out.'

'That sounds like it might not be salad.'

'Don't bet on it.' She bent across the bed and kissed Jessica on one sleep-crumpled cheek. 'Sorry about yesterday, sweetheart. Forgive my big mouth.'

'I won't, because there's nothing to forgive. Your life is an open book to me from now on.'

Norma groaned. 'Put your mascara on,' she said, 'it's easier to pick the right clothes.'

The thought of any sort of make-up first thing in the morning was exhausting. Standing naked after her shower, Jessica stared into the full-length mirror and contemplated the vision she had become through the years. About three months after the operation she had decided (quite surprisingly really, considering her lifetime devotion to avoiding such issues), in an upward sweep of mood and tentative enthusiasm, to try and work some magic on the downward pull of gravity on her face and neck. Not quite believing the many adverts proclaiming the miracles that would occur if she used certain products, she still sent away for what creams were suggested, and felt at the very least it would please her therapist and keep herself occupied for ages in the bathroom every night before retiring. This in turn would sober her up just the right amount to fool Bill when she climbed into bed late enough for him to be feigning sleep even more convincingly than she did herself these days.

Not that it worked, of course. She would stare quite ruthlessly into the cruel morning light and every line, every droop was still there. She got quite irritated, and if she could have been bothered, would have asked for her money back. But of course she didn't.

Wasn't it only yesterday she longed to be an adult? She wondered when that magical time had happened. It seemed it never had. Not in the way she'd been led to expect. You were young. Then suddenly you weren't. And the time in between had got so busy there had been no time to say, 'Hey, this is it! You're all grown up. Enjoy!' What a cheat. What a swindle.

Once, for a while, every day was an adventure. She was the mother who convinced her sons that each new day might bring something wonderful. Charlie still greeted the morning like that, so it worked for him, or so it seemed. Sam was always sceptical, middle child's survival instinct drawing on the cynical side of his submerged flamboyant nature. Stephen pretended. He's the one that really suspects that life is the villain. He's the one that needs the cherishing, the tenderness, the courage. He was like her. He had that tendency to pull towards the dark side of the moon.

'Was I ever depressed at school?' she asked Norma as they sat and waited for their food to arrive in the open air café in the shopping mall.

'Good God, no! You were moody. But then that was our age.'

'I remember myself as someone that took every-thing and everyone in their stride. I was always intensely curious.'

'That's how I think of you. Other people's business was the hub of your life.'

'My God, I've changed,' Jessica sighed. 'I'd like that back. My own life has become stupendously bland. My own making, of course. But how do you stop that? You know, that relentless slivering into mediocrity?'

'Don't ask me.'

'I won't. Your existence may be a little bizarre, but at the very least it gives you something to work on apart from the WI and the villege fête.'

While Norma was deciding an amusing retort the brunch arrived. Jessica smiled with delight at a plate groaning with bacon, fried egg, sausage, hash browns, and pancakes with maple syrup.

'American food was invented for you,' Norma

shuddered. 'Look at you – every taste bud in your body has been waiting for this trip across the Atlantic. What took you so long? And please don't try and make me believe it was the WI and the fête; you have never stepped into that village hall in all the years you've lived there, apart from picking the boys up from Brownies or whatever they call themselves.'

'For your information, the Brownies are what *we* belonged to. The boys join the Cubs.'

'Then go on to the Scouts! How could I forget!'

'You couldn't. I seem to recall you were all but deflowered on a Scout and Guide's camping trip to the Isle of Wight.'

'And delicious it was, too.' Norma pushed the remains of her fruit salad away from her. 'Oh God, Jess, I miss sex more than anything else in my life. Is that frightfully immature of me at my age? My mother would be horrified.'

'And I miss motherhood. Makes you wonder, doesn't it?'

'What d'you mean?'

'That glorious mixer in the sky. He takes away sex from *your* life, before you tired of it, I mean, and motherhood from mine just when I was getting into my stride.'

'Oh, come on, Jess, three sons is hardly "just getting into your stride". You've had your share. And soon there'll be grandchildren.'

'You sound like my therapist.'

Jessica was quite suddenly overwhelmed with a

homesickness and misery that not even the sunny-side up of her egg could abate. She too pushed her plate away.

'Let's shop,' said Norma, and she stood up, eager for a diversion, determined to move before apathy settled on either of them.

And getting up, Jessica thought, 'To hell with this! I'm in California. And the sun is shining. Maybe the relentless pursuit of happiness will rub off. Maybe the oh-so-English cynicism that is entrenched in my nature will wither in the glory of a Hollywood spring.'

'D'you want some Levi's?' Norma asked.

'I don't know. You tell me. Where do we start?'

There was a smell of flowers in the air, and suddenly, from nowhere, she remembered she'd miss the flowering of the wisteria back home. The one that for the last hundred years had climbed and grown over the stone walls of the house in Sussex, and scented the air with its pale purple blooms in late spring.

Norma read the look on her friend's face as sadness. 'Come on, Jess,' she said, 'throw yourself into it. This has to be better than a wet morning in Chichester when there's nowhere to park except where you'll obviously get a ticket.'

Jessica laughed. Difficult to stay down when people around you smiled, and wished total strangers a 'good day'.

Then suddenly, loaded with all sorts of things she'd bought without thinking and didn't need –

the only way to shop without guilt, according to Norma – which didn't convince her for a moment, laughing at the silliness and extravagance of them both, enjoying herself to a degree she couldn't fail to recognize, and just for once not accompanied with 'well, nothing that feels this good can last long', she heard her name called. 'Jessica?'

She turned, frowned – surprised, confused. Who else did she know in California, for God's sake? Norma smiled. Nodded. 'Where are you looking?' Jessica said. And then she saw her friend from the party. 'It's Lilian,' Norma waved. They stopped, and Lilian came towards them, wearing a hat that was even more outrageous than that first evening.

'It *is* you,' she said, and bent forward to kiss them one by one on the cheek.

'How nice to see you,' Jessica shifted the weight of her packages. 'Are you shopping as well?'

'Killing time before the afternoon movie,' Lilian said. 'Playing hookey from work, if you must know. There's an actor I was keen to catch. Prefer to see him in action than put myself and him through the miseries of the audition process.'

'We're about ready for coffee,' Norma smiled, 'why don't you join us?'

'Houstons?' Lilian took two of the parcels without asking and strode off with Norma towards the restaurant in the corner of the mall near the cinemas. Jessica followed, weak from the confrontation of such assertiveness. She remembered what Norma had told her; wished she hadn't; recalled the embarrassing remark she'd made at the party at the mention of homosexuality. Finally, she hoped Ms Peterson's memory was worse than her own.

'D'you want to eat?' Lilian asked as they were shown to an alcove by a window in the busy restaurant.

'We had a late breakfast,' and Norma breathed a sigh of relief as she threw her packages into the corner of the leather seat, 'I'd just like coffee. My friend here eats for the Olympics so I can't speak for her.'

'Just coffee,' Jessica said.

As they waited for the drinks, and a sandwich that Lilian ordered without glancing at the menu, she took off her silly hat, ran her fingers through her hair and said, 'I was going to call you later.'

Jessica looked surprised.

'Are you interested in art?' Lilian went on.

'I don't know. Why?'

'There's an exhibition opening on Friday. A friend of mine. Santa Monica gallery. I wondered if you'd like to see some of what they like to call the "bohemian life" on this piece of the Pacific.'

Jessica looked at Norma, who raised her hands above her head. 'Don't look at me, Jess. Do your own thing.'

Lilian said, 'Both of you come.'

Jessica wondered why was it still so difficult for her to make even the simplest of decisions? Here she was, a grown woman, in her fifty-second year, that was once a girl that leapt wilfully into every valley of life without so much as a glance behind or in front, hesitating about a perfectly innocent invitation to an art gallery. When she caught Norma's eye for the briefest of moments, to her horror she felt herself blush with embarrassment as if Lilian could read her mind, and jump to conclusions about the hesitation. Norma laughed, and Jessica had an overwhelming desire to kick her swiftly and silently under the table. But her resistance to behaving like a schoolgirl kept her sedate and convinced that the reddening of her skin would pass for a combination of sunshine and the 'change of life'. Hating to admit it, even to herself, but she was aware of being afraid of dealing with Lilian. Treating her almost like a separate sex. As far as she knew, she'd never actually encountered a lesbian, except the incident that had intrigued them all at school. But who knew? Why should she assume they all walked around dressed in male clothing and cut their hair short? Now here they were, with this delightful, intelligent woman, behaving, in her own mind at least, like one of those men who, on hearing another of their species is gay, starts to make remarks like, 'Better not tie my shoe laces while he's behind me (chuckle, chuckle)' and throwing out names like 'shirtlifter' and the like, all because of the terror of the unknown. What the jokes were about lesbians Jessica didn't know. Except the quaint, old-fashioned idea of a lot of men that 'All they really need is a good man to see what they're missing'. In all innocence, she couldn't really believe that Lilian was making a pass, despite Norma's insinuations of the previous day.

'I'd love to come,' Jessica said firmly.

'We both will,' smiled Norma.

Lilian's sandwich arrived, looking so delicious Jessica was unable to resist asking the waiter to bring her one 'just like it', which made Norma groan and laugh, and before they knew it Lilian had ordered wine and a side order of 'french fries', which turned out to be a very large platter of chips.

'We can share,' said Lilian, and Jessica dug in very cheerily remarking, 'French fries don't sound half as dangerous to one's cellulite as "chips". I feel a strong love affair building up in me for America every minute I'm here.' And it was all so easy, just the three of them, women, content that the conversation was purely female, enjoying the art of throwing words and sentences between themselves without having to fight for listening time, let alone supremacy, dipping french fries into tomato ketchup and then the salsa that Norma ordered as an afterthought. Lilian calling for blueberry cheesecake, 'Make it a big piece and bring three forks,' and Jessica was aware of enjoying herself more than she'd done for too long a time, basking in the kind of talk that even a few years ago would have been outside her energy and vocabulary because the pain of her life had been well on the way to self-destruction.

It was somehow, that lunchtime that spread into afternoon and made Lilian abandon her trip to the movies, the very beginning of the breakthrough for Jessica. It could have been simply the easy companionship of women after so many years of loving and pandering to the men in her life. And when the three of them parted, plans made for Friday, she and Norma made their way home in the Los Angeles' rush hour and talked about Lilian.

'How come I've managed to miss almost the most fascinating woman I've come across in Hollywood since I arrived in this city? I should have gravitated towards her the moment she appeared on the horizon.' Norma bent forward to put a cassette into the car stereo, took her eyes off the road, and Jessica braked gently in her capacity as a passenger, hoping her friend wouldn't notice.

'I saw that,' Norma said, eyes in the back of her head as always, and swerved just in time to avoid a truck swinging out from a side street.

'What?' Jessica said, pretending to stretch her legs.

'You, back seat driving. Or side seat driving in this case. You still do it.'

Whitney Houston loud in their ears. Music to strip the years from you. Dialogue between them, straight from their familiar past.

'I don't think Lilian hangs out with your usual crowd,' Jessica said.

'Don't I know it! D'you know, I'd all but forgotten how much women laugh together. Where did men get the idea we take each other too seriously?'

'You remember my neighbour at home? Betty?'

'Ooh, yes.'

'Remember Peter, her husband?'

'The one with a gin and tonic welded to his hand?'

'That's the one. Well, he once told me in all seriousness, years ago this was, and with what he believed was sincere affection, that he felt really sorry for women because they didn't know how to enjoy themselves. Not like men.'

'God help us. But then he *is* married to Betty what's her name. Not exactly everyone's idea of a ball of fun. She got me in a corner one New Year at your place. Do you still feel obliged to give those awful parish get-togethers on high days and holidays? She talked about the royal family without stopping for at least thirty minutes. Is Di's marriage in trouble already, etc. etc. Who the hell cares any more? I kept sneaking looks at my watch, as one does when you've been waiting for that particular midnight since Boxing day. She relayed every detail of some story in that dreadful magazine that devotes itself totally to the trials and tribulations of the world's royalty. I was immobile with boredom and reluctant fascination that the poor woman obviously had nothing in her life except the vicarious thrill of the misery of the rich and famous. We both missed twelve o'clock when it came, thereby cancelling out the whole point of the evening.'

'That's Betty.'

'I wonder what came first, his gin or her banality?' They pulled into the drive. 'I'm not surprised you caved in with misery,' Norma said as she parked the car. 'Village life has been a refuge for you. And in all probability better than triteness. But for God's sake, darling, there must be someplace else to hide that is less vapid.'

A verbal message from Bill when Maria opened the door to them. 'Just to say hello and send his love,' she smiled, struggling with the very Englishness of the words in her strong Spanish accent. It was too late to call him back. With relief, she postponed the phone call until the following day, just in case the 'blues' she believed for that moment had retired back to Sussex would by some devil's trick seek her out as she dialled home. She went upstairs instead to put away her new purchases, and then came down for tea, served in a silver pot from a silver tray brought to them in the living-room.

She waited for the down after the lunchtime wine, but to her delight it failed to manifest itself and invade the comfort of her day. Dinner that night was not nearly as uncomfortable as the previous experience. Finding herself without much of an appetite after the indulgences of lunchtime she wasn't so cynical about her hosts' healthy supper, packed into such small and un-interesting portions, although still unconvinced that one's vanity was worth any such deprivation.

As the three of them sat there, she was almost able to convince herself, had she been a total stranger to the truth, that all was well in her hosts' somewhat bizarre marriage. Even the pictures of Chuck's cavorting had subsided a little from her imagination.

'Why don't we play tennis tomorrow?' Norma suggested later. A couple had arrived after dinner for coffee and drinks. 'Jessica used to be rather good at school,' she explained to a slender, face-lifted Beverly Hills matron who seemed less than remotely interested in anything the English guest was doing now, let alone almost half a century ago. Jessica had begun to feel sorrier for Norma than herself, so surrounded was she, or so it seemed, by a multitude of inadequate acquaintances. If this was what wealth brought, simply a splattering of sycophants, then you could keep the luxury and the seemingly endless availability of gold credit cards (I want this now and nothing's going to stop me syndrome), because as far as Jessica was concerned, the solitary confinement of a clinical depression seemed like an oasis in that sea of bullshit.

Sitting in one of the enormous armchairs, she put her head back and let the music from the stereo wash over her, mixing with the small talk of her companions. The clink of ice against crystal. The talk reverberated with topics unfamiliar to an English ear. She was content to sit. Content. A word she'd almost forgotten in her indecent haste to be unhappy. She could feel the feathers of her spirit unruffling in that bizarre fairyland.

For the first time in a very long time it felt good to be herself. Had she really merely needed a break from everything that was familiar? Was it just that familiarity that had become the trap? If that was true, returning would be difficult. The memories would still be there when she went home. Sooner or later the reality of her life at home would have to be faced and understood. That afternoon, that lunchtime, with Lilian and Norma, it had been the laughter, the easy communication with someone who came as a stranger to her and her past. A few hours of female companionship that, for some reason, lit up the landscape of her life again.

No wonder Bill had felt inadequate lately. He couldn't win. He knew her too well, what had happened and what to expect. And so she alienated him.

The weeks ahead stretched before her without the predictability that had stifled her at home. Determination and contentment. So quickly. She'd been told that she could turn from despair to living again in almost a moment. She hadn't believed it. The time seemed to have begun, just as she'd been promised.

'I could come to the gym with you tomorrow, if you liked,' she threw at Norma on her way to bed later that night.

'You are beginning to sound like a girl I once knew,' her friend smiled.

'From your lips to God's ears.'

But when she woke in the morning she found she'd overslept. 'Let Mrs Wooldridge sleep till ten, Maria,' Norma had said. 'Take some juice and coffee up then. She'd probably like a Danish as well if you can find one in the freezer!'

And she was right because by the time Jessica opened her eyes and smelt the coffee and tasted the pastry she was in such a good mood that the usual morning miseries had scarcely got wind of her awakening.

And so it was. A new start. Not to be examined and pulled apart in case it fled in fright. But it was definitely there. A bubble inside her that wasn't related to panic. Still a little tentative, maybe even bewildered, but determined to hang around and wait for her to nurture that small crumb of happiness. And change it into a feast that would stay, and maybe find the strength to ward off the invasion of those latter day blues that common-sense told her might only be hiding somewhere out of sight, taking a breather from the tyranny of memories.

When Bill called that morning, Jessica was able

to say, 'Hello, husband. I'm feeling all right. Everything OK at home?'

If she'd told him how sure she was she'd turned the corner he'd think her crazier than ever after such a short while. In Bill's book it took time to get over a nervous breakdown. In hers, it seemed, sanity was a mere breath away. Too fragile to be mentioned out loud, afraid of 'Take it easy, Jess, these things take time. Be careful of yourself.'

'Everyone sends their love,' Bill said.

'How are the boys?'

'I think Stephen's in love again.'

Jessica's heart missed a beat. She said calmly, 'What makes you think that?'

'He's coming down this weekend with her. A certain tone in his voice. You know what I mean. You've mentioned it before.'

'What's her name?'

She shouldn't have asked at this early stage of the game. Time enough to be miserable for him later.

'Her name's Linda. She's a nurse apparently. I'll take them to the pub for lunch on Sunday. Bit of a loss without you, really.'

'You can make up your own mind about her and then tell me.'

'Right.'

She hated the telephone. So much so at that moment she found herself wanting to put the receiver down and get on with her present and frivolous life. If her eldest son's heart was to be broken again she could cry for him from America as well as the garden in Sussex. And maybe she didn't want to know this time. Maybe they could get on with it themselves. But she'd interfered in all their lives for far too long for them to keep secrets from her. It wouldn't even cross their minds that one day she might even lose interest in their comings and goings.

But, of course, she hadn't. Not really. Not yet. She just didn't want the bubble inside her at that moment to even be dented. Time enough for all that when she was home.

'Are you enjoying yourself?' Bill said.

'Yes, I think I am rather.'

'Is the weather good?'

'Wonderful.'

'It hasn't stopped raining here. You're not missing a thing.'

'This is costing a fortune,' Jessica said, eventually, wondering why after all these years all they could find to discuss was the weather and the children. 'You'd better ring off.'

'I love you, Jessie, look after yourself. We all miss you, even Butch is off his food.'

'He needs to lose some weight. Tell him he'll be able to catch those rabbits if he slims down.'

'I will. Goodbye, darling. Don't forget my postcard. Oh yes, and one to Betty and Peter. I'm going in for dinner tonight. They intend to rope me in for the Rotary's annual get-together if I can bear it without you.'

And he was gone. And she wanted to tell him 'I love you too'. She knew she'd probably feel guilty all day because of her negligence. She hoped he hadn't noticed. They'd been married too long to doubt each other.

She said a small and hasty prayer for the preservation of her gentle eldest son's too loving and easily-led heart, then went out to join Norma in the Hollywood sunshine.

Chapter Eight

As it turned out just she and Lilian went to the art gallery that first Friday. Norma had retired back to bed after breakfast with 'one of my frightful migraines, darling, please forgive me. I'll see you both this afternoon.' Jessica had overheard the muted violence of the marital quarrel during the night – keeping their voices down no doubt for her benefit, and she rigid with not wanting to be part of that particular fabric of their lives, but curious enough to wish she could hear the words coming discreetly yet passionately from the master bedroom.

Chuck had left town before Jessica rose. 'Flying East to see his daughters. New York, then Connecticut.' So Norma would nurse her bad head and she and Lilian would go alone to Santa Monica.

The weather cleared by midday, and sunshine, hot on Jessica's unmade-up face, washed over them as they found a parking space near the beach and walked to the gallery. 'Santa Monica is where most of the British seem to live,' said Lilian.

'Probably reminds them of Brighton,' Jessica

said, 'without the candy floss and winkle stalls of course.'

'What in God's name is a winkle?' Lilian asked. And Jessica laughed. The beaches were almost empty. 'I'll bring you down one Sunday,' Lilian smiled, 'it's busier and quite like nowhere else in the world, I suspect. As a reserved and well-behaved Englishwoman you should see Venice beach on a weekend at least once.'

The gallery was packed. The paintings nothing special, but everyone made the right noises. And Jessica was impressed that the artist was a woman of her own age and this was her first exhibition.

'What's she been doing up till now?' she asked Lilian as the reception drew to a close and they said their goodbyes and congratulations.

'She was an actress. Parts dried up, but she didn't intend to follow suit. She hopes she's found another career.'

'And has she? I mean, will people buy them?'

'It's likely. In case she turns out to be successful. They may not understand or even like the work, but a lot of the people here were invited for their well-known fear of being afraid to miss anything. Buy her while she's cheap and unknown, especially if the painting goes with the decor, then you can boast when she's famous and sells for millions.'

'How very clever.'

'It's another form of ambulance chasing.'

'If I had the money I'd buy one just to celebrate her wonderful audacity.'

Lilian smiled and squeezed her hand.

They went for a late lunch. Two other women came with them and they made their way back to the beach and settled into a café on the boardwalk at Venice. The other two were obviously a couple, and this was a first for Jessica, ignorant, or even innocent as she was. She found herself relieved they didn't make it obvious, but then chastised herself for her bigotry, even though unspoken. It was a new world, and she would surprise herself by taking it in her stride.

They ordered white wine and after a couple of glasses Jessica loosened up and began to make them laugh about life in a typical English village.

And while Lilian watched her, liking her for the way she saw the black and funny side of other people, Jessica watched Lilian. She was quirky and amusing, quick witted and with just the right amount of cynicism to make her fascinating to an Englishwoman who had been reared to distrust everything and everyone until proved otherwise. There was so much they both instinctively felt they could have said to each other, even on that first occasion. Weeks later, Jessica wondered how even then, at that early stage in their relationship, she knew there would be time for them. What she didn't see, acknowledge, in those tentative times of a new relationship, was what it was that drew her so quickly and eventually so passionately towards that life-enhancing and joyfully cryptic personality that sat so comfortably in Lilian. Her strength was obvious. Her sureness of her place in the world delightful. But the attraction was more. Deeper. How could Jessica have guessed immediately that what she did was fall in love with herself? Not the self she'd drifted into at that time. No. It was the rest of her. The part she'd suffocated. The part she'd dreamed of being and never realized.

But that day by the beach, feeling the sun too hot on her face and borrowing Lilian's silly hat to stop her redhead's skin from burning, all that Jessica knew was the indisputable fact that something was happening to her, and Lilian knew it, like no man ever had or could. It was disconcerting. With a man Jessica could have pretended, played games, thrown down her ace at the time she chose, and the male of the species would have flung himself into a blind panic while trying to keep control of the situation. Not this time. Lilian was a woman, and the kind who only appreciated direct and truthful confrontation. What was the expression she used? 'Say it like it is, babe.' Very American, but it made its point. And there was Jessica. Heterosexual as far as she knew, and had been, very much so, since puberty. Now, treading on hot coals, wondering if she could still get burnt at her age.

Lilian watched Jessica often as conversation tumbled together, her eyes smiling at her at times a shade too long. A romantic farce played itself out, drawing them into a spell they had no desire to resist. Wilfulness, a characteristic of Jessica's she believed she'd abandoned on becoming a mother, raised its flirtatious and arrogant head as it had always done in her halcyon days of irresponsibility. And just when she'd begun to believe she'd been up so many paths in her lifetime that there was no exploring left for her.

She was wrong.

The afternoon began to melt and merge into a warm and muted evening, shadows playing on the sand, orange sun settling into purple clouds. 'Don't get romantic about it,' Lilian said, 'I think it's pollution.'

They said goodbye to Lilian's friend, Rochelle, and her companion, the girl's name had long since fallen from memory, along with the colour of hair and eyes, kissed on cheeks blushed with a day's sunshine, found the car and drove east to Beverly Hills.

It was hard not to feel a little guilty about Norma, leaving her alone all day. 'They had a row last night,' Jessica said, 'she and Chuck, I mean. They fight a lot.'

'I'm not surprised.'

It was obvious that even Lilian had some idea of the state of her friend's marriage by the tone in her voice, but Jessica was not in the mood just then to delve into it.

The traffic going east was bad and the hold-ups made worse by endless roadworks. 'We might have been better on the freeway,' Lilian muttered.

She could feel Jessica's growing agitation at the lateness of the hour. 'Sorry about this. Should I feel bad about monopolizing you all day?'

'Norma won't mind. This holiday is supposed to be therapy for me. Make me better, so to speak.'

Lilian glanced at her quickly, then moved her eyes back to the road. 'And?'

It was time to tell about the depression, even so early in the friendship. It would get it out of the way. Besides, Lilian was easy, she would listen, and every nuance of the day had lead Jessica to believe this woman's comments would only be wise.

'I think I've been having a kind of nervous breakdown. A vacation with my best friend thousands of miles from home was the only thing left we hadn't tried.'

'What happened?'

'To cause the depression?'

Lilian nodded.

Jessica cleared her throat, grimaced and hoped it would pass for a smile, even if somewhat watery, then said weakly, 'It all seems rather trivial now I'm here.'

'Don't tell me if you'd rather not.'

'But I do.'

It seemed important somehow that she knew and accepted the dark side of Jessica as soon as possible. They came easily then, the words that had been hiding themselves from most others. The tedious traffic-stopping car journey back to Norma gave her all the space she needed to explain what had been crippling her from getting on with the rest of her life.

'I seem to have built a prison for myself from the tangle of emotions I've nurtured out of the stupidity of an imagination that withered without a baby to nurse. That's all it is really. Said out loud it makes me feel pathetic. Then before I could locate the key to this self-delusionary hell, they dragged me out by force and removed one of my breasts. It seemed to my warped mind the final aggressive action of a male chauvinist society. Silly of me. But I'd ceased to think straight.'

'Cancer?'

'Yes. You're almost the only person to say that out loud. Apart from Norma.' She put her hand to her heart. Talking about it could propel her into a dip of familiar misery. She fought against it.

'I liked being a woman, you see,' she said lamely.

Lilian glanced at her again. 'What sex do you consider yourself these days?' she said quietly.

For a moment Jessica had the terrible thought it might have crossed Lilian's mind she'd been alluding to her. Then she laughed. 'I know,' she said, 'I really had begun to think there was nothing for a woman after motherhood, so besotted am I with my kids. I'm only just beginning to feel angry with myself about it all. I've wasted so much time. It seems the only way I might be able to cut that damn cord is not for *them* to leave, they've done that already, but for *me* to get away. Is that silly enough for you?'

They parked in Norma's drive and without persuasion Lilian came in to offer any apologies that seemed necessary.

'Martini time,' smiled Norma, standing poised in her kitchen, pretending she'd heard the car and only just found the vodka bottle. Jessica suspected her cocktail time had started a lot earlier and she squirmed with guilt. She should have stayed with her friend. Her selfishness knew no bounds apparently. Norma's migraine had gone by lunchtime and she'd fled to the hairdressers to cheer herself up, and lingered a while in Neiman Marcus to stretch the cheering into ecstasy. Her obvious, deep-rooted unhappiness softened Jessica's heart and she went to kiss her, relieving her of one newly poured martini, not that she particularly felt much like drinking but it seemed the least she could do. Lilian helped herself to red wine. 'I cook with that,' said Norma.

'It'll do. I'm not staying long. How long's Chuck away?'

Norma said, 'He'll be back Monday. Why?'

'I'm having a dinner for a friend leaving for Europe. Join us, on Sunday.'

'I'd love to.' Norma smiled at her. Lilian glanced at Jessica, but there was no need for words. Her presence at the dinner party was confirmed in that look. Lilian's smile across the room was warm and brave. Jessica felt safe.

By eight-thirty Lilian had gone. Too much drink had left Norma unwilling to make dinner and 'Maria's out for the night'.

So they ordered in. One quick phone call and an entire Italian meal for two appeared thirty minutes later at the door.

'Amazing,' Jessica said, surprised at how hungry she was. She groaned with guilt later as the remains of Norma's pasta marinara found its way down the waste disposal.

'There's not still a war on, you know,' Norma laughed.

'You're so spoilt,' Jessica groaned, 'you're all so spoilt!'

'Compared to whom?'

They went to bed. And she listened to Norma pacing the floor of her bedroom before finally falling asleep while she was trying to make up her mind whether to go and comfort her friend. She dreamed about Lilian and Norma doing the most extraordinary things to each other under an eiderdown, which filled her with embarrassment when she greeted the morning and Norma bending over her, trying to persuade her to join her at the gym. 'Get lost,' Jessica muttered, and closed her eyes again.

'You're feeling better,' Norma said. 'I'll see you later.'

Jessica lingered on in the dream, surprised at the depths of her own sensual imaginings, dragging it out before it slipped forever into the subconscious. Surely it wasn't jealousy she felt as she dwelt on images of her two friends? Shades of that emotion followed her into the waking morning. Lilian's smile had held secrets. Her touch tentatively sexual. Jessica wondered if she was more starved of passion than she realized. Or had a curiosity for the unknown taken an unbelievable hold on her? Maybe she'd just become lazy and bored. Becoming aroused was too much of a performance where Bill was concerned. Perhaps she needed a certain stimulus that was sadly lacking after thirty years. She lay with eyes closed and remembered the games she and Bill used to play to turn them on, in those days when she was trying so hard to make even more babies, and leaping into bed when her temperature had reached the crucial figure was not necessarily conducive to an immediate and lasting erection. What a performance it had all been. And to no avail. Why on earth couldn't she have been satisfied with three children? No wonder people had thought her crazy.

She thought again about Lilian. Thinking how soft she would feel, how unlike a man her body would be when touched. The perfume of her would be as familiar as her own. How easily she would know about those certain places of a woman. How delightful it would be not to issue instructions. A deep feeling of eroticism crept unheralded across her body, the fine hairs of her skin tingling as memories of past and sometimes forbidden pleasures rose like the headiness of ripe fruit into her nostrils. The fingers of fantasy touched her breathlessly on damp and open thighs.

Embarrassed, as if someone were there to read her mind, she forced herself from bed and went downstairs to find some breakfast, falling already out of the English way of early morning tea drinking, allowing Maria to stop her work and make toast to eat with the coffee already brewed.

On the way to Lilian's on Sunday evening Norma said without taking her eyes off the road, 'Will this place be full of dykes, do you think?'

Jessica squirmed, unhappy with her friend's choice of words. 'Why d'you use that word?' she said.

'There's worse used. You should hear Chuck and his friends.'

'Must I?'

'He calls them "carpet munchers". You can guess what that means.'

'Thank you for sharing that with me!'

Norma laughed, glanced quickly across at Jessica while they waited for a light to change. 'You like her, don't you? Lilian, I mean.'

'Yes, of course I do. So do you. I really don't see what her sexual preferences have to do with anything.'

'They haven't, and you're right. I think she's

adorable. Let's enjoy the evening. At least there's no going home to a quarrel tonight. I rather like the bed all to myself. I guess we can adjust to anything if we put our mind to it.'

Jessica asked what they'd fought about the night before Chuck went away, but Norma had shrugged and muttered something like 'the usual' and made some crack to make her laugh, and changed the subject.

Jessica suspected that her friend had no intention of leaving her husband, but would stick it out until the humiliation became bigger than Chuck's wallet. Jessica herself wouldn't have lasted half the time. God knows what sexually contracted diseases he'd exposed his wife to in the last few years, because they still did occasionally try to make love in that sterile and emotionally barren, well-pillowed Californian king-sized bed of theirs. 'He gave me crabs once,' Norma threw at her one evening over coffee while Chuck was taking a phone call. It made Jessica splutter into her drink so much there was no time for further explanation before Chuck came back in, appearing so genial and normal it was hard to imagine. There was something of the farce written all through their bizarre union. And the thought of the fastidious Norma having to deal with crabs was hysterical in the short term. It was hard to see Mr and Mrs Sarrison growing old together.

Lilian's house was just as Jessica had imagined. True to what she'd been told the first evening they'd met, Lilian's approaches to 'housework' consisted of books and magazines removed hastily from chairs and surfaces just before they were used or sat on, and dishes from a previous meal put quickly into the dishwasher as the first guest of the evening wandered to the kitchen to help themselves to more wine. But the walls were covered with oil paintings and watercolours, lovingly gathered through a lifetime so obviously filled with warm adventures. No decorator had designed Lilian's house. It was all her, and only her. It shone like a beacon of reality in a town devoted so thoroughly to pink shopping malls and homes that looked like film sets.

There were six of them to dinner that night. They ate outside on a terrace smelling of mock-orange and jasmine standing in over-sized Mexican clay pots. Ficus trees covered in white lights glowed and twinkled around them as they sat. There was a married couple and one other single man to make up the numbers. Norma knew no-one, except of course, Jessica and Lilian. That fact seemed to relax her and as the evening wore on she became more like the girl with whom Jessica had shared her schooldays. Money or no money, her marriage was smothering her, imprisoning her, and eventually would change her for the worse.

The food was home cooked, with little or no concession to fat-free or sodium-lite. Without being asked, Jessica stood as they finished each course, as if to follow Lilian each time to the kitchen gave her once again that feeling of safety that enveloped her when they were together.

Norma was enjoying herself, flirting with the single man on her right. 'I hope she's not set her heart on it,' whispered Lilian on one of the trips indoors to get more wine, 'Rocky's gay.'

'With a name like Rocky?'

They touched hands as Jessica turned and smiled. 'I feel much better,' she said, rather lamely, feeling embarrassed, but wanting Lilian's hand on her own.

'How long are you here for?' Lilian said.

'I guess as long as I need, and as soon as I feel better.'

'Does that mean you'll be going home any minute?'

'No.' Jessica's voice was firm. 'No. I'm actually beginning to have a really good time. And I'm not ready for the return of the killer miseries yet. No doubt they've decided to scuttle back to England until further notice. They'll be waiting at Heathrow for me when I return, or maybe, even now as I talk, sitting like a coven of witches in the cupboard beneath the stairs at home. When I open the door they'll fall all over me along with the rest of the rubbish I'd stored away for years. Other people's mostly. Sons' rubbish, I mean. There are times I feel I'm drowning in other people's debris.'

Lilian said nothing, but put one hand out to

touch Jessica's face. 'How brittle you are,' she said, 'but so wonderfully wise. Is it only because you're sad?'

'I'm not sad, I'm angry. I just don't know what about.'

That evening Norma was too drunk to drive home, and she had to call and get José out of bed and tell him to take a cab to the valley and take them home in her car, which Jessica was too terrified to drive. Norma eventually caught on to the truth about her flirtation with the young and virile Rocky, which made her giggle quite uncontrollably all the way home. 'Look at me,' she said, 'I can't even tell whether they're straight or not these days!'

'When are you coming home?' Bill asked towards the end of the fourth week. 'You must confirm and book the ticket darling.'

'Not yet. It's all doing me so much good. You were absolutely right to think of it, you clever old thing, you. And besides, Norma needs me. I'll tell you about it when I see you.'

His answer came across the impersonal international telephone lines, making her feel guilty and angry at the same time because he could make her feel that way. 'Are you really feeling better? I'm glad the time away has worked out for you. You sound almost like your old self again. Has Stephen called you? He said he wanted to. This girl he's

175

seeing seems to be turning out quite serious. He's looking forward to you meeting her.'

She wanted to say, 'Don't tell me, I'm not ready yet, don't pull me back too soon into that life. Not yet. Let me fly a little longer.'

She believed she didn't know the reason for her uncharacteristic behaviour. Not even to herself could she explain such an alien emotion as the one she felt towards Lilian. Not that the emotion itself was alien. Not at all. She'd been there before. With Bill. Maybe even a few others. It was the part of Lilian herself she couldn't, or wouldn't fathom. But Jessica? She was bewildered, ecstatic, confused and terrified. And happy.

It was weeks before Bill put his foot down. Days that flew past in a flurry of poolside breakfasts, dinners on lighted terraces, pizzas eaten in Lilian's car on the way home from the movies, or visits to art galleries and museums. A journey before dawn one Sunday to the Rose Bowl in Pasadena, and brunch on Venice beach watching the parade of eccentrics and out-of-towners filling their gaping mouths with frozen yoghurt and chocolate dough-nuts.

Jessica listened while her husband used Stephen's romance to lure her home. 'Why do I have to be there?' she said. 'It's too short a time for this affair to have got serious.'

'Jess, you will have been gone almost two months. I miss you. I need you.'

'Isn't Ruth coming in?'

Bill said nothing, and as soon as she spoke she regretted it. Perhaps the remark would go right over his head, used as he was to her nastiness these last few years. She was strongly resisting the return to the fold. 'Let me talk to Norma,' Bill said.

God, she hated it when he got that 'I'll be patient and understanding new-man tone' in his voice. 'Don't treat me like a child, Bill. Norma has nothing to do with this. I love it here. I'm not sure I love England right now.'

Was that a metaphor, she thought? Was it Bill that had faded so rapidly from her heart? That morning was the first time she admitted to herself, as she argued with a husband who merely wanted a wife to come home, that this particular wife didn't actually want to leave her friend. And it wasn't Norma that sprung so energetically into her mind. Not a bit of it. Not the soul-mate of her youth. It was Lilian she couldn't bear to part with.

'Oh God, Bill,' she thought, 'I know I'll have to go back. Back to being that nice Mrs Wooldridge who's having such a hard time coming to terms with you-know-what, and maybe if she joined the wives' fellowship or even the choir it would take her mind off her troubles.'

So at last, guilt-ridden, feeling that eventually even Bill might tire of her, after two months of playtime, vacation with the girls, she rearranged her flight back. She would arrive home almost three months after she'd arrived.

'Maybe this is better,' she muttered to Norma when she put down the phone, having organized the journey with British Airways.

'Better than what?' Norma said.

'Well, before I was so negative. Now, at least, I'm *positively* miserable. I just don't want to leave and I have no reason except I'm having such a good time. That must at least be a step forward.'

'I wish I was coming with you.'

'What's to stop you?'

Norma shrugged and didn't answer. It was still a battle for her, with no solution to the state of her marriage and her life, not one that she could face, anyway. Jessica went to her, and they held each other. Life gave you merely moments it seemed, and just when you were getting the hang of it all, it threw sand in your eyes to blind and distress you.

'I was right all along,' she said, 'life *is* the bitch. But I have enjoyed myself. America, California, whatever it is, has totally seduced me. I won't hear a bad word said about it ever again.'

Chapter Nine

Chuck said, 'Bring Bill next time, he's one great guy.' And Jessica wondered how he knew that when their relationship had been sporadic, to say the least.

'He mouths words,' murmured Norma. 'There seems to be no connection with his brain at times,' and she nodded disparagingly towards the departing back of her husband.

'Come back with me,' Jessica said. 'Just for a while. If you hate it you can return. And the boys would love to see you.'

But it was no good. Fear was deep rooted in Norma. Fear of getting old alone. The terror of poverty and old age creeping up on her after she'd grown used to so much comfort. 'It's amazing how quickly one gets used to a higher standard of living,' she said plaintively.

A part of Jessica understood. And a life of pretence was maybe after all an easier option. Leave the bravery where it belonged, in the capable and unveined hands of the young.

*   *   *

All she had to do was tell Lilian.

'I have to go back.' She said it as soon as they sat down.

It was two days after the reservations had been made, and she'd arranged that Bill and Stephen would meet her that English summer morning when she arrived home. She was trying hard to conjure up a degree of enthusiasm, and the thought she might still be able to take her new-found cheerfulness back with her, to reside in the warm damp atmosphere of a Sussex garden, and nestle in the fledgling spirit that seemed to be at last inhabiting a small space in her heart.

'To England?' Lilian said, her voice un-emotional.

Jessica nodded. They were standing in one of the art galleries she was constantly being dragged to, Lilian longing for Jessica to share her passion. It was the big one on Wilshire, not the little private ones where salespeople hover. They both wanted to take a look again at the painting of David Hockney's that hung with such confidence in one of the galleries. It had been Jessica who'd used the word 'confident', because that's what it was.

'The road to the studio', it was called. Apparently Mulholland Drive. Not obvious to un-cultured eyes. Understanding was not the emotion she'd found when standing before the picture for the first time. It was the colours, tumbling and dancing around each other and, it seemed, right off the canvas and into her heart when she'd walked with Lilian into that special space. For that was it. It summed it all up. If she had the talent it would have been exactly that painting, those brushstrokes she would have pulled out of herself if confronted by that virgin canvas. It was what California had done for her. Filled her soul, her heart, her eyes, with unadulterated colour, and had dragged her from a black and white existence into the seductive fairyland of reds and greens and blues. Primary colours. Not the elegant and whimsical shades of pastel that were so symbolic of the life she'd left behind. Not the grey of good taste and understatement, but the colour that life should be. Red. Life's blood. Washing over and in her again, filling her with a flowering of hope, spring-like in its erotic budding, driving the weight of the winter and the gloom it stood for away, so that she could stand and see the life ahead instead of listening to the cynics who had blocked the view for too long in their attempt to keep her silent and undemanding.

'When will you leave?' Lilian did not turn as she spoke. Both of them remained with their eyes on the painting. Jessica longed to sit on the bench behind them. She could feel the edge of it pressing against the back of her knees as she stood there, but to move would break the spell, and there were times to break spells and times to wait.

'In five days. At the weekend.'

'Is it all arranged?'

'Yes.' A pause. And Jessica's heart was suddenly

straining and beating as if to leap out of her body and towards the woman by her side. Towards her love. Because she was. Her love. And there were no words she could find, even though now at last she could admit to herself how she felt. It was strange how she knew, when nothing in her life until then had led her to believe she could ever love another woman in the same way as she did a man. But it felt the same. The heart beating faster. The fear of making a move in case the spell was broken. The waiting to see, hear, whether the object of all this elation in you felt the same way. But she knew the answer. And had done since the beginning. At last, it was the right time.

Lilian said at last, 'Do you want to go? Are you ready?'

'I don't know,' and then, immediately, 'the answer's "no". Of course I don't want to go. I'm afraid of what's there. I have to remember what I was running from. It's still there. Things that I saw as gravely important don't seem to matter when I'm here. Reality.' The words tumbled. Still they didn't look at each other, didn't draw near for comfort. Jessica could feel the heat from Lilian's body, smell the musk from her perfume. She knew without the touching that Lilian's hands would be cool on her arm, her forehead, her breast.

'You know I love you, don't you?' Lilian said, her head still turned away.

'Yes.'

There was so much else that needed to be said, but Lilian seemed to understand she would have to lead. Deep waters were closing over Jessica in her panic to stay afloat. She was used to the lifebelt of conservatism. This was whirlpools, swamp. Something alien. Something Lilian could deal with. Jessica waited.

Lilian said, 'I've loved you since you drank the raspberry-flavoured coffee at your first Beverly Hills' party, and swallowed that chocolate cake without a thought of your waistline. I realized quite by chance you were the one thing I'd been hoping to meet in this crazy town. Someone without an image panic.'

'And what about all the other panics that I'm sure by now you've noticed make up a good part of me?'

'I can live with those. They're familiar. They're a part of life. Not to be talked out of us by therapists. Something we learn to live with if we want survival. They make you beautiful because I see them on your face. Your life laid out for me. You just have to stop being afraid of yourself.'

At last, Jessica sat down. On the bench behind them, waiting, it seemed, to support her excited and fearful desire. She sank down to hide the shaking of her limbs. Lilian came and sat beside her. Took her hand. There were two other people at the other sides of the room. A man and a woman, not together, making their respectful ways around the walls in solitary enjoyment. Silence all around them. The way an art gallery compels you. Like church. A place for confession. A time for declaration. Jessica glanced at the young man in sweats making his way slowly towards them, his eyes on each painting. Her hands were damp with perspiration.

'I don't want you to go,' Lilian whispered. 'Stay with me. Even if it's not for ever. I can't bear the thought of seeing you off on that plane, making noises like, "Have a good life". Give me a little while. Then go back if you must. But make this your time. And mine. You are the funniest, the most endearing, unexplored territory I've ever known. And the angriest. And I love you for it.' She paused and at last Jessica looked at her, saw she was smiling, saw the silly hat that had slipped sideways on her newly washed hair.

'Well?' Lilian said at last.

'I love you too.' It had been easier than she'd imagined.

'You'll stay?'

'What will I tell Bill?'

'Anything you want.'

'He'll not understand any of this. I'm not sure I do. What's happening to me?'

'Love's love, Jessie. Across the genders, love's love.'

She didn't mind the 'Jessie', forgetting Bill's old pet name for her in the passion of the moment. They stood without another word and left the gallery. Took with them the sensations of the Hockney painting and carried them back to Lilian's doll-like house in the valley, and placed them lovingly on each other's bodies as they undressed one another in the heat of that Californian afternoon and laid on the patchwork quilt that covered Lilian's big bed. And it wasn't strange, or tentative, or less joyful than any other love experience of Jessica's youth. Their bodies held no secrets from each other, the excitement came with the knowledge of each other's hearts. Just the two of them. Making love. Because of love.

'I love you, Lilian.'

'And I you. Stay with me.'

'I promise.'

'Always?'

'Always.'

Well, what are promises for, anyway? Jessica must have broken hundreds, probably thousands, on her unenterprising journey through the first fifty years of her life. Promises to herself as well as others.

She called Norma at ten-thirty that night. 'Sorry to call you so late. I think I'll stay at Lilian's tonight. There's been a dinner party, and it hasn't begun to break up yet. Do you mind terribly?'

'Shall I come and get you?' Norma said. 'Or I could send José.'

'No, no! Everything's fine. Truthfully. Saying

goodbyes is taking me longer than I expected. I'll see you in the morning. Is Chuck home?'

'Not yet. Late business again.'

'Are you OK?'

'I'm watching TV. You see how enterprising I've become? Finding things to do when I'm in bed?'

The brittleness of her sarcasm was not lost, and Lilian saw Jessica's reaction to it on her face as she said 'goodnight' and turned back to the sofa where they'd been sitting.

'What is it?' She reached up and pulled Jessica towards her.

'I feel guilty. About Norma, and leaving her alone. She's not happy, and I feel I should be helping somehow, but for the life of me I don't know how.'

Lilian handed her a glass of wine. Silence hung tentatively in the air. Jessica said quickly, wanting no hidden agendas between them from the word 'go', 'You know what that marriage is all about, don't you?'

'I know Chuck, so I can guess. Why doesn't she leave?'

'Fear.'

'Of what?'

'Being alone, poverty, or anyway, having a lot less money than she's grown used to.'

'And that makes up for the humiliation? She can live with what he is because of what he's got?'

'Well, it's all a bit pathetic really, isn't it? Tacky,

but hardly earth-shattering. I mean, I'm sure he's only doing what loads of men dream about. Specially as they get older. We all need a little stimulus, something different to speed the pulses and convince us we're still in the game. I couldn't live with it personally, I think I'd laugh and ruin his performance in any shape it came, but then Bill's always been as straight as a dye. I can't imagine what it must be like to be married to someone who isn't.'

Lilian laughed, and Jessica blushed at the realization of what she'd said. They listened to the music from the stereo. Finally Lilian spoke, 'What has Norma told you about Chuck?'

'Just what he likes to do, and how he's the one who organizes the so-called "parties". I suggested she dressed herself up. You know, played games. Lots of relationships go through this sort of thing. I've read about it. She didn't seem to think it would help, or anyway, didn't respond enthusiastically to my suggestions. I wanted her to come home with me. Back to England.' Jessica smiled, 'I'm glad she didn't take me up on that idea. God knows how I would get out of it as things have turned out. I don't know what else to say to her.'

Lilian's eyes hadn't left Jessica's face as she listened. After a pause she said, 'I'd better tell you all of it.'

Jessica stared at her. 'What d'you mean?'

'It's not just any old hookers that Chuck arranges for these parties of his. That's how it started, I guess, but like most things in this town he got bored and kept stretching the limits. The hookers got younger and younger, and I'm told that both sexes are involved.'

Again Jessica stared, and then, 'I'm an innocent, Lilian. Explain yourself. Just how young *are* these hookers, and are you telling me that Chuck is queer?'

She could have bitten her tongue off at the use of that particular word, but Lilian, blessed at times and with those she loved with a sweet tolerance, merely smiled and went on holding her hand.

'It is said some of the youngsters are fifteen, maybe sixteen, though willing. And no, Chuck is not "queer" as you so quaintly call it. He's merely rich and bored, and believes money can buy him everything, even youth. They all are. The ones he caters for, that is. The kids don't complain. They either need the money, or even live in hope that one night they'll meet a rich producer and they'll be just what he needs for his next movie. Pathetic. He is living on borrowed time as far as the law and this town is concerned. He's started to believe his standing and his "old" money can protect him. They can't. They won't. He's made enemies. Most people that stay rich during recessions do, and he's been too indiscreet of late to stop that many guys from talking. Except I believe it will more than likely be the wives of some or at least one of his fellow partygoers that will eventually pull the plug on him.'

'I have never really believed those sorts of things went on. It's revolting.'

'I thought that might make your hair curl. And I don't believe your friend Norma wanted you to know. She told you a small area of scandal. Just enough to get your sympathy. She knew the truth would only rouse your anger and not your under-standing.'

'For God's sake, Lilian, the man's practically a child molester! I don't care if they're willing or not. How can Norma bear it?'

Silence. Lilian shrugged.

'Do you think she actually knows? I mean, the details?' Jessica knew the answer to her own question even before she'd voiced it. She began to wonder what exactly she'd got herself into, coming to this extraordinary town in the first place. And was Norma really living with such shame that she couldn't even tell her oldest and dearest friend?

'I suspect she must,' Lilian said. 'She's not a stupid woman. And I do know that the reason his previous wife got that enormous settlement was to keep her mouth shut. So tell me, why doesn't your "best friend in all the world" leave?'

Jessica paused for just a moment, and then, 'She signed a pre-nuptial agreement.'

Lilian took both her hands. 'What an innocent you are. Everything still surprises you. How on earth have you remained so childlike all these years?'

'We live in Sussex.'

Lilian laughed loudly. 'Don't tell me you haven't come across anything slightly dissolute in Chichester. Not even a mild bit of wife swopping? The place seemed ripe for it to me. All those pretentious good manners. Hiding their secrets behind a veil of hypocrisy.'

'I haven't. Or anyway, I haven't noticed. My life has been so occupied up until these last few years. When do people have time to organize or even think about things like that? And anyway, we don't mix in those sorts of circles.'

Lilian laughed again. 'Each time you open your mouth you surprise me even more,' she said, 'I love you very much Jessie, and I am truly sorry I've handed you something to make you even angrier with life than you are already.' She reached behind her and picked up a box of Hershey kisses. Jessica shook her head. For once her appetite had abandoned her.

'What shall I say?' she said at last. 'What do I say to Norma when I go back tomorrow? She has to get out of there. She must go home to England. The whole thing has corrupted her. She's not thinking straight. I don't recognize her. Where did principle and honour go?'

'Out of the window, ground into the dirt as soon as she muttered "I do". Trodden underfoot, easily forgotten along with all the other little tribulations the rich discard, like unpaid utility bills and never having to wait for the January sales. Good God, woman, have you no notion what the power of money is? You know people kill for it, you read newspapers I presume, so why are you so shocked if it buries even nice people's integrity?'

Jessica couldn't answer. Couldn't tell her about the young, sweet Norma, crying in her best friend's arms over lost teenage love, driven by passion into the most unlikely and irredeemable love affairs, with no hint of sensibility. And now here she was, if all this was true, and there was no reason for her to doubt Lilian, sacrificing her once-gentle self yet again, only this time not for love or even lust, this time for the strongest cliché of all. Good old money. The final ideal out of the window. Who would have believed Norma could turn out to be so predictable; and so damn stupid.

'I'll tackle her tomorrow,' Jessica said as they prepared for bed. This time to sleep. The developments of the latter part of the evening had driven all thoughts of passion out of her mind. The joy of realizing she had no reason to explain her temporary loss of sexual drive when the affair was still so new was music to her soul. To be held in affection without desire. To be stroked for only comfort until her eyes could hold out no longer against sleep. All this without guilt. To be understood and not feel silly. To be free, to be utterly and completely female without a hint of apology, this Lilian gave her. And when they awoke in the morning, she was still in Lilian's arms. And she was still in love.

'Shall I drive you back?' Lilian said at breakfast.

'Thank you.'

And they smiled at each other.

Norma had been to the gym and was sitting by the pool when Jessica helped herself to coffee and joined her. 'So?' She took off her sunglasses and stared up at her friend as she approached.

Jessica sat down on the lounger beside her.

'So?'

How was Jessica supposed to start the conversation? Excuse me, 'best friend in all the world', but I've just apparently come out of the closet and spent a loving and sexy night with a member of my own sex for the first time in what I've come to realize has been an extraordinarily sheltered life, oh yes, and during this affair I've learnt you happen to be married to a man who can only get it up with underage hookers of both sexes, which I have been told you know all about.

'What happened to you?' Norma said.

'A lot.'

'Don't tell me. I think I've guessed and I'm not sure I'm ready for it.'

Jessica stared at her. 'What?'

'You and Lilian. Am I right?'

'Yes.'

Norma leaned back in her lounger and started to laugh.

Jessica said, 'I would prefer shock. Or at the very least, surprise.'

'I'd seen it coming. And I've been too long in this town to be surprised at anything.'

'You should have said.'

'Well now, that would have been one of life's interesting confrontations I must say.'

They sipped their coffee, embarrassed, a certain coyness they were both too old for settled uncomfortably into the stillness that sat between them as one or other searched for words appropriate for this sudden madness of spirit.

Norma said at last, 'Are you still going home?'

'I don't know. No. I can't. Not now. I must talk to Bill.'

'Jesus Christ, you're not going to tell him, are you?'

'You think I shouldn't?'

'Definitely. I definitely think you shouldn't.'

Jessica looked at her carefully. She said, 'You think it's part of my depression, don't you? Just a little crazy with my menopause.'

'Well, now that you've said it, that's my first reaction, yes. What else are you going to say? Norma, I've fallen in love, and we're going to spend the rest of our lives together in the smog of Los Angeles? Is that what you want me to believe?'

Jessica put down her coffee cup. The reality of the situation was catching up with her at last. She wished Lilian had been there. Maybe she really was just a silly woman at the mercy of her out of control hormones.

Norma went on, 'I've known you too long, Jess.

This is not you. The extremes of this silly town have captured you in a very bizarre fashion. It can do that. Specially if you're off balance to start with.'

'Is that *your* excuse?' The question was brutal. Direct. It took Norma by surprise. She didn't move, not even to replace her coffee cup in the saucer. Jessica saw the perspiration break out on her top lip. Panic had always done that to her, even as a child.

She said at last, too brightly, too fiercely, too defensively, 'What d'you mean?'

Confrontation was inevitable. Jessica said gently, 'I know about Chuck, I mean the rest of it. The part you felt you couldn't tell me.'

'Oh.' There was nothing else she could say for a moment. And then, 'We both need a drink,' and rang a small bell to summon Maria. It made Jessica wince, that bell. It seemed to stand, at that moment, for every worthless thing that her friend was so desperate to hang on to. And she realized that for the first time in years the last thing she actually wanted was a drink. Her mind needed all its faculties. It was time to decide what to do, at least in the immediate future. Maria brought wine.

'I'm going to move in with Lilian for a while,' Jessica said. 'Do you understand that?' She hadn't planned it that way. The words were simply there and then they were said.

Norma didn't smile. 'Is this the first time in your life you're finding it difficult not to judge?'

It was hard to look at each other. Then Jessica said, rather fiercely, 'Why can't you just get up and leave? I'm not suggesting you report him, or anything like that. I can see that would be an impossible situation. But sooner or later someone will, and then what the hell do you do the rest of your life? All the money in the world won't sweeten that. For God's sake, get out now, while you still have some small wisps of dignity intact. I just fail to understand how not only can you stay married to him, but that you are still sharing the same bed.'

Norma said nothing. Eventually she shrugged. 'I don't want you to go to Lilian, but I guess I'm too late. It's all been so much more bearable with you here. I should have told you everything at the start. I just couldn't find the courage. I have no bravery left. But I guess you've gathered that.'

'Yes.'

'You, on the other hand, seem to have found a mountain of it in these last few weeks. I envy you.'

Jessica remained silent, aware she still wasn't quite brave enough to simply come out and say, 'Well yes, but then I'm in love, you see, and we both know how courageous that makes a girl.'

She packed her belongings and Norma didn't stop her. Jessica said she would call the next day, tell her what she'd said to Bill, 'I'll phone him tomorrow.' Norma promised she would think very thoroughly about leaving, but both of them already knew about the history of promises. The unknown territory of Jessica's future stretched in front of her. It was hard not to be afraid. What had Lilian said that morning when she'd dropped her off? 'Don't rush yourself. Just do what your instinct tells you. Commonsense will follow. Trust yourself. Things will be just dandy.'

Well, Jessica's instinct had told her she couldn't spend one more night under the same roof as Chuck Sarrison and remain polite, pretend she didn't know. She thought of her sons at fifteen and shuddered. She could only thank God she was not his wife, and the miles to the sanctuary of the house in the valley were scarcely enough to shield her from the repulsion she felt for him, and the confusion in her heart about Norma still living with him.

Above all, Lilian was waiting. And ahead of her, the telephone conversation with Bill. But that was tomorrow. Now was the time to start living in the present. How else to survive these next few weeks and the days ahead when she would still ask herself what the hell she was doing? Was she still expecting a knight in shining armour? Only the knight was a dame, and Jessica was no longer a girl, her decisions would affect more than just herself. All she knew was that suddenly her life was far from over. It beckoned with an enthusiasm she thought no longer existed for her.

Norma drove her to Lilian's office, and then she cried a little. First on Jessica's shoulder, then on Lilian's over lunch. She left them both sometime in the middle of the afternoon, tired and a little drunk, not so much from the wine as from her emotional outpourings. Lilian abandoned her office and took Jessica and her belongings back to the valley. It had all been so quick. So final. It seemed to scare them both, and that night they both slept restlessly but were unable to confront or explain their fears.

And at six a.m. the following morning Jessica rose, leaving Lilian still in bed, and called her husband. Plunging in without too much preparation, 'I want to stay a little longer Bill. I've cancelled my reservation. I'm not ready.'

'Cancelled? Not ready? What's happened? I called Norma last night. She said you were staying with a friend for a while, and that you would call me with the number. What the hell is going on out there?'

'I can't tell you on the telephone. But I can't stay with Norma any longer.'

'Then come home, for God's sake. Have you fallen out?'

'Not really. Sort of.'

'Make up your mind, Jessica. I swear to God you seem worse than ever. And as for Norma, she was being extremely secretive.'

'I'm perfectly fine. Very strong. That's why I can say to you I'm staying longer. Let me write to you.'

He sighed. Across the miles, not understanding. But if she'd told him everything just like that he would have understood even less than she did herself.

'A letter is on its way,' she said. 'Or at least it will be after today. I'm sorry Bill.'

He was silent for a long time. The thought went through her head, 'Well, you've blown this one girl,' but eventually, across the frantic beating of her heart which seemed to thud right into the telephone and across the miles, Bill said very quietly, 'All right Jessie, all right. Let me have your number there. I'll phone in a few days. Just take care of yourself and don't make decisions that are impossible to reverse. Let me know if you need money.'

She wished fervently the subject of money had not come up. She hadn't thought. She said to Lilian, 'I can't take from my husband when cavorting so enthusiastically with another.' But what else? Here she was about to slip into a second dependent relationship like some wretched middle-aged playgirl.

Clever old Bill. Had he guessed that something stranger than anyone at home could have imagined was happening to his crazy wife? But then, as Lilian pointed out to her later, 'You're not really crazy. You know that in your heart. And menopause or not, I'm sure Bill probably finds you just as exciting as you were thirty years ago.'

Jessica laughed for the first time that day. 'Now who's being naïve?'

'It's simply that you no longer see yourself with

any clarity. You've blurred your outline. Take away the wife and mother and you believe there's nothing there. *You're* there. And you're screaming at the top of your voice to get out.'

'Supposing when I do get out I'm absolutely horrid?'

'Then you'll be horrid.'

'I see.'

'And I will still love you.'

And Jessica believed she would.

Chapter Ten

Four days later she talked to Bill again. This time, he called her. He believed he'd given her time to think things through. In the last few years he'd learnt to live with a wife who found it hard enough to decide what to wear each morning; now she seemed to be leaping from one decision to another without any thought whatsoever. And Bill was worried. In his love for her he was sure he could take anything her confusion threw at him, and he had up until then. Her lack of response, her surprising self-absorption after a lifetime of living through others, and her humour, which lately had become more acerbic and even hurtful. He had taken it all. Everyone had assured him it would pass. 'It's the shock of the operation, Mr Wooldridge, the counselling will help.' They'd dismissed her longtime pain of not having a fourth child, seeing the desire as a silly whim embarked upon by a woman in the throes of early meno-pause. And he'd not wanted more babies, and Jessica knew that. It remained unspoken between them. Not confronted, like so many of the painful moments of their life. Norma had been his last hope. Surely she would pour out her heart to her oldest friend. After all, women had this thing going, this bonding that everyone went on about so much these days. So she'd gone to America. He would give her a month, and then she'd come home.

But she didn't. And now she didn't want to, and on top of everything something had happened between her and Norma. Bill was almost at the end of his tether. He missed her. It was time she came home.

It was dawn. She and Lilian, still holding each other. Together, loving, the passion awake immediately, and the love pouring over them, pushing away the doubts, and making them strong. To Jessica it seemed she'd walked so quickly into this strange and wide-awake new existence. Almost run. Without thought, Bill would say. But thinking no longer mattered, no longer seemed that important. The compulsion for sensibility no longer drove her insane with its demands. Only instinct. What she wanted. What she needed. Because at long last it seemed she knew. Wilful as it was, at least she realized what would make her happy at that time. To be with Lilian, to enjoy the surrender, to lie in the sunshine on the unmanicured lawn in the afternoon in the valley, and count the hours until Lilian returned, knowing that when she did, there would be no dread in Jessica about making conversation if she didn't want to, knowing that even if she found her moody, Lilian would wait in silence and tolerance for her to get through it, without entertaining the thought she herself might be to blame when it was abundantly clear it was merely a passing phase on Jessica's part. And they both understood it *would* pass if it was left untended. Unworried. Unirritated. Jessica was never to hear from her lover's lips, female lips, 'Is it something I've done? Or haven't done?' If the life they'd embarked on so quickly was wilful, Jessica did her best to push the thought aside, even in those early tempestuous days, holding on to Lilian's warm and slender body, throwing off one of those ridiculous hats, 'I hate them, but don't stop wearing them now, I've grown so used to the face beneath.'

And Lilian's retort, laughing, assertive, American, East coast, 'Don't worry, babe, I don't intend to do anything you tell me, you'd be impossible with power. Worse than that, you might stop being angry, and then life would be so much less exciting!' She would stroke the angry scar on Jessica's breast every morning, making it beautiful with her touch, looking with compassion into Jessica's crumpled, dawnlit face as her eyes creaked open, stopping the old misery before it even got a foot in the door. 'I have you,' Lilian would say, 'I have you.' And she did. For that time they had each other, and the world was an easier place to inhabit. And no-one else was necessary. They never talked about the future. And despite the phone call, despite Norma, despite even the mess Jessica was about to leave behind in England, along with the confusion and unhappiness, for that glorious time it was worth it. Lilian was worth it.

The first morning they woke together Lilian had said, 'I think I've been waiting for you a long time. I always knew there must have been a reason for me to have moved from the East coast, to come here, the worst city in the world, God help me, I'll probably die here without ever seeing New England again!'

And Jessica, serious, thoughtful, 'Have I always been gay, d'you think? Have I just not realized?'

Lilian had laughed and hugged her, untidying grey-red hair with onion-stained fingers from cooking supper, shaking her head, 'No, no, Jessie baby, we'd just not met yet. You had your Bill, and that was right for then. This is right for now. Don't dwell on it. Let it happen.'

But it was Jessica Wooldridge she was talking to, not some brave and hopeful, young American girl with remnants still of the pioneer blood left lovingly in her genes by a weatherbeaten Victorian great-grandmother. Jessica Wooldridge née Byfleet, whose ancestry could only be traced back to Surrey, with a little Baptist church-going on the paternal side of the family and too long ago to worry about at the time of her confirmation. No aggressive bravery from the women in Jessica's background. Her mother's silent struggle and eventual surrender to cancer had a certain resignation about it that more than likely helped her through the whole process of dying. Perhaps it had been easier than living, specially with Jessica's father and the orderliness of the life he had, in his turn, inherited from *his* parent. Childhood memories remain for ever. Jessica remembered it all so clearly. Everything so cut and dried. So predictable. Worthing had been the place for vacations. Never ventured anywhere else. It never crossed his mind. If they'd lived in Lancashire it would have been Blackpool. The one year they went to Ireland had been her mother's idea, and Stanley Byfleet in a fit of largesse had agreed. No-one ever knew what had come over him at the time, but it didn't become an option for the future. Dad said the Irish enjoyed the drinking, and the fighting that followed, too much for their own good. 'Not a place for children, Sarah. Dublin is not a place for children.'

Jessica remembered thinking it was *just* the place for children. All that poetry and singing, which was the reason her mother had wanted to go in the first place, starved as she was in that marriage of anything much to do with selfish pleasures, let alone the joy of poetry. And what was the point of alcohol if you didn't enjoy it? Years later Jessica had visited again with Bill, and been very surprised to learn that their writers could live there without paying tax. A tax haven for writers. Mum would have been impressed, and if Dad had known at the time there is no doubt they would never have crossed the channel for that holiday. Never have put their feet on the soil of a country that was governed by such frivolity. Poor Dad. He never could see the point of shelves full of books, and Mum loved them so. 'But Sarah, what's the reason for hanging on to them when they've all been read?' She had no answer to that. So eventually all the books in the house were merely borrowed from the library because Mum could never have borne to throw them away, or even hand them on, loving as she did, not only the reading of them, but the feel and smell of living one's life surrounded by them. Besides, their friends were mainly Dad's, and club nights at the British Legion was their pastime (not reading – 'that's for sissies or old maids with too much time on their hands with no man to tend to'), or cricket on the Surrey village green every summer Sunday when it wasn't raining. There were times when Mum must have prayed for a wet weekend. Rain meant no sandwiches to prepare, no urns to fill with tea for half-time, no mindless chatter with other wives – 'The little women are gossiping today, tea will be late again, have to put a stop to that, bless them.'

It must have destroyed her mother's soul. She escaped before the onslaught of the menopause, in the only way she would have dared. She died, and left a space in Dad's life he found he was never able to replace. He'd believed all his days that it was merely her housewifery that he would miss.

That the practical side of domesticity had been all a woman needed, and so therefore he'd made her happy. The sweetness of her loyalty and devotion to his ego left him bereft when he was finally alone, leaving him with the nagging thought that he'd shared in giving her a life less than perfect.

But by then Jessica had been convinced by her parents that for a woman marriage was the only path to happiness, that her fulfilment would be children, or a new washing machine, and a house of her own.

And for Jessica it was. Then. She was joyfully fulfilled for years. Wouldn't have had it any other way. And if she had her life over, she'd do it again. She'd lay odds on it.

Each generation in England had moved forward a little in spite of the love of conservatism. Just not as fast as they should for the salvation of the middle-class wife and mother. No wonder she was angry. That they were all angry. Hiding it well behind those stiff upper lips and those small glasses of very dry sherry.

'No wonder we rant in our middle years,' she said to Lilian. 'We find the excuse at last, just when there's no-one to listen. Typical. We were never allowed to learn good timing, I guess.'

Lilian picked up the telephone at the same time as the answer machine. She talked rapidly across the recording of her own voice. 'Hang on, hang on, the machine's working! Serves you right, whoever you are, shouldn't call at this hour, we could have been up to god knows what, and that's god with a small G!' And then, eventually, 'Sorry about that. Should have realized it was Europe. Will you hold, I'll call her.' And her hand across the mouthpiece, eyes wide in pretended horror, laughter suppressed in her hissing voice, 'Jesus Christ, sorry babe, it's the old man!'

Jessica snatched the phone, amused at the English expression Lilian had picked up, and waved her downstairs, 'Get some coffee you fool, you're behaving like an idiot.' And Lilian kissed her, butterfly-like, then left, dancing gracelessly out of the room in a very good imitation of Jessica herself.

'Bill? Is that you? Sorry about that. People leave the answer service on permanently in this neck of the woods.'

'Who was that who answered? The friend you mentioned?' He didn't wait for the reply, and Jessica knew he was irritated, and that he must have heard Lilian's badly disguised hiss. He said, 'Are you all right, darling? Are you feeling better?'

'I'm absolutely fine, I told you. I'm having a great time. Parties and everything.' He said nothing, forcing her into prattling mindlessly, giving herself away, making it obvious that everything was as far as could possibly be from being 'absolutely fine'. After all, a round of partygoing was the last thing she would embark on if she was her old self. It was hard to believe she could have said anything quite so trite. And she didn't stop there. Couldn't stop. Driven on by his silence and the desperate need to fill the gap that was widening by the second, she plunged into a medley of banality that could only have driven him to the conclusion he finally arrived at as her voice and reason petered out.

'I've fallen in with this fascinating crowd – darling you would love them we go everywhere Norma doesn't really get on with them and as the atmosphere between her and Chuck is so horrendous I felt it beholden on me to leave them to it to work out their own salvation – after all Norma never did listen to anyone specially if it was for her own good anyway I'm living with this really fabulous woman called Lilian that's who answered the telephone and this is her own house well of course it is if I'm living with her – silly of me what I meant was she isn't renting it which is what so many people do over here she owns it so she's delighted I've been able to move in because we get on so well and she makes me laugh and stops me drinking and introduces me to all these wonderful people the like of which one would never encounter in West Sussex – but I'm sure you'd approve and if it's as all right with you as it is with me I'd like to stay here for a little longer.'

She must have paused for breath somewhere along the way, it just didn't feel like it. The lie about Lilian stopping her drinking was thrown in for good measure in the vague hope he would be pleased that at least her new life was sobering her up. It was a bad bending of the truth.

What went through his mind at that moment she could only begin to imagine, knowing him as she did. Apart from the obvious, of course, that the wife he'd known, loved, and cherished for thirty mostly happy years had finally slipped over the edge and regressed into insanity or even senility.

He was quiet for what seemed for ever. Jessica tried to breath normally. Well, what should she have said, she asked herself? 'Darling husband, I'm having an affair. There's no need for you to feel threatened. It's not with another man. It's a woman this time, and I still love you, I would just like you to leave me alone for a while so I can enjoy this adventure?'

But then he would have still thought her crazy, and still said what he finally did say, in that tight voice of his he had taken to using when she got particularly impossible. 'I'm coming over. Where are you exactly?'

And from years of habit Jessica gave him the address after only a breath of hesitation, and then she finally put the phone down, discarding it with indecent haste from sweating and clammy hands, for she'd been steadying herself with both. As Lilian came back into the bedroom she was greeted by Jessica's shocked face, lit by the dappled sun struggling through the branches of the large ficus trees outside the window. Later in the day the sun would be strong enough to show up the dust left by undomesticated hands too busy with a fulfilled life to bother with rags and spray polish.

'What's happened? You've told him?'

'He's coming here.'

'So you've told him.'

'No. I sounded crazed, I guess. So he's decided to rescue me. I'm sorry. There's a godawful mess looming ahead of us. D'you mind?'

'Confrontation.'

'Exactly.'

'Fun.' She put down the coffee and smiled.

'I'm not smiling,' Jessica said. Lilian came to her then and put her arms around her, kissed the side of her neck, and they stood together in stillness.

Jessica said, 'I'm so afraid. What do I tell him? How d'you explain all this to a husband without destroying him?'

'I don't know. I'm not sure you can. Destruction is part of every rejection. It's worse if you do nothing. At your age you must know this. I'm patronizing you. I'm sorry.'

'It's all right.'

Lilian had never loved a man. Except as a friend. She'd also never had a relationship with a married woman before. Jessica still found it hard to use the word 'affair', conjuring as it did the passion and pain of Cary Grant and Deborah Kerr. She wanted another word to describe the magic there could be between women.

'When will he arrive?' Lilian asked, pulling away and running her fingers down Jessica's worried face with her special gentleness, understanding easily the panic that inhabited her lover so rapidly.

'I can't let you go,' Jessica whispered. 'How do I deal with this?'

They sat on the side of the bed. Outside the sun was well on the way to winning its battle with the morning clouds. It would be hot again. Lilian said, 'You're shaking Jessie. Don't. I'll be here. It's not something you have to face alone. No-one can force you to do anything you don't want. Life shouldn't work that way.'

'He's my husband,' Jessica said weakly.

'That's not all he is. And you're more than his wife. Nothing is that cut and dry, whatever your upbringing.'

'I know. But knowing that doesn't always help.'

'We'll work it out. I love you. Gird your loins, babe. Nothing will turn out as bad as you're feeling right now.'

She lingered in her imagination over what she would say to Bill, tried without success to see the expression that would pass over his face when she told him the truth. There are no rules for telling your husband that you're cheating on him, that you're in love with someone else, that you want to live with her, and would he please find the courage to tell the children because you wouldn't know where to start. If the scene had been played out before, it hadn't been documented in any book or magazine Jessica had ever read. Time to make things up as she went along.

Lilian went to work. Jessica decided to sort through their clothes closet in an attempt to fill the long hours of the day while she was alone. If they were to live together for any length of time they would have to find more space. The house was tiny, particularly for California where people were allowed to spread themselves in spaces that would have sheltered a visiting army back home. Or was it just that every room in Lilian's picket-fenced-nearest-thing-to-a-cottage-that-America-could-get type house was so delightfully cluttered with no sense of a proper place for anything? Jessica was beginning to feel a little like that herself; confused, with no sense of where she'd been or where she was heading. She wished now Lilian had stayed home. But it was time to think about living with one's own decisions. Grown-up time. Life seemed to get no easier, even when it started to get interesting. Jessica could still remember a time in life when she believed she knew all the answers. She must have been crazy. Or young. Both.

The day dragged, and as if to match the somewhat jaded melancholy that had joined her in her solitary state, the sun went in unexpectedly at midday and stayed there for the rest of the afternoon. She had rented a car only the day before as neither Norma nor José were any longer at her beck and call. She had begun to see how easily one slipped into being utterly spoiled. All she had to do was find her way around. She called Norma and asked for the name of her hairdresser at the salon in Rodeo Drive. It would give her something to do. Something to take her mind off the drama that inevitably lay ahead.

'Are you all right?' Norma asked. 'So unlike you to go to the hairdresser.'

'Bill has decided to come over. I think he intends to sort me out and take me home.'

'Does he know what's waiting for him?'

'No. I'm still a coward.'

'No, you're not Jess. What you have to tell him is better done face to face and you realize that. It's kinder and he'll prefer it. Why don't I come and pick you up and take you for the hairdo?'

She sounded so like the old Norma, Jessica suddenly wanted very much to see her. 'Come and meet me for tea,' she said, 'I want to drive myself. Get to grips with this town once and for all. By "grips" I mean turning left, and running the red light the way everyone else does.'

'Good for you! I'll pick you up at José Eber's at five. We'll go to the Beverly Wilshire and drink tea and pretend we're at the Ritz.'

It wasn't the time to say that she was happy where she was and where her life was taking her at this time, and had no desire to be at the Ritz.

213

In fact, she was as contented as a person could possibly be who had the prospect of a very unhappy and justifiably angry husband about to descend to ask questions she had no idea how to answer. In fact, she could say with some ill-concealed joy she was as pleased as punch with the prospect of the Beverly Wilshire. With or without Warren Beatty, for sadly Lilian had told her he had ceased to live there some years ago, and 'Thank God for that, because no way am I taking you star spotting at your time of life.'

Charlie would be sad she'd not met one single famous person all the time she'd been in Hollywood. 'Perhaps I haven't been looking,' she thought as she valet-parked the car in the Rodeo Drive underground car-park. God, what bliss, no wonder Norma can't go home, and she propelled herself into the plush reception at the hairdressers.

It had been years since she'd had a really decent haircut. There were a few trims by the local woman in Sussex, but as her depression had made her more and more immobile the thought of even that short trip with all the predictable dialogue over the basin – 'Going anywhere special?' or 'Been for your hols yet?' – would bring her out in a panic. Running to the telephone even to call Bill's office and get him to cancel the appointment from London. His secretary, to whom he no doubt handed over the problem, must have thought her quite hysterical. Jessica shuddered now at the memory.

'Don't pull me backwards, Bill,' she thought to herself as she waited for the stylist, 'let me go. I may yet return. If you want a different person, that is.' But of course he didn't, and he wouldn't. He merely wanted 'the old Jessica', and Jessica suspected she'd gone for good.

Norma's hairdresser, Patrick, appeared, and without once dropping the smile, studied the neglected hair thoughtfully. 'It's a mess,' Jessica said apologetically, 'what can you do if anything?'

Patric shrugged as only a Parisian can, and sent her to be shampooed in a flurry of instructions that left the girl who washed it nodding with understanding because she was French too, and Jessica completely confused.

By the time she was ready for Patrick again, she'd been conditioned, and oiled, and coloured. She suspected that Norma had talked to him when she made the appointment for her, because she had no memory of asking for a tint, unless she'd reached the stage of agreeing to everything because it seemed easier, so different to what she was used to, and rather exciting. She'd never felt really like a frivolous girl, even at her most wilful, and this was definitely trivia of the highest calibre.

'I'm not sure I could grow to love it,' she said to Norma over afternoon tea later in the day, 'but it made me feel almost glamorous and frightfully important.'

'You look wonderful,' Norma said.

Not terribly like herself, which unnerved Jessica a little, fearful as she was that Lilian would hate it on sight, forgetting for the moment, in her new-found independence that changing her hair was her own decision and needed no other's approval.

'What's the colour like?' she said somewhat tentatively. 'Have I gone crazy?' She touched her straightened and newly tamed hair with nervous fingers.

Norma laughed, 'You've simply gone Hollywood,' she said. 'Enjoy it.'

'I love seeing you,' Jessica said, and reached across the table to touch her friend's hand. And despite the fact it was as difficult for Norma to ask about Lilian as it was for them to mention husbands, it was pleasant to sit in elegant surroundings pretending for a few brief hours they were nothing but girls again, with little else to giggle about except colour rinses for the hair, and their last manicure. And eventually they ordered two glasses of wine to go with some sort of exotic-looking edible the waiter had just placed on the alcohol drinking tables. For all her dread of the forthcoming confrontation, Jessica's appetite was as insatiable as ever, and she was loathe to miss out on a new eating experience in a strange country.

'They're cheeseballs,' she said with disgust after the first bite, 'just rotten old cheeseballs, for God's sake. I prefer Betty's radishes!' And they smiled at memories of afternoon tea and Betty's small caprices. And Jessica's old life seemed even further away than ever, and the meeting with Bill merely a hiccup in a new existence.

'Call me when he arrives, Jess. He may need a little tenderness. If it gets really sticky he can stay with us.'

'What do I tell him about Chuck?'

'I'd rather you didn't.'

Not to tell Bill exactly what had driven his wife out of that Beverly Hills mansion seemed to Jessica to give him a decided advantage from the beginning. To leave on a mere whim and set up home with a female lover for no good reason that he could see would most assuredly convince him of her increasing madness. 'Not fair,' she said.

But then Norma looked so miserable that Jessica relented and promised to say she'd fallen in love from the start and it had become inevitable that Lilian and she would have to be together. It was easy to understand Norma's panic. To lose Bill's goodwill as well was too much. And after all, Jessica was the happy one these days. Happiness filled in the cracks of a less than perfect existence even more than wealth. 'Hang on to that, babe,' Lilian said when she got back to the valley, amused with the thought of capitulation for the sake of a friend's already lost integrity.

'I can't change all of me,' Jessica said, delighted to know Lilian was there at the end of her day, and she wouldn't dream of mentioning, let alone noticing, that the dishwasher was still unloaded from the previous night, and most of their clothes were still thrown all over the bedroom.

'You've done something weird to your hair,' Lilian muttered as the porch light caught the gleam of the 'vanilla haze' hair tint when they answered the door to the pizza delivery boy later that same evening.

'I like it.'

'I'm glad one of us does.'

Bill phoned the next morning. 'That was quick.' Jessica could think of no other greeting. 'He shouldn't be coming,' she thought unreasonably, 'creasing up the tranquility of my mind with all those demands he's entitled to.'

'I'll be arriving on Sunday evening,' he said, 'I'll get a cab at the airport and meet you at the hotel I've booked.'

'I'll pick you up.'

She regretted the offer as soon as the words left her mouth. To find the way to the airport would be a hurdle that was silly to attempt when one needed a clear and serene mind to face an irate husband.

'On your own?' Bill said, with just enough attitude in his voice to irritate her.

'There's no need for that amount of surprise in your voice. I'm doing very nicely, thank you.'

'I'm not suggesting otherwise. Don't get so defensive.'

'Damn him with his brilliant ability to make me feel less than capable!'

'You're being unfair,' Lilian said when Jessica relayed the morning telephone conversation.

'Why? Why am I being unfair? I *am* doing nicely and I think he should be aware of it. I'm not the wife he sent so graciously to America, having set up the whole caboodle with Norma beforehand, believing she would be my salvation, and ultimately his.'

'He doesn't know what's happened. Let him at least try to understand. Give the poor man a chance. He looked after you for long enough. Didn't make too bad a job of it. You're still here to tell the tale. Wait till he arrives. If he behaves badly you can feel absolved by taking care of him for a change.'

'Norma's offered to do that.'

'Good for her.'

'Why are you suddenly being so spiky? What have I said?'

'What makes you think it's you? It's not automatically your fault you know, Jessie. I'm nervous as well, you know. Or did you think you had the monopoly on guilt as well as misery?'

'Ouch.'

'Well, either think before you speak or don't take a drink until you've spoken.'

Jessica shut up then. For a moment. She didn't want to quarrel. Fighting with Lilian was more nerve-racking than therapeutic because Lilian suffered with asthma, and when she got angry, which was not unknown, it could bring on an attack.

But old habits have a nasty way of showing themselves at inopportune moments, and Jessica had always insisted on the last word, even though she knew it infuriated everyone who had ever loved her. She tried to throw the remark away, muttering as she did, 'I don't know why you're sticking up for him suddenly. Thought you had no time for men.'

Lilian turned and flicked water from the tap where she'd been washing her hands. It caught Jessica full in the face, and she thought for a moment Lilian was angry, but as she dodged the drips, she realized she was laughing.

'You idiot. I have loads of time for men. Don't be fooled by that old cliché. I like them, I just don't want or need to spend my life tending to their poor battered egos. How about you? Aren't you enjoying the break?'

'I'm sorry.'

They kissed on the cheek, then on the mouth, hugged, and Lilian pushed a plate of Chinese chicken salad into Jessica's hands.

'I'll drive you to the airport,' Lilian said later.

'I don't expect it.'

'You should. You should expect everything from the people who care about you. Make demands of me, Jessie. I want to love you well.'

'You do. And I'll try.'

Chapter Eleven

They had two days before Bill's arrival. Jessica could at times feel Lilian's fear that somehow they would lose each other, that Bill would find a way to tempt her to go home. 'But it's real, I promise you, Lilian,' she said. 'I'm not going anywhere. Don't be afraid.'

Lilian would smile at the words. Hold her. 'I know,' she said, 'you don't have to hunt for the words. I know. But he has years on me. An importance I understand. Falling in love doesn't automatically come with the right to sweep aside all others.'

She wanted no influence on any decision that would finally be made. It had to be Jessica's choice, and only hers. But Jessica knew her mind had been made up from the moment they'd stood before that painting and said the words that for the weeks before had been so difficult to even confront. This wasn't anything she could turn away from. Not yet. This deserved at the very least a chance.

But Lilian said, 'I seem to know the world better than you. Your life so far seems to have revolved round the supermarket and – what did you call it?

– the "Harvest Festival"? You don't have any idea what's going on out there. When, and if you do, you'll want to run like hell back to the sanctuary of that marriage, however jaded it's become.'

'Give me a chance, Lilian. That's what I'm doing.'

'I know, babe. And I'm sorry. It's your life.'

Jessica said tentatively, 'Have you ever been with a woman before who'd only ever experienced men?'

'Yes, of course. It happens frequently. Sometimes out of curiosity on their part, or an easily bored sexual nature. Sometimes because they've been badly treated in male-female relationships. Sometimes out of sheer persistence and persuasive power on my part.'

'Really?'

'Really. I can behave very badly if I'm unbelievably attracted to someone.'

'You didn't with me.'

'I fell in love. The form seems to change when that happens.'

'No chat-up line to me then?'

'If you mean something like "I suppose a screw's out of the question," then no. Once at a party I did say to a woman I wanted and had been working towards for weeks, "Have you ever thought about making love to another woman?" '

'Very well behaved of you, I must say.' Jessica's curiosity out-weighed the jealousy that suddenly surged through her.

Lilian smiled broadly, 'I do *know* how to be-have,' she said, catching hold of Jessica's hand as if she'd read her thought, 'I just don't.'

'What was her answer?'

'This woman?'

'Don't irritate me. Of course this woman.'

'She said, "No, but I haven't ruled it out." ' Lilian laughed again, and Jessica wanted to ask her all the usual questions that jealous lovers have wanted to ask since infidelity was first conceived as an option. Like, how much younger was she, and was her pubic hair still soft, and did she make a noise when she had an orgasm, but of course she didn't. She said what anyone says at times like those, man or woman. 'Were you attracted to her more than me?'

As if there could ever be a truthful answer in those circumstances. 'Please please my love, lie to me if it makes it easier.'

Lilian said, 'I wanted everyone more in those days, babe. It was love I had the problem with.'

Ah well, nothing's perfect.

'What shall I wear?' Jessica asked at brunch on Sunday. They were meeting two of Lilian's friends at a bistro on Larchmont and they had arrived early. Surprising really, because she had dared to suggest Lilian looked in the mirror before she left the house and so have no doubt about that particular straw boater she'd thrown on without a thought.

'I've looked,' she said.

'And you still think it goes with jeans?'

'Everything goes with jeans.'

Jessica loved it – the whole thing – their life together, which had taken on such easy familiarity in so short a time. Jessica had laughed so much at the straw boater, and felt so happy, they went back to bed there and then to make love, and Lilian insisted on keeping the hat on.

So that was the reason they were surprised to still arrive at the restaurant before the others. Lilian was in a wonderful mood, despite the obvious traumas ahead. She said, 'Before we discuss what one wears to tell a husband you've become a lesbian do you want champagne or mimosa this hot and steamy morning?'

'I think mimosa. It's less alcohol. And would you mind keeping your voice down, you idiot.'

'Good for you. It means you'll drink double the amount.'

'Oh shut up, you fool.'

They ordered the drinks and sat back. The restaurant was busy. Brunch was the time you could order maple-syruped pancakes with your sausages and eggs and swill it down with champagne without feeling guilty. It was Hollywood. Guilt was something to be ignored or talked out of you by your own personal therapist, and sweated out of you by your own personal trainer. Here, in this glitzy, audacious, silly and delightful town everyone let you get on with anything your heart desired without comment. You want to screw up your body? That's OK. It's your body. Feel like painting your house pink and green like the shopping malls? Going to work on a skate-board? Insisting your dog wore hat and sunglasses and had his own psychiatrist? That's OK as well. Whatever turns you on.

Jessica loved it. It made her laugh. It gave her courage and time to think about what she wanted. And at that time, under those skies, she wanted a life with Lilian. They could hold hands across the table as they did that morning, and no-one around them would bat an eyelid.

'Well?' Jessica said, when the drinks had arrived and Lilian had disappeared behind the enormous menu so that only the boater was visible.

'Well, what?'

'What shall I wear to the airport?'

'Something you've bought here. Something I like you in.'

'You like me in everything.'

'Exactly.'

The friends arrived. Lilian asked them for suggestions about the outfit to confront Bill. She was teasing, and they were no help, but it kept Jessica from taking herself too seriously, and keep-ing the situation ahead of her, for a while anyway, in proportion.

And before she could draw breath, let alone make a decision on anything, it was seven o'clock and Bill's flight was due at eight-thirty. Lilian drove, using the jeep. Jessica shook and sweated too much in wide-legged jeans and sneakers. She had decided on a shirt of Lilian's as it was impregnated with her favourite perfume and Jessica felt it might give her courage for what was ahead. The aroma of Lilian in her head, on her skin. Not that she believed for a moment that Bill would be difficult or aggressive as soon as he came through the barrier, it was simply not his way, whatever the situation, but at least the sight and sound of the strange woman by his wife's side would force them into a kind of mutual attempt at light-hearted niceties. He would more than likely find Lilian a strange enough sight as it was. What with her insistence on the straw boater still on her head, now unable to even sit straight after a full day of trying to suppress her head of unruly hair.

'Every time you catch sight of me you'll remember this morning and he'll never be able to persuade you back,' Lilian said.

'He won't anyway.'

'I'm just making sure.'

He was one of the first people through the barrier. No luggage. Just a hold-all. Flung across his shoulder, making him look like Charlie, except for the expression of worried tiredness on his face, which reminded her so much of her first-born. Loving, gentle Stephen, with all his frailties and insecurities that made him so accessible to the cruelties of this world.

Jessica's heart sank, and then went out to him. 'There he is,' she said. And without waiting to see if Lilian had seen where she was pointing, she hurried forward to greet him.

'Bill?'

For a moment he seemed to stare right through her. 'Jess.' He bent forward to kiss her on the mouth. 'I didn't recognize you for a moment. You're quite brown. I think even your hair's caught the sun.'

'Hello Bill.'

Behind them, Lilian's voice, warm and low, one hand outstretched to him. He took it, his eyes studying her, taking in the hat, the earrings, the smile, wondering what part she played in the changing waters of his wife's life.

'I'm Lilian.'

'My wife's house mate?'

'Right first time.'

'Thank you for picking me up. Both of you.'

Lilian went to get the car, and Bill and Jessica were left to wait, standing there in the cooling air of a Los Angeles evening with suddenly, it seemed, nothing to say to each other except everything, and no way in to the sort of conversation they were destined and compelled to have.

'I missed you, Jessie.'

She said, 'Did you book a hotel or what?'

'Yes. I have the name in my bag. I presume you're coming with me.'

It hadn't occurred to her. Or Lilian.

'Of course.'

Lilian, once in the car, the other two in the back, said, 'My place?'

Jessica leaned forward, unable to meet her eye, speaking urgently into her ear, begging her to read between the lines, and understand, 'I'll go to the hotel with Bill. Is that all right?'

Not an eyelid did Lilian bat. Merely a whisper of hesitation showed on her face, discernible only to a lover's eyes. 'Naturally. Will you need a toothbrush?'

'That's all right.' The words "I can use Bill's" were hard to say. Jessica sat back and stared miserably out of the window, letting her husband and Lilian talk the usual trivia of 'How was the flight?' and 'You must be jet-lagged', while all Jessica could think about was 'I'll have no clean knickers for the morning'. She had always worried about the most irrelevant things in any crisis of her life.

Lilian dropped them at the entrance to a large hotel just off Sunset, shaking Bill's hand – 'Hope we'll meet again tomorrow' – and kissing Jessica's cheek while he went to check in at reception. 'Call me when you can, babe. I'm at the other end of the telephone when you're desperate. I can be here in twenty minutes. I love you.'

'And me you. He looks so confused.'

'It's going to get worse.'

'I need a martini.'

'More than likely.'

And then Lilian was gone. Oh dear God, Jessica thought, why, oh why hadn't either of them realized that Bill would obviously want to spend the night in a hotel with his wife? How could anything so obvious have been overlooked when she'd imagined all those other scenarios? She'd planned on Lilian in the kitchen, waiting to pick up the pieces that she and Bill would be shedding, then holding Jessica close while together they watched a tearful and brave rejected husband disappearing into the night with the words, 'I'll wait for ever Jessica. Have a good life.'

To her relief, immediately they'd seen the room, Bill said, 'Shall we have a drink in the bar?'

'Aren't you jet-lagged?'

'I'd rather talk than sleep.'

So they ordered their drinks, and Jessica devoured the assorted nuts and the olives they put on the table, then drank her martini too quickly and called the waiter over to order another without considering Bill. He said, 'Can you line up another for me while you're about it?'

'Sorry. I'm getting selfish in my old age.'

He smiled. And for a moment it seemed like every other drink in every other bar they'd ever shared, with nothing different in their lives to worry them except maybe the boys' schooling, or Sam's individuality upsetting the teachers again, or Charlie bunking off maths for the third time in a row and forging Bill's signature on an excuse note.

'How are the boys?' she said at last.

'They're fine. Looking forward to you coming home.'

'Stephen still in love?'

'Yes. She's a nice girl. You'll like her.'

'They have their own lives,' she said weakly, guilt washing over her.

He was silent. Then, 'They miss you.'

'You're playing dirty.'

'All right. *I* miss you. I want you home. It's been too long.'

'You said as long as it took when you sent me here.'

'You say you're better.'

'I am.'

'Then come home. Do as arranged. You can't hang around this place indefinitely.'

'What's wrong with this place?'

'For God's sake, Jessica, there's nothing real here. We always said that. We said it was great for the odd holiday and little else.'

'I hadn't lived here then.'

'You don't live here now.'

'I feel as if I do.'

He stared at her. 'What's happened, Jessie? *Something's* happened. It's written all over you. I thought on the phone you'd gone quite mad. You were making no sense. Going on about people you

231

were mixing with, falling out with Norma after all these years—'

'I haven't fallen out with Norma.'

'Well, moving out of the house then. Without a phone call or an explanation. Not even Norma could or would shed any light on it.' He leaned towards her, tried to take her hand. She pretended not to notice and he leaned back again with a sigh.

'I know things have been tough these last years, Jess, but depressions sometimes take their time to go away.'

'Are you referring to the one in England itself, or my own personal depression? Anyway, I couldn't wait any longer. For either of them. There were no green shoots for me either, despite what I was told. My life was disappearing before my eyes and I'd never noticed. Something's happened to me here. It feels good. I don't want to be sad again.'

'You're stronger. A fool could see that. So come home. Be the old Jessica again. Where you were always happiest. At home.'

Her eyes, to her chagrin, filled with tears. A thing they'd not done for weeks. Now she let him take her hand. He thought he'd won. Thought for a moment he could recognize the old frightened Jessica he'd grown used to handling, and what with the tears, and in her momentary confusion, she looked at him and believed he was pleased. Believed her unhappiness made him more secure. The sudden tears had put her safely and forever back where he believed she belonged. She pulled away. Abrupt. Irritation large on her face. Coldness and strength in her eyes. Bill frowned. Seemed to steel himself. She didn't let him down. 'I'm in love with someone else.'

The silence was long and cold. The piano player in the bar too soft to drown out the sound of Bill's sharp intake of breath. People talking around them, ice crushed and noisy against long glasses, a scent of French cigarettes in the air, and to make the memory complete for ever the pianist began to sing 'These foolish things remind me of you'.

Jessica hated herself at that moment because she almost laughed out loud at the sheer dramatic impact of the whole damn scene. Even then, instead of feeling sorry for the shock she'd given him, she began to work out how she would describe the scene eventually to Lilian. Irrelevancies again. Just when a clear and compassionate head was needed above all else.

He didn't deserve this. Not Bill. He'd been the cause of none of the pain through the last years. But what else could she do? Whatever way it was handled was cruel. No way to save his pride. No salvation for his dignity.

'I'm so sorry, Bill. I never meant or ever dreamed I would ever say anything like this to you.'

He remained silent.

She said, 'Please say something. Anything. Ask

me questions. Just don't sit there. I feel dreadful as it is.'

'Who is it? What's his name? What else does one say after all these years? What are you going to do?'

'There's something else to tell you.'

'Good grief, it's not Chuck, is it? Is that the trouble with you and Norma?'

She threw her head back and laughed. It was a wonderful excuse to let the tears flow and blame it on the mirth. Finally, 'No, Chuck is not my lover. That's a promise. One day I hope I can tell you how funny that is.'

'Lover? Has this affair of yours reached that stage already?'

He'd gone quite pale. Jessica said quickly, while the fire was in her, while the memory of Lilian's straw boater was sharp in her head, while the two martinis made her brave and not yet unpleasant, 'I'm in love with Lilian. And she's in love with me.'

She had never believed it when she'd read the novels but it was true. His jaw almost dropped to the ground. What with all her mixing with film people the last few weeks she was tempted to call, 'Cut. Perfect. Print.'

Eventually, 'I don't understand. What does that mean? How the hell can you be in love with Lilian? Is this some sort of weird joke?'

'I'm not cruel enough to tell jokes at this particular time.'

'Then explain, for Christ's sake.'

'Please keep your voice down. People will turn and stare. They're not politely uninterested in other folks' business over here. It's not England. A good domestic fight would probably make their night. They find the Europeans most quaint.'

'I don't care a fuck what the American protocol is for when your wife's just told you she's decided to "come out"! That is the expression, isn't it? I believe that's the hip thing to say, isn't it?'

Jessica reached across to take his hand. 'I'm sorry, Bill. I was as shocked as you when all this happened. I didn't look for it. I'd no idea I wanted it. It happened. I don't know whether I've "come out", as you call it. I just fell in love, and it was with Lilian. That's all it is. It's not something I've been dwelling on for years. It's nothing you've done, or not done. I want to spend some time with her. I don't know about the future. I haven't thought about it. It's not like that. This is just for me. I can't let it go. Can you understand at all?'

He put his head down and remained still and silent for a long time. The customers in the bar had turned back to their own conversations, realizing that nothing spectacularly interesting was going to happen in the English corner after all. The piano player had swung into 'This could be the start of something big'. Jessica was aware of a yearning for this night to be over, whatever that would take. To be back in the safety of Lilian's arms. Not to have a husband before her eyes fighting back anger. Or was it tears? There was no way of telling how to deal with it. She tried to imagine her own reaction if Bill had fallen in love with a man. It was beyond her. As much beyond her as it would be to him. Yet Lilian believed that love was love. That it had nothing to do with gender. There were just men and women, and everyone looks and tries to find happiness, fulfilment, call it what you will, wherever and with whoever they can. 'Whatever works for you, babe.'

Many of Lilian's friends believed wholeheartedly that once you'd changed, made love with a woman, you'd never go back. Jessica didn't understand any of it, let alone herself. All she *did* know was that it was all so much more than just sex. It was so undramatic and easy. So tender and liquid. How could she explain to even an intuitive and understanding husband the thrill and comfort it gave her to look into another's eyes and see herself deep in the soul of the person she was holding in her arms. Lilian would say, 'It's a girl thing, babe. Just a girl thing.'

'Say something, Bill. Please talk to me.'

He looked up. The bewilderment and pain in his eyes brought tears again to hers. 'I don't quite know why, Jessica, but I believe you. I can't pretend to understand, but I believe what you're telling me. I just don't know where we go from here.'

'I'm not coming home.'

'Obviously. And I must go back.'

236

'What will you tell the boys?'

'That's up to you.'

'I should tell them. It should be my job.'

He stared, and then smiled. 'My goodness, you have changed. I wish I'd been able to meet this Lilian before.'

'Will you stay tomorrow and talk to her?'

Silence again. Then he laughed. Briefly, with more pain than mirth. 'Confrontation, eh? Which one of us, man or woman, can give my wife what she needs most. Quite a thought. I'm not absolutely sure I'd be able to get through that without either laughing or screaming.'

'She's nice Bill. You'd like her.'

'Would I now?'

'Please don't patronize me.'

'Is that what I'm doing? I thought I was being gently understanding like a man is supposed to be.'

'You're patronizing me. Using that man-to-little-woman voice.'

'Oh. I think I'm beginning to see which direction you're heading. I would have thought feminism was a bit old-hat these days. Or am I getting a little long in the tooth? Isn't it post-feminism these days? I seem to remember reading that in the *Guardian*. That's what's happened, isn't it? You've become a feminist.'

'Become one? I've been one for years. I never believed I wasn't equal to a man. It just didn't come up. I'd just put it on the back burner while

I've had you and the kids to take care of. I want it back now. I want myself back now. The boys are fine. I'll come home sometimes. If you want me that is. What *do* you want? Tell me. What about you?'

'*Now* you're thinking about me? Now? All these years of devotion to "the boys", as you call them, suddenly it's what do I need? I'd like *you*. I've waited for years to get you back and just when it was within my grasp you fall in love with someone else. And a woman, for Christ's sake! I must tell you, I feel bloody ridiculous, to say the least.'

'Oh Bill, forgive me. For everything.' Her eyes were still full of tears. She held his hand and they finished their drinks. The table next to them had obviously heard the most fascinating part of the conversation and were keeping still and silent in the hope they would hear some more. Jessica couldn't blame them. She would have inveigled herself under the cocktail table if dialogue that intriguing had ever come her way when she'd been out at a bar. She could never have imagined in her wildest dreams that she herself would ever have been part of such extraordinary entertainment.

'Now what?' she whispered. 'Where do we go from here?'

'I think upstairs and call room service if you don't mind. Another martini somewhere a little more private would fit the bill very nicely. Will you join me?'

So that's what they did. And after the fourth

martini she was too tired anyway to go back to the valley, and knowing Lilian by now would be dying of curiosity and nervous exhaustion, Jessica phoned her while Bill was in the bathroom. In fact, he knew she would want to make that particular call, he guessed, sensitive as he was, despite the circumstances. 'You'd better call what's-her-name hadn't you? It's late. She's probably worried as hell, wondering if I've become the furious husband and let fly with my fists.' The attempt at a joke hung heavy between them. She smelled the sarcasm, but merely smiled rather weakly.

'Her name's Lilian,' she said, 'and yes, I should call her.'

'I'll use the bathroom and give you some privacy then. I would like you to stay here tonight if you can find your way clear to do that. I might think straight in the morning, and then we can work something out. I hope she's the understanding type. I guess as she's female she probably is.' His voice sarcastic.

Jessica said nothing as he left the room. Confusion, jealousy and pain bring out things in each and everyone's nature, things they bury so they're able to show an appropriate face to a society that doesn't notice or care anyway, as long as it isn't happening to them.

'Lilian, it's me.'

'How're you doing?'

'I'll be back in the morning. Is that OK?'

There was a pause. The briefest of moments. Then understanding came quickly. 'Yes, of course. Come home when you can. If I'm at work call me.'

'I'll get a cab.'

'I love you, babe.'

Jessica replaced the receiver loudly, hoping Bill would hear and know he could come back in. She wished she'd said 'I love you too', for Lilian's sake, but it seemed inappropriate at the time. Tonight she would be with Bill.

'All right?' His voice slurred. A mixture of weariness and alcohol. She had not seen him so drunk since they were young. He'd stayed sober in the last few years, probably to keep a wary eye on her at social gatherings. Two of them finding comfort in a bottle would have been unbearable. Surprisingly, the martinis seemed to have had very little effect on Jessica that night. She put it down to sheer terror. It was still hard to realize she'd come this far.

'I said I'd see her tomorrow. Are you sure you have to go straight back?' She knew the question was redundant before she heard the answer.

'I think so. Not very modern of me, I know, but if I hang around my instinct tells me I'd just make everything worse than it is. If that's possible.' He sat on the side of the double bed. 'I think I'd like to eat something. Can we order? It's very late.'

She looked at her watch. It was two in the

morning. 'We'll get a sandwich,' she said. 'I'll do it. You sit quiet.'

He said nothing. Just sat back against the headboard of the bed and closed his eyes. She felt suddenly very hungry.

'We could send out for pizza,' she mused. He laughed, without opening his eyes.

'Whatever, Jessie. Whatever.'

So there she was. There they both were. Sitting, half-lying, on the over-sized bed in a strange hotel off Sunset Boulevard, waiting for, and finally eating, one enormous sent-out-for Hawaiian pizza. Bizarre. On any other occasion, given a different set of circumstances, it would have been fun. But they ate almost in silence, out of necessity, Bill eventually eating very little, her with a greed that would have put Butch to shame, finishing every last crumb, and even making short work of the pieces of pineapple that Bill had meticulously put aside from his small share. He began to fall asleep towards the end of this less-than-glamorous early morning feast, and Jessica lifted the pillow from his back and began to help him off with his clothes. Caring for him was the most natural thing in the world.

He tried to stay awake. 'We should be talking,' he said, struggling to keep his eyelids open.

'We'll talk at breakfast.'

'Thanks for staying. I'll be back to normal tomorrow.' As if he would. Would either of them ever be normal again, whatever that was? And then he was asleep. Snoring gently, completely still, the way he always slept when he was overtired.

Do you forget all those little things about a person eventually if you separate? Those things that are knitted into the fabric of both your lives for so long. No wonder so many people stayed together long past their own personal sell-by date. It was easier than starting again with someone else. And the pain doesn't get any cleaner as the years pile up on you, despite what you believe in your youth. Jessica was hurting almost as much as him, and there was someone waiting for her. Someone who would blunt the edges of her memories. Someone who would work hard to begin a new history for the two of them.

She hated herself that night. Hated the whole idea of change and growth. She longed for the old contentment back, conjured up pictures of Stephen, and Sam, and Charlie. But they were pictures of them as babies, as toddlers, as school-boys. And now they were men. No longer hers, or Bill's responsibility. Unless they asked to be. It was over. And with the long overdue acceptance of that had to come the discarding of her old life. She couldn't help Bill, just as he had never been able to help her at the height of her severe misery. Maybe she'd known that all along. Maybe that was the reason it had all been such a struggle. She still loved him. He was still her best friend, her greatest ally. But there was no going back. She knew what lay behind her. She'd lived through all the good of those years, and then the bad. If she went back it would be the same. And she wasn't. Things had happened. Things had been said. Time to move on, and she could only take Bill along if he accepted that change. And how could he? His life had simply progressed the way he'd expected, the way he'd planned. He was successful, popular, long married, and he'd waited patiently to have the wife he adored place him in the centre of her life again, and after all those years that wife wanted something else. Something he would never understand, because neither did she. There was nothing to do except undress and lie down beside him and cradle him in her arms to help him feel safe for just one more night before he went home and tried to find his pride and put himself together.

There was no rest for Jessica that night. And, as always, when sleep was alcohol-induced, Bill awoke long before he was refreshed enough to face the day, and found her lying beside him in her slip, staring red-eyed at the ceiling, praying for the hours, days, weeks ahead to go by quickly for him and so ease his pain.

They lay in silence for a moment, unable to find any words to express or alleviate the misery they both felt. 'Thanks for staying, Jessie.'

She turned her face to him, held his eyes in her gaze, hating herself anew for feeling nothing but pity. 'I'll always love you, Bill. You know that, don't you? Nothing will ever change that.'

'I know.'

'What will you do?'

He sat up. 'I'll go home today. If you could call Stephen I'm sure he'll meet me. I don't want to explain too much at the moment. It'll be easier if you phone him when I'm on the plane. Will you do that?'

'Of course.'

They sent for breakfast in the room, and left it to go cold as they could only manage coffee. She found two Tylenol in her purse and gave them to him for his hangover.

'Not very dignified,' he smiled. 'Me last night, I mean.'

'Not true.'

'Will you let me leave things as they are for the time being? I mean, homewise and moneywise. Let's not be hasty. Give us both time. I'll wire you money each month. Will you let me do that?'

'I don't know what to say. I don't deserve it.'

He took her hands then. 'Yes, you do, my darling. You deserve the world. If this is the only way you can find it right now I'll leave it at that.'

'You are still the nicest man I've ever met. I'm glad I had the sense to marry you. And I'll accept your offer. Until I get on my feet. I don't know what's going to happen. I just want to go.'

'Then go. You must do what you have to do, Jessie.'

She had never been so pleased with the man she married as she was that morning. He released her in the most loving way a person could. She wondered at his strength, and wished she'd found it in herself when it had been time to cut the umbilical cords that had held her too long to the children she'd reared. It would have saved them both many years of weeping.

Bill left to catch his plane. She watched the cab pull away from the hotel. He didn't look back. She'd said, 'I'll phone each weekend.'

'When you want. We'll keep in touch. You take care. My love to Norma if you see her. You never did tell me the story there.'

'Not the time. I'll write. Tell the boys I'll call them. They'll understand.'

And he was gone.

Jessica went home to Lilian and called Stephen. Time for him to take care of his dad.

Chapter Twelve

'Mum?' His voice jumped enthusiastically across the miles to sharpen the dagger of guilt she'd prepared for her own heart.

'Hello, darling. I'm phoning for Dad. He's on his way home and he'd like you to meet him at Gatwick. Is that all right?'

He hesitated. 'Sure. Aren't you coming home yet?'

'Not yet, darling.'

A moment's silence again. 'Something up, Mum?' He got more like his father every year.

'Your dad and I have a problem right now. We need to spend some time apart. I'm not sure I can explain any more.' It always took her by surprise the way most people revert to clichés as soon as they find themselves under pressure, and she was no exception. As if she'd come from the womb with the dialogue for all the battles in life already embedded in the innocent baby computer of the mind.

Jessica heard her eldest breathing heavily in the pause that followed, knew he would be biting his bottom lip, and her heart ached for him from sheer habit. How long would she bear this? How long before she threw in the towel, did what was easier all round, went back to making everyone feel comfortable except herself?

'Are you all right, Stephen? Are you still there?'

'Yes. Just a bit shocked really. Is Dad all right?'

'Look after him. I'll write to you.'

'Shall I tell Charlie and Sam?'

'If you like. They can call me here.'

She gave him the number. When the phone went down, she was crying. She called Lilian at work. 'I'm at home,' she said to the answer machine in the office, unreasonably annoyed that the one person she needed right then was at a meeting or even off somewhere for lunch. She wondered at Lilian's composure. Or steeliness. Whatever it was at that moment, it threw Jessica off balance. She went upstairs to shower again and change her clothes, muttering furiously under her breath, 'Typical of a woman without children. Totally unable to comprehend what kind of state I'm in.'

She didn't hear Lilian call out because she was standing in the shower for a long time. Tiredness was so reminiscent of her old life it was hard to hang on to the fact she was not still in Sussex trying to pick up courage to face another day. She watched a shadow through the shower curtain moving across the sunlight from the open window and pushed the drape to one side. 'Jesus Christ, Lilian, don't do that! You nearly gave me a heart attack. It was like bloody *Psycho*, for God's sake!'

'You had no sleep.' Lilian's tone summed up the mood, her knowledge of Jessica was, for once, irritating more than comforting.

Jessica stood on the bathmat and dripped. Lilian wrapped her gently in one of the large, warm bath sheets and then patted the moisture from her skin with so much tenderness Jessica began to cry again. 'It was the worst night of my life,' she stammered almost incoherently. 'And where were you the morning after?'

'On my way home to you, you fool. Where else would I be?'

She let Lilian dress her in the new nightdress they'd bought together in 'Victoria's Secret' only a few days before. It fell in soft silk pleats to the ankles, touching the body delicately enough to ease some of the tiredness.

'Go to bed,' Lilian said. 'I'll bring you some tea, and if you can stay awake you can tell me all about it. You can even blame it all on me if you feel like it.'

'You can't *make* tea,' Jessica said, disgruntled, unreasonable.

Lilian laughed with delight at the expression on her face. 'I promise to make sure the water's boiled,' she said.

'And warm the teapot.' They chorused together, and it was hard, but not impossible, for Jessica to smile back weakly and punch Lilian ineffectually on the arm. 'I've broken hearts today,' she said tearfully, 'and I don't like it. It's worse than my own unhappiness. How do I face the days ahead, let alone myself?'

'Let's get through this day first.'

'Make the tea, woman. And for God's sake, put more than one teabag in.'

Lilian kissed her softly on the mouth, still salty from tears, and then pushed the wet strands of hair from Jessica's neck and away from her eyes.

'I love you very much, Lilian. I'll be braver after a sleep.' She could scarcely bear the tenderness of her lover's touch, so little did she believe at that moment she deserved it.

'You're brave now, babe. Stop underestimating yourself. Do you want something to eat with your tea?'

'No thanks. I ate pizza at three o'clock this morning and it hasn't worked it's way through yet.'

'Good God, why are the Europeans so obsessed with their elimination problems?'

Jessica kept putting off writing to the boys. She had no idea where to start, how much to explain, how much was their business. As it turned out it was more or less taken out of her hands.

One week after Bill's rapid departure, Charlie phoned. She'd got through the seven days better than she would have thought possible. Lilian had offered to take time from work, she was at a very early stage of a project and felt she could afford a break. But Jessica had resisted the idea. 'No, don't. I'm fine. I want to do this on my own. Find my feet. Let me wing it.' So Lilian had taken herself back to the office, and left her to avail herself of a few obvious Hollywood occupations. Like going to a nail clinic for the first time in years. She took her split and broken nails to Norma's recommended manicurist and placed them in front of her as if handing her the booby prize.

'This may look like "Candid Camera",' Jessica said, 'but I assure you that load of chipped varnish at the end of those liver-spotted fingers is no joke.'

The remark passed coolly over Anna's beautiful Romanian head. She'd lived in Hollywood for too long to see anything but tragedy in a person's self neglect. 'Will you have a pedicure as well, Jessica?' she said.

She'd rapidly grown used to the way everyone, even short-term aquaintances, called her by her first name. It was very American, and Norma said she'd never really got accustomed to it, preferring the British way. 'You know,' she said, 'back there where everyone knows their proper station in life!' It made them both laugh at the time because the one thing Norma had never been in the past was a snob. But for Jessica, the sound of her Christian name so quickly on a stranger's lips made her feel young and single again. Herself again. Not having to answer to anyone, and not merely known as that 'nice Mrs Wooldridge', which had come to make her feel, in the last few disgruntled years anyway, like another's property.

She had her pedicure as well, and waving pale pink toes and fingers in the air to dry she lingered in a bookshop for hours before going home. Sheer unadulterated hedonism. Self absorption. Delicious. Her father would have turned in his grave. 'This is what comes of having no man to care for, my girl.' She could almost hear his voice. 'No socks to darn.'

'You can darn mine,' Lilian would say.

'You can darn your own bloody socks.'

Bliss. Sometimes the delight of sharing a home with another woman was merely the simple pleasure of living with someone who knew what a lavatory brush looked like, and best of all, what it was for.

She even went to see Patrick again and insisted he put a grey tint on her hair so it wouldn't show as her own colour grew back. He looked disappointed, but feeling more relaxed the second time in the salon, she said she loved the cut, and he'd made her look so much younger anyway with only a slight snipping of his magic scissors that there was no need whatsoever for any kind of colour change. She even bought a hat with a sunflower on it which made Lilian roar with laughter and insist that they both went to bed that night and wear nothing but their hats, which made it totally impossible to make love because they were both laughing too much to concentrate. Jessica was as happy as was possible.

Charlie phoned on Sunday morning while they were still in bed.

'Let me call you back, darling,' she said, 'this is too expensive for you.'

'OK.'

She put the telephone down. 'Who was it?' Lilian said, not bothering to open her eyes.

'Charlie. I said I'd call him back. He sounded strange.'

'What did he say?'

'OK.'

'Excuse me?'

'He said, "OK".'

'And from that you decided he's strange?'

'Yes.'

Lilian sat up and swung her legs over the side of the bed, tousling her hair where it had flattened in the night. 'I'll make coffee. Give you some privacy. Plenty of space for a mother's angst. Could this be why I never wanted children?'

Jessica dialled his number as Lilian disappeared from the room. She could be heard singing on her journey to the kitchen. 'The sight of last night's dishes piled stickily in the sink will put her in a less Pollyanna mood,' Jessica thought gleefully, 'wipe the song from her lips and the smile from her face.'

'How are you, darling?' she spoke immediately her youngest son picked up the telephone.

'I'm all right Mum. How are *you*?'

'Have you spoken to your dad?'

She couldn't bring herself to tell him she was

fine, blooming, whatever. Somehow it seemed less than appropriate in the circumstances. In all honesty she had no idea how to play it. If she was 'feeling great' it might be construed as callous; if in the depths of misery, what was she doing here in the first place?

'That's why I'm calling,' he said.

'Is your dad ill?' Her heart leapt into her throat.

'Not as far as I know. I tried to call him last night and he was out. Again today. But I spoke to Stephen and Dad had told him.'

'Told him what?'

There was the briefest of pauses, then, 'I don't know, Mum, it all sounds so peculiar. Stephen was crying, you know what he's like, and I don't know whether one or other of us has got the wrong end of the stick.'

Jessica knew immediately she'd been thrown in at the deep end. She played for time, as brief as that was. 'You mean about your dad and I splitting up for a while?'

'I knew that a week ago. It's your business.' Her baby was always the wise one. Born upright. He came into the world feet first and that's the way he remained. She waited. He was silent. One of them had to start the conversation, and she thought in her innocence it might be possible to avoid the complete truth as far as the boys were concerned, choosing to forget in that instance the closeness that had once been part of their family life.

'So what do you want me to say?' she asked gently.

'Stephen said that Dad said you'd gone very odd and decided to shack up with a woman.'

She winced. 'He's right,' she said at last. 'Maybe we could leave it at that,' she thought, 'maybe he won't want anything more explicit.' Stupid of her. The pragmatism of her youngest son was hard to suppress.

'Are you gay, Mum?'

She said nothing for a moment, trying hard to answer him in a way that he wouldn't find too confusing. At last she said, 'I'm in love with someone, and it happens to be a woman.' Her voice was unconvincing. There seemed no way she could explain herself, either to him or herself.

'How can you be gay? I'd have noticed.'

He sounded so cross. Put out. It made her laugh. 'Oh Charlie, I haven't been gay before, don't be silly.' She wished someone would think of an alternative word. Lilian preferred lesbian, but somehow Jessica hadn't quite got her mind in gear for that yet. There's a kind of finality about it she wasn't quite ready to embrace.

The conversation with her son was taking on the cloak of high verbal farce. 'How can my mother be gay?' he said. 'When did you decide? How long have you known?'

'Listen, darling, I realize it's hard to understand but it wasn't like you're imagining. Things happen. I'm not sure I expect you to understand.

I don't think I do. But I feel good about it. I don't expect you to, I'd just like you to accept it when or if you can.' There was a long silence. 'Charlie, are you still there?'

'Yes.'

'Do you want me to speak to Stephen?'

'I don't know whether he wants to talk to you at the moment.'

'Oh dear.' Her heart sank a little. It was hard to think of any one of them turning away from her. 'He'll come round,' she said, hope more than conviction in her voice.

'Probably.' His voice was brisk, his answers short. She felt he had little left he wanted to say to her at the moment. Lilian came into the room mouthing the word 'coffee', and Jessica nodded. Standing with the telephone in her hand, wondering how either of them were ever going to end this conversation, let alone make sense of it, she watched Lilian throwing off her short robe and disappearing downstairs again completely naked.

'Have you spoken to Sam?' Jessica said.

'Yes.'

'And?'

'He laughed.'

'I wish *you* could.'

'I'm not Sam.'

'No.'

There was really very little left they *could* say to each other. He said work was fine, that Stephen had taken time off to stay with Dad for a while,

255

and that her eldest son was still in love with the same girl and it looked like marriage was in the air, and finally he wondered if she would be home for Christmas.

'It's too early to say.'

Then she promised to write, to all of them, to tell his father she would call him, and she would also speak to him, Charlie, again very soon, and please would he work very hard at forgiving her for all this confusion she'd flung into their lives. He told her he loved her, that he'd try, and then he was gone, and Lilian came back with coffee and cream cheesed bagels saying she'd burnt her breasts bending over the toaster to fill the coffee machine and that it would never have happened when she was younger because everything above her waist in those days stood upright on its own accord and it meant she would have to start cooking with clothes on which meant more washing in the long run. And Jessica laughed too much and too long in case she cried and undid her good intentions.

Over the following weeks whenever Lilian asked, 'How are you, babe?' she would get the reply, 'I'm surprisingly fine. A little spaced out but I expected more remorse.'

Jessica began to believe it wasn't just 'a standing *cock* that had no conscience'. She'd felt guilty all her adult life. Her mother's death (as if she could have prevented it), her father's final days in a home (which she *could* have prevented but the boys were small and she wanted them the centre of her life, not marginalized as his creeping senility would have demanded if the family had made room for him), her sexual neglect of Bill in the latter years and, of course, the years of personal depression that had corroded all their lives. Guilt was part of her life. It was hard to imagine functioning without it. Now, when the family's confusion and unhappiness was totally her fault, it was time to feel guiltier than ever. But all those lives going on in merry old England seemed no longer to have any direct connection with her. As if they were all second cousins twice removed. When you thought of their pain all you could muster was, 'Oh dear, I *am* sorry, thank God time is such a healer.'

She made friends with Lilian's nextdoor neighbours. She felt it time to find a kind of niche within the neighbourhood, the way she did back home. But now she needed to try and think of California as home. If that was possible. Not that the two young men living next door reminded her of Betty and Peter. Hardly. Jeremy and Harold were a couple. Harold stayed at home and tended house, while Jeremy worked as a production assistant. He was away quite a bit on location, so she and Harold became quite close in a very short time. He was fascinated the way she'd turned her life upside down so rapidly and still seemed so sane.

'I'm still not sure I am,' she'd said. 'It all seems

to be happening to someone else. I'm just looking on and rather enjoying it.'

They went to the mall together where he threw hats at her to try on trying to find at least one that was even sillier than some of Lilian's, and sprayed himself with women's perfume in the pretence he was trying it out for her. 'I'm the "wife" you see, dearest. Jeremy brings home the spoils and I look after him. I love it!'

Of course, it wasn't the full story, as he eventually told her. Harold was HIV positive, and had been for the last year. He and Jeremy had talked it over, and both decided it would be best for him to give up work and take good care of himself at home, away from the stress of a fulltime job. Jessica was amazed at his – their – bravery, and their confidence that if Harold took great care of himself they would have many years together.

Lilian had known all along. 'I'm glad he told you himself,' she said. 'It wasn't my place.'

They were the most unusual neighbours she could have imagined. She loved them and the evenings the four of them shared. Life was good. More than that, life was interesting, and because of that she began to feel she might be.

Bill went on sending her money, which didn't please Lilian, feeling that she would remain trapped by him for ever.

'Be patient,' Jessica would say, 'he wants so much to stay close. Maybe he'll meet someone and release me.' Not that she believed that for a moment. She sometimes felt that everything in England was merely on hold, which was disturbing to dwell on, and not wise to share with Lilian. They loved each other. That was never in dispute.

Bill's letters, when they came, were always short and merely businesslike. They contained usually just necessary news of the boys, and sometimes the news in the village. There was no dissent in them on his part. It was Jessica too that didn't want that final break. Bill would always be in her life. Her fourth child. Her life's blood that kept her forever and silently close to her sons, albeit that the apron strings were free of knots. It was the one thing that she and Lilian couldn't discuss. Lilian knew when and at what she was licked. It was her great strength. A lesson Jessica wished she'd learnt a long time ago. She, of course, usually worried at confusion like a terrier with a bone.

But 'her darling Lilian' made her laugh and cry more than anyone else had ever done. She knew every shade of every mood Jessica would find herself in. She demanded nothing of her except what she was. And with Lilian Jessica began to find out what and who she was for the first time in her life. Lilian made her trust herself. She made her free. She made her safe. And most of all, she made her glad she was who she was.

'You're my road to Damascus,' Jessica said to her once. 'What am I to you?'

'Everything,' she smiled. 'I can only pray you'll

never be my Helen of Troy.' Her undoing. She'd never be quite sure Jessica wouldn't leave. Marriage, children, all that was unexplored territory to her. Nothing she could rationalize, so it was best to ignore.

'I'll not leave you,' Jessica would say. 'Where would I go? I love my life here. You've made it perfect.'

She saw Norma at times, but they mixed in different circles, and the couple of occasions she came across Chuck when she was visiting and he was unexpectedly at home Jessica found herself totally at a loss as to what to say to him.

'They breathe a different kind of oxygen,' Lilian said. 'It's what money does for you.'

It was sad, but Norma was suddenly a part of the past. Her particular kind of present was not something Jessica could cope with, so she too was put in the box with the rest of that old life. She could think of their girlhood together with affection. Their middle years seemed to hold no mutual meeting point. They'd moved on, both of them in directions the other one could not follow or deal with.

They met in the hairdressers or the shopping malls. They had lunch and talked about the past. Places where aquaintances meet to catch up on each other's lives. The subjects of both their private lives was touched on briefly, but then postponed until an easier time, which was long in coming. Almost as if both of them were in some kind of middle-aged limbo. Waiting for a life to be resolved, pushed into a direction they could recognize and embrace. The difference between them was, of course, that Jessica was enjoying the romance of her interlude, was hanging on because she dreaded seeing it end, hoped it never would, but too old for such fantasies; and Norma's unhappiness got worse, but she was scared to burst that final bubble, and kept praying it would solve itself, which is the dream of the very young.

She came to dinner sometimes and drank too much so that Jessica was sure José had to carry her from the car when she got home, as she and Lilian had to carry her to it sometimes when she decided it was time to make the journey back to Beverly Hills.

Lilian suggested that Jessica take up tennis again and she remembered how good it used to make her feel, and maybe it would again. She would start to enjoy the winning as she had when she was a girl. They began to walk every weekend. Long, often uphill hikes, strengthening her physically as well as emotionally, sometimes a number of them, rather like a group of middle-aged Girl Guides, knee-length khakis and baggy shirts.

'Who said Hollywood has to be glamorous,' Lilian shouted once, from the top of a hill overlooking the valley, lining all of them up so she could take a photograph for posterity.

They went to Palm Springs and Jessica said she hated it. All those neat estates of houses and bungalows, not a hint of weeds or trash. 'Like *Stepford Wives*,' she grumbled, which made Lilian laugh, and then promise they would never retire here when Los Angeles wore them out.

One long weekend, on the spur of the moment, they got into the jeep and drove to San Francisco, stopping overnight at San Simeon at a shabby little motel because they hadn't booked ahead and it was the only vacancy in town. They could hear the ocean once the traffic had died down for the night, but not actually see it because they were on the wrong side of the Pacific coast highway. There were cobwebs on the bushes outside the door of their motel room, and Jessica was so used by this time to the almost obsessional cleanliness of the Americans that it took her by unreasonable surprise that they weren't dusted into oblivion by the morning.

'Time for the rainy season,' Lilian had explained, 'that's why the shrubs look dusty.'

They ate that night in a restaurant Jessica had chosen because it was right on the beach and was totally covered in what Lilian insisted on calling Christmas lights.

'Fairy lights,' Jessica said, 'they're fairy lights, for crying out loud. It's not Christmas all the year round, even in America!'

'Fairy has a totally different connotation here, babe. You could well be insulting half the male population, let alone the "little people". Anyway,' as she dodged the punch on her arm, 'it'll be dreadful food.'

'Not necessarily.'

'I bet I'm right. No place needs to draw that sort of attention to itself if the food's great.'

Lilian was wrong for once. It was the very best of Italian meals, and kept them going when Lilian wanted to press on the next day and skip lunch. Jessica had wanted to stop at a small town called Castroville. The billboard erected to welcome travellers passing through informed them they were entering the 'artichoke centre of the world', and Jessica laughed because Lilian refused to park the car anywhere in case they could find no other sort of sustenance except the one vegetable she detested.

'And I've never tried artichoke ice cream,' Jessica teased. 'You are so mean.'

'There's the "garlic centre of the world" just down the highway,' Lilian said. 'We could stop for flavoured donuts. That sounds to me like your idea of a culinary masterpiece.'

'Yuk.'

And there was Norma blindly insisting the Americans took themselves too seriously. No-one who decides to put up posters like that does so without a sense of the ridiculous. Lilian said, 'Don't you believe it. This is California!' On one stretch of road there was a billboard set up high for the world to see, advertising brazenly:

'Vasectomies – money back guarantee!' which seemed to prove a point somehow.

'I love this country,' Jessica shouted through her mirth, and caught her breath as they turned a corner and saw another spectacular view of Big Sur.

'Jessie darling, if you're impressed by the South Pacific Highway I must take you one day to New England. Next fall maybe.'

'I'd like that. America still hasn't let me down.'

'It may. One day. But there's so much of it, you can choose where you want to settle. If that's what you want to do, that is.'

'Settle?'

'Yes.'

Jessica said nothing. Simply stared out of the car window and pretended to herself Lilian probably didn't notice the lack of response. It wasn't that Jessica couldn't see the rest of her life in their relationship. It was simply that she didn't *see* the rest of her life. She wanted her future to be forever an ongoing surprise. And more than that, maybe remove the word 'settle' from her vocabulary for ever. If that was possible. She'd *always* been settled. Had always wanted it. It had meant husband. It had meant children. It had been her whole life until the day she'd got off that plane at Los Angeles. Now was the travelling time. Now was the gypsy time of life. She'd done her bit. More than her bit. She'd had half a child more than the average and been utterly fulfilled for a lot of years. Now she was out. 'In more ways than one,' Lilian said.

They drank just enough wine that night in San Simeon to make Jessica a little on the wild side. They finished their pasta, and she was suddenly full of the joy of being alive, of being in love, and loved, and simply delighted with everything in her immediate world. They walked at midnight on the dark beaches behind the motels. The lights from bedrooms and chalets were gradually going out all around them. they could hear the sounds of the waves as they broke against the sand and pebbles. The stars for once were quite clear. The moon half full, brighter it seemed than Jessica had seen it since she'd left England. She took her hand from Lilian's and, head thrown back, she ran towards the sea.

'What?' Lilian watched, called out, laughing, her voice following.

'I want to paddle,' Jessica called out, without looking back. 'I want to run and splash, and do all the things I wouldn't dare do before! Come with me, Lilian, come with me,'

'You'll ruin your shoes,' Lilian called, still laughing, half following, half-hearted, waiting to see what was happening. Jessica's staid old Sussex soul drowned in a kind of glorious madness and she waded into that dark starlit ocean until the night feeling of the sea came shivering to her waist, splashing above to her eyes and mouth as the waves broke against her, lifting her gently half off her feet as she struggled weakly to stay upright, feeling as she did now the sheer delight at being alive.

'Come in, Lilian! Come on!'

And then Lilian too stood there, and they were holding on to each other beneath that Californian night sky. And there was no need for words of love. It was in them, and around them, keeping them warm as the spray splashed against their faces, leaving them to lick the salt from each other's lips.

They stood for a long time. No sound but the sea to soothe the ears. Faint and distant, a radio played from one of the motels. Rocking gently as the changing waters of the turning tide pushed and dragged, making them unsteady on their feet.

It was the best night of her life. Not the birth of the children. Not her wedding day. But the glorious freedom of spirit for which there were no words. And it wasn't because of Lilian. Not because they had met and fallen in love. But it was all her own work. Jessica's work. She couldn't pin it down, or begin to understand it, and the reasons didn't matter. But inside herself, she was free. The door had opened, and the years stretched ahead of her with promise and not despair. A second life to embark on, with more wisdom than she had started on the first. And she knew she was better. Well again. Because she'd found the courage to see the light at the end of the tunnel, and propelled herself towards it with a passion she thought she'd lost. Now she felt her own roots in the earth. Her own universe she could explore without asking permission.

She did ruin her shoes, of course. Lilian had had the sense in her more sober demeanor to slip hers off before wading into those Pacific waves. Their jeans felt disgusting when they started to dry on their legs as they walked back to the motel, entwined with each other like children, silent with tiredness.

'We'll buy you sneakers in San Francisco,' Lilian said, helping her peel the blue denim from damp legs when they undressed each other later. 'You'll have to wear your shorts tomorrow.'

'That'll be a sight after all that pasta,' Jessica said. And then, 'Should I feel this happy when I've burnt so many bridges?'

San Francisco was crowded. 'Must be tourist season,' Jessica said.

'Not a bit of it. It's like this all the year round.'

They walked, and shopped and went to all the places every tourist goes to. Lilian had been many times, had lived there for one year when she was younger, but she put up with the trailing round on the trolleys up and down the hills, trying to ignore the pan-handlers after Jessica had emptied her pockets for them of all small change, the inevitable trip to the wharf, laughing at buskers singing lustily and off-key 'I left my heart in San

Francisco', taking a trip round Alcatraz, and then, before they started the journey home, after two days of seafood suppers and too many glasses of Chardonnay wine, Lilian called in for her telephone messages.

'Any for me?' Jessica asked, stuffing panties and socks haphazardly into their mutual travel bags without a thought of clean or dirty.

'Two for you,' Lilian said. 'Bill and Norma.'

'Can they wait till we get back?'

Lilian paused. Looked at Jessica without expression. 'They both sounded like shit if you want me to be honest.'

'Oh hell, bubbles still being burst all round me. Who sounded the most desperate?'

'Hard to tell. Call from here. Use my card.'

Jessica sank on to the bed beside her. 'I still feel you might disappear from my life at every phonecall,' Lilian said.

'I'll never disappear from your life, Lilian. But you will always have to share me. I'll not love you less, but Bill and I have jumped too many hurdles together for me just to abandon him. When he calls I'll answer. Do you understand?'

'Do I have to like it as well?'

'No. Please believe that I love you.'

'That will do.' And she bent forward so they could kiss, before going into the bathroom and leaving Jessica alone to use the phone.

It would never fail to surprise her that she'd captured the heart and imagination of Lilian

Peterson. A woman so full of the joy of life, so crammed with the tricks for living, that friends and even short-term aquaintances sought out her company to bring what could only be termed as her particular kind of sunshine into their hungry existences. 'You're a life-enhancer,' Jessica said to her time and time again. 'What did you ever see in me with all that miserable baggage I pulled around with me? Was it just my body you were after?'

'I guess that was the last thing I wanted,' Lilian said, and then laughed when Jessica pretended to take offence.

'Well then, what? What did you see in me?'

'The same as all serious lovers. I could see the potential. It would be fun watching you climb out of the swamp.'

'Is that how you really saw it? As a swamp? It's a good metaphor. At times I've wondered if I deserved you.'

'What makes you think you do?'

Bright, loving, cynical, passionate, and aware of others with a talent that put most people to shame. She'd never said a really bad word about anyone. Except maybe to get a little tight round the mouth if the subject of Chuck Sarrison raised its ugly head. Little else seemed to disgust her. She let people live their lives without interference or uncalled for criticism and if at times something came up she found unbearable she merely walked away. She seldom complained about anything, however many so-called projects fell through at the last moment after weeks of hard work. 'Another Hollywood bullshitter's screwed up,' was all she'd say, and even that was with a smile on her face. The only things she owned were the furniture she had picked up through the years at yard sales and thrift shops, her beloved paintings, and the hundreds of second hand books she'd collected over a lifetime of moving across the States, being more likely to throw away a diamond ring than a book of poetry. Not that she'd ever wanted a diamond ring. Or a Donna Karen dress. Nor any of the things that Norma could no longer live without. She let others breathe their own air, gave advice only when asked, and never took offence when her words went unheeded.

'You are unbelievably tolerant,' Jessica would say, 'you'd get on with the devil himself. How d'you do that?'

'It's easier.'

She was capable of teaching a lot, though she insisted it was a mutual exchange. Jessica doubted that someone as easily irritated and cynical as herself had much to give in the way of gentle understanding. 'I used it all up on mothering,' she would say, 'you would shudder if you really knew what Bill has put up with over the years. And look how easily I've discarded my very best friend in all the world. I believe at times I'm the queen of bitches.'

'That's what I love. It makes me laugh. It's

so damn honest. And Hollywood is so full of sycophants. They all lie to themselves. A very dangerous occupation.'

'I love you, Lilian Peterson. You are an A1 person.'

Chapter Thirteen

It was evening when they'd got the messages. Too late to call Bill. 'I'll do it before we leave in the morning.' Lilian planned to start the journey back to Los Angeles about 6 a.m. 'Miss the worst of the freeway traffic,' she said.

Jessica called Norma. 'We're in Frisco. We picked up the messages. Are you OK?'

'I'm sorry, Jess. I needed to talk. Something's happened. I'm frightened.' Her voice was shaky. Like a person hanging on to self-control by her finger tips. She sounded sober and like a child.

'Tell me.'

'The police have taken Chuck in for questioning. He's been gone since midday. His attorney's called me once. I don't know what's going on. I've heard from nobody since about three this afternoon.'

'Oh, my God.'

Lilian looked up from her packing, taking in Jessica's shocked voice and suddenly white face. 'What is it?'

Jessica spoke across to her, letting Norma hear, 'Chuck's been arrested.'

'No!' Norma's voice, quick to correct her, 'no.

Not at all. Not yet. Just questioning. Our attorney was adamant. I just don't know what to do. What shall I do?' She began to cry quietly, in that resigned kind of way that people have when they've come to the end of their tether. Lilian was standing close and heard the sounds.

'Let me talk to her,' she said, and took the telephone. 'Norma?'

The crying stopped. The sound of a nose being blown, the pulling together of one's shame rustling softly across the miles. Jessica sat on the bed. Looked up at Lilian. Watched her deal with the extraordinarily alien situation. 'Can you call your attorney's office?' Lilian spoke gently, balancing the timbre of her voice to soothe the tension that could be heard even in Norma's breathing. 'Somebody there might know something. He must have called in.'

'It's a her. Our attorney's a her.'

'Will you call *her* office then?'

'I'm afraid to find out anything. They went to Chuck's office. The police, I mean. His secretary called me. I haven't spoken to Chuck direct. Do I just sit here? Will anyone tell me what's going on?'

'Don't go to the precinct. Just wait there. I know it's tough, but there's little else you can do. Is there anyone you can call? A friend or anyone?'

There was the briefest of pauses. Then, 'No. No-one knows. About everything I mean. Just Jess. And you, of course.' Jessica could hear what she said, and the thought of her old friend so bereft of a close confidant at this point in her life made her feel sad, and inevitably guilty, thinking of her own desertion. She took the telephone from Lilian, who noticed the tears and sat down next to her on the bed, one arm round her shoulders.

'We'll be home tomorrow,' Jessica said, 'I'll come round straight away. I'm sure he'll be back by then. Surely they can't hold him all night unless they intend to arrest? Try to get some sleep. I love you. Muster your strength.'

They tailed off their goodbyes, Lilian speaking as well into the telephone, trying to send support and understanding. Not that Jessica did understand. Not just the law system in a strange country, but the whole damn circumstances that Norma found herself in.

'I don't know what to say to her,' she said at dinner that night. Neither of them had much appetite, and apart from Norma, Jessica kept dwelling on what might be the reason for Bill's call, and whether the little paradise she and Lilian had found was strong enough for any cracks that might appear at any moment. She had hoped for a longer period of peace of mind. The rest of the world was catching up with her all too rapidly and she found herself not yet ready to relinquish this different life that had swept her up.

'We'll get home fast,' Lilian said, taking Jessica's hand in both of hers. Large hands for such a small person. Almost manly in their strength. They were comforting. The way Bill's had once been. Still were, if she'd been able to give him a chance. Had she swopped one partner just to lean on another?

'We'll take route 5,' Lilian went on. 'Not so pretty, but we'll be in LA early afternoon, even in my old jeep.'

Jessica didn't answer. Neither of them brought up the subject of Bill's call. Their sense of doom seemed too mutual not to come true, and that night in bed they fell asleep in each other's arms without making love, too afraid to voice aloud their separate fears, alone suddenly in their anxiety, fearful to show with selfishness, even to each other, that their idyll had been interrupted, and hoping it would all be of a temporary nature. And during the night Jessica woke abruptly to hear Lilian having one of her asthma attacks, searching in her large travel bag for her spray that she never could remember to keep at hand.

'Here,' Jessica whispered, taking the bag, finding what was necessary immediately, holding onto her until she began to breathe normally again, listening to the pounding of both their hearts, close to each other, still unable to say the words to make Lilian secure, still unsure of what they actually were.

When the attack was over, Lilian calmer and breathing easy, they tried to fall asleep again. Turning away from each other quicker than they intended, each one pretending the night was too hot to cling to each other, yet wanting nothing else. Love was still difficult, Jessica thought, even in sisterhood, it was still so bloody difficult. To be satisfied with permanent solitude would be lasting bliss. To grow beyond neediness as well as desire was the only solution. Eventually she slept, without dreaming, or at least with no waking memory of it, and at 5 a.m. she called the bank in London, and was told that 'Mr Wooldridge was at home that day and would she like to speak to his assistant?' So she called Sussex, heard the telephone ring in the house that had delighted, then imprisoned her for so many years. And when Bill picked up the receiver she could hear Butch barking in the background, heard Stephen call out to him to 'keep it down', and before her husband said 'Hello' she heard him tell someone to 'Check the light under the soup for lunch.'

'It's me,' Jessica said quickly. 'What's wrong? Are you ill? Why is Stephen there? Is *he* ill?'

'Hang on, darling, I'm in the hall. Let me close the kitchen door.' She heard his footsteps crossing the hardwood floor, pictured him at the kitchen, saw in her mind's eye the pattern of the sun as it came through the lattice windows of the hall, and then, in the distance, his voice, 'It's your mother. Do you want to talk to her?' The reply was inaudible, but when Bill picked up the phone again she presumed it had been 'no'.

'Is Stephen all right?' She tried very hard to keep the panic from her voice. It didn't work. Lilian was up and pouring the coffee she'd ordered from room service which had been delivered while Jessica was waiting for Bill's return to the telephone. Lilian looked up anxiously, brought the coffee across, stirred it, stroked Jessica's cheek, and then turned back again to her packing.

'He's had some bad news, Jessie. He's staying home for a while. I'm sorry to thrust all this on you. There's not a lot you can do really, not from so far away, but I thought you'd want to know.'

'I couldn't call back when you phoned. We're in San Francisco. I'm sorry.'

'I've interrupted a holiday. Forgive me. But I'm not sure how to comfort him. What to say. Thought it was all best coming from you.'

'What's happened?'

'It's Linda. You know the girl I told you about? The one he had become serious with?'

'Yes. You said you liked her.'

'I did. I mean I do. Well, darling, to put it as quickly and painlessly as I can, she managed to get herself pregnant.'

Stephen's voice suddenly from the room somewhere behind Bill – '*We* got pregnant, Dad. It was a joint effort, for Christ's sake!'

'All right, son. You heard that, Jessie? *They* got pregnant. That apparently is what happens these days.' He sounded exasperated, tired, unable to cope.

'Don't, Bill. Don't be like that. He's right. It

takes two. Go on. I presume it was intentional?'
Her heart started to beat. To be a grandmother.
It felt good at that moment.

'No.' Bill spoke softly. She could hear the
confusion in his voice.

'What d'you mean, no? It was a mistake? An
accident? I thought a wedding was likely anyway.
So Charlie told me.'

'Oh yes, indeed. They just hadn't planned on a
baby yet, apparently. She's still taking nursing
exams or something. I don't know.'

'How could it have been an accident? In these
days? I thought I'd talked enough about condoms
when they were growing up to make them believe
I had shares in a rubber company.'

'She's on the pill, I'm told. Something went
wrong.'

'Ah.' Jessica waited for him to go on. He cleared
his throat.

'Tell her!' Stephen's voice, coming nearer to the
telephone. He sounded angry, near tears, as he
always was at times of fury. Like her.

After the briefest of pauses, impatient to know
the cause of all the drama, she spoke again, 'I don't
understand. Surely this is all no reason to get
upset. They will just have to make other plans.
Ones that include a child. It's been done before.
It's not the end of the world. Is the girl there? Is
Linda there? Let me talk to her.'

'She's not here.'

'Let me speak to Stephen then. Will he speak

to me, or is he as angry with me as he is with the rest of the world, by the sound of it?'

'Hang on.'

Bill passed the telephone over. It was good to hear her son's voice, hear his breath. She waited for him to speak, knowing he was holding back tears.

She said at last, 'Darling? Why the drama? This should be wonderful news. What's wrong? Tell me. I'm here.'

'She got rid of it,' he said, 'just like that. She just went out without discussing it with me and got rid of the baby. As if I had no say. She's had an abortion.'

Jessica had no idea what to say to him. Her heart, her head, everything that made her who she was or had become, filled with guilt. It rushed to stamp out all other emotions that she'd been learning to accommodate in her ruthless obsession to re-invent herself. She should have been there to hold him. At least her arms would have been some comfort. Or would they? It was no longer a mother's arms that held that sanctuary for him. He'd become a man, and all she had to offer as his mother was an ear and a shoulder. The words 'I know what you're feeling darling, it will soon be better' were only believed by childlike ears. Her time was completed. His life was his own to waste or fulfil. Bill knew that with a kind of wisdom she was still struggling to learn. The pain of inadequacy was strong inside her when she felt his anguish. At that moment she longed out of all proportion for the days when she could march to the school playground and tackle the bullies that were making his then six-year-old life a misery. How proud he was of her in those far away days, fighting his battles while he was too small. Now there was only silence, a drawing in of breath, the knowledge she must not take his pain into herself. It was not her place. 'Oh darling,' she said. 'Oh darling, I'm so very sorry.'

So the questions she longed to ask remained in the silence of her heart. 'Shall I talk to Linda?' formed on her lips, but died there before they lived. Stephen suggested nothing, merely told her the details. As much and as coherently as he was able, then handed the phone back to Bill.

'D'you want me to come home?' Jessica said. Lilian looked round from her stretching exercises, then turned back again without a word.

'I don't know, Jess. We'll keep in touch.'

'How's the girl? Have you seen her, or spoken since any of this happened?'

'No. I feel strongly we mustn't interfere, whatever my feelings are. It's her decision surely.'

'I don't know what to say. Whose side I should take.'

He fell silent. She felt appallingly detached from them all, and sensed that Bill knew it. Her heart began to ache with a pain she couldn't place.

'Bill?' she said at last, 'I'll come home if you want me to.'

'I'll keep in touch with you. Stephen's going to stay here for this week. I'm back at work tomorrow. I've suggested he tries to at least talk some more with Linda. God knows what she's going through.'

She said no more. They seemed to be slipping away from her and she was powerless to stop them because she'd caused it. Bill, alone at last in the hall at home, told her what he knew, or at least their son's side of the recent events.

They hadn't planned a child. Still, when it happened, Stephen was pleased. 'He's your son,' Bill said, at that point in the story, and Jessica almost drowned suddenly in the rush of memories.

'And Linda?' she queried, aware that already the timbre in her voice sharpened when the girl's name was mentioned, the school bully still large in Jessica's head. 'Did Linda seem pleased at first?'

'So he says.'

'So what went wrong?'

Apparently, as far as Bill could decipher from Stephen's angry explanation, it took a few days for it to sink in with the mother-to-be, and then she began to realize exactly how much she would be sacrificing at this stage in her life and career, and not only her, Stephen as well. They had plans for their future. Needed more financial security before they started a family. It was the wrong time. It would drive a wedge between them instead of a bond. She pointed this out, believing in his love for her that Stephen would understand and, however painful, would stand by her and support her decision. She had misjudged him. Stubbornly, his mother's child in this respect, Stephen refused to understand. So Linda went ahead anyway. Thinking, feeling, that he was bound to come round. When he didn't, and that barrier of fury and bewilderment went up around him, Linda obviously went under, unless she was tougher than Jessica could ever imagine. No-one wins. Except that old bitch once again. Life. Laughing up her sleeve. Just when you thought it was safe to stop holding your breath. Zap. Pow. There goes another one, stumbling to her knees, wondering how to get up when there was no-one in sight to help now she was playing with the grown-ups.

So Linda had made her choice.

'And it was *her* choice,' Lilian said when they were in the jeep and driving back to Los Angeles.

'And his.'

'Not ultimately. *Her* body. *Her* choice.'

'And he had no say in the matter? He should just stand by and watch his seed thrown into the incinerator and simply smile understandingly? Is that how it's done these days? That's liberation, is it? Is that what you're telling me? They loved each other, for goodness sake. It's not as if she'd been abandoned.'

'Sweet Jesus, you come out tops in over-reacting, babe! I think "his seed in the incinerator" is a little on the dramatic side! This is not a personal attack on you. That's not what the girlfriend intended. You didn't come into it. You weren't there, thank God.' And Lilian laughed, then spoke more softly, trying to push the anger away as it started to settle between them. 'I'm simply saying that in the final analysis it's *her* decision. If she regrets it later, it's still her right and no-one else comes into it.'

'I can't bear it.'

'You don't have to. Stephen does. Don't take that from him.'

'You don't understand.'

'So you keep telling me.'

Driving back to Southern California, Stephen and Norma took their individual turns at churning her pointless and wasted guilt. She was angry with the spoilt and wealthy Chuck and also with a young girl she'd never met and had already passed judgement on, and she hated it that the woman she loved, Lilian, could see everyone's point of view except hers.

'Our first fight,' stated Lilian, surprisingly cheerful as they arrived back home in the middle of a stupidly hot October afternoon and dragged the suitcases into the unairconditioned, jumbled house. It never ceased to amaze Jessica how this woman she was living with in such glorious dishevelment, could turn even the stickiest of moments into a life-enhancing experience. Less acerbic wit and she'd be suspiciously like any old Pollyanna.

'I'm just tired,' Jessica said. 'And I'm sick and

283

weary of wearing sneakers every day.' Lilian roared with laughter. 'I want the fucking leaves to fall,' Jessica went on, knowing how unreasonable she sounded but totally unable to stop. 'I want to wear boots and see grey skies that are genuinely filled with rain and not just car fumes.'

She was hurting Lilian deliberately. Knowing her heart would be pounding with the fear that the words she was hearing meant 'going back to England'.

'Go and lie down,' Lilian said quietly. 'I'll call Norma. I'll bring some tea.'

Jessica felt pathetic. She lay on the bed as Lilian pottered downstairs, and made some phone calls. She tried to relax the knots in her neck and shoulders, and began to work on an apology before the tea was ready.

She didn't want to be angry with Lilian as well. She didn't want to be angry with anyone. Except maybe herself. For not coping. For going to pieces at the first hurdle. For taking it out on Lilian. It had been that inadequate conversation with her son, knowing she should have been able to help, and not just presuming her pain was as great as his.

'I'll write to you, Stephen,' she'd said. 'You must forgive her. Listen to what she has to say.' Words that were hard to understand, mouthed to comfort him when he had no desire for comfort, needed the pain to feed the anger to get him through. Then the receivers had gone down. And

Jessica was still in California. Living her life. Knowing too much about his. Mixing his sorrow with her existence. Knowing at last that Lilian was right. About everything.

She went downstairs and stood silently beside her while she made the tea. 'You're watching me in case I don't boil the water,' Lilian laughed.

'No I'm not. I wanted to be near you.'

'Good.'

Jessica threw an extra teabag into the pot just before the water was poured, put some milk in her cup before the tea – 'the way I like it', she said – and watched Lilian pull a face because the extra bag made it too strong as usual, then Jessica kissed her and sat back in comfort with her selfishness, wondering how long this woman would put up with her, and knowing they would love each other for ever, whatever happened.

'You're better,' Lilian said.

Jessica nodded. They kissed, and their lips were cool in the heat of the early evening.

'I just wanted the leaves to fall,' Jessica said, after they'd sat for a while in companionable silence.

'They take their time.'

'It's difficult to find the dark side of the moon when you wear sneakers all the year round.'

Lilian laughed at her, delighting in her foolishness and irascible behaviour. Jessica went indoors to answer the phone and raid the cookie jar for the chocolate Oreo's.

It was Norma on the telephone. 'Chuck's back. I went to pick him up. The attorney seemed to think it would be a good idea if I showed the loving face of a devoted and worried wife.'

'And?'

'It seems it's only Chuck's word against one other. And it also seems that Chuck will get out of this by the skin of his teeth. Our attorney says they have no real evidence. Not against Chuck, that is. Some fool made a video of one of the parties. My husband wasn't in it, and denies all knowledge of so-called sexual romps, and was then sent home saying he would be willing to testify if it came to it.'

'Well.'

'Exactly.'

'How is he?'

'Quiet. Scared. Clinging.'

'Shall I come over?'

'No. I'll call you tomorrow.'

'Take care of yourself.'

'Oh, believe me, I intend to.'

'Good girl.'

Lilian was opening a bottle of wine and shuffling in the cupboard for a clean glass. 'I'll get two from the sink,' Jessica said. 'They're all dirty. We left in a hurry. Remember?'

'Why couldn't I have fallen in love with some-one domesticated?' Lilian grumbled. 'Why am I always attracted to the mirror image?'

'Bloody cheek.'

They sat on the weed infested grass and drank the wine and talked until it was dark. The sky was clear, and the moon new and sharp. It was one of those perfect Californian nights straight out of a Nora Ephron movie. They let the machine pick up the messages, got giggly and a little drunk, made plans, or rather suggestions for Thanksgiving, and skirted the truth in their hearts as best they could. Jessica was aware that night how important it was to live for each moment as it came, to keep oneself in the present so as to preserve one's sanity. Each moment, each day of her life was to be appreciated for what it immediately was and not what it had been or might become. There was today, and nothing else.

Norma called her again the following morning. 'Will you be going home in the near future?' she asked. 'Back to England?'

Jessica was surprised. 'What brought that up? Have you spoken to Bill suddenly? Did he call you?'

'No. I merely wondered because I think I might go back for Christmas. See my mother. Do the family thing. Take presents. It's been so long. I thought we might travel together. That is, if you're thinking of it.'

'You must be psychic. I need to see the boys. Sort some things out with Bill. But I haven't really made up my mind. Lilian doesn't know yet.'

She hadn't known for sure either until that moment, but she knew it was time. Time to see if the healing hands of America would still keep her safe in the land of her birth, or whether she would once more slip into that slough of despair that she was afraid might suit her husband at least more than the new assertiveness that had become so much a part of her.

'Will you go with Chuck?' she asked Norma.

'No. I've told him we need some time apart. I'll get him through the next few weeks. Stagger through Thanksgiving as I said, and then go.'

Jessica made up her mind. 'I'll come with you. But say nothing till I've broken the news to Lilian. She's dreading it. Believes if I go back she'll never see me again. Nothing will convince her otherwise.'

'Will you? Come back I mean.'

'I've changed so much. Maybe no-one will know me any more at home. It's the first time I've liked myself for years.'

They made plans to have lunch the next day and then, in a fit of unprecedented domesticity, Jessica began to clean the house.

Lilian called at lunchtime. 'I'm at the Dome on Sunset Plaza,' she said. 'D'you want to join us?'

'Who's us?'

'A writer we want to adapt that new book I told you about. Come and join us. I miss you.'

'I'm in the middle of cleaning the house.'

'Are you ill or simply feeling guilty about something?'

'I just feel better.'

'Put the mop down and throw on your jeans and that silly hat you bought. I want to take you somewhere after lunch. Don't bring your car. Get a cab. I'll drive you there.'

'Where?'

'The place I want to show you. An oasis in this desert of hysteria.'

Jessica laughed. 'I'll be as quick as I can. Order me a turkey burger. Cleaning house has made me hungry.'

'Excuse me?'

It was almost two before she arrived at the Dome. Lilian sat near a window with her two partners and another woman who was obviously the writer. Lilian stood as Jessica came to the table, and kissed her cheek, winked at the hat that had been thrown on at the last moment, more to hide hair dusty from cleaning than a certain person's request. They were on coffee. The burger arrived, along with a king-sized portion of french fries. Jessica had, by that time, managed to devour the entire basket of sourdough rolls before the waiter reappeared.

'Incorrigible,' muttered Lilian. Jessica kicked her under the table.

'Are you involved in the industry?' the writer asked. Her name was Marjorie. Jessica shook her head, her mouth full of bread and butter.

'She's thinking about it,' Lilian said.

Jessica looked surprised. 'Am I?'

'I thought you could be my assistant on this next project. If you're starting to clean the house you must be getting more bored than I realized.'

They all laughed. Jessica said nothing, and wondered if Lilian was even slightly serious, or was it some ploy because she'd guessed already about the intended trip back to Europe and needed something, anything to tempt her to stay.

'Are you going to tell me where we're going?' Jessica asked as they drove west towards the beach after lunch.

'Sanctuary,' Lilian said.

And then they were there. Just at the end of Sunset Boulevard. Near the ocean. Into a drive and what looked at first like somebody's private garden. 'What is this place?'

'I told you,' Lilian said, 'it's a sanctuary. For meditation.'

They went through the shrubbery, past the inevitable gift shop, by the statues, and then found a seat overlooking a lake. Stillness. There seemed to be only two other people in view. Both reading. Then across the other side of the water a woman in shorts sat down on the grass and promptly fell asleep. The sound of traffic seemed further away than it actually was. Even the police sirens were gentler, or so it seemed. Birdsong was the closest sound in their ears.

Lilian stretched out her hand to touch the face of the woman by her side. 'It's a place to make you think straight. And we need to talk.'

'I can't believe we're still in Los Angeles.'

'Talk to me, Jessie. Tell me what's on your mind. In your heart.'

There was no hesitation. As usual, Lilian had made things easy. 'I need to go home. Just to tie up a few ends. I can't explain completely, I just know I must see the boys, try to make them understand. Maybe help Stephen – no, don't say it, I don't mean interfere. But there are times, there always will be, when I'll be needed. I love this life, but as strong as I now feel, I can't abandon everything that came before. There'll be moments I'll need to draw on those years to keep me stable.'

Lilian nodded. Jessica felt the sweat in the palms of their hands as they held each other. They were both afraid.

'I love you, Lilian,' she said. 'D'you understand?'

'I have to share you.'

'Yes.' She looked across the lake for a moment then back to Jessica with a smile that no longer seemed to hold so many secrets. She said, 'It was always on the cards.'

'I didn't know that. You should have said.'

'Darling babe, your other life will always pull

you back. All the love in the world can't change that. What you are is your past.'

'I've changed so much. I can't be what I once was when I was young. I'm not sure I'm even afraid of growing old any more either. It would be nice to get to an age when people applauded you for just getting up in the morning. But I would have liked to sleep through the middle years. The idea of going home, even for a while scares me a little. I'm afraid it will pull me backwards again.'

'It won't. I don't believe you'll let it.'

Jessica wondered why they were both so sad. They loved each other. She was coming back. Home was in both places. In all the hearts of the people she loved.

'I'll phone every day,' she said.

Lilian laughed. 'That'll be nice for Bill.'

'He'll have to share me as well.'

So then it was November and a few leaves fell reluctantly. Everyone changed the colour of the clothes in their wardrobes. Made Jessica feel very English again. All those browns and greys and ambers. She bought herself boots and a felt hat. 'When you come back,' Lilian said, 'bring a raincoat. It goes crazy in the rainy season.'

She told Bill she would be home a few days after Thanksgiving. 'Butch will be pleased,' he said, thinking he could hide the way he really felt. Jessica smiled to herself at the familiar subterfuge. She'd spoken several times to Stephen. It upset her that he'd not forgiven Linda. She had, but kept the thought to herself.

Lilian would have raised her eyebrows at the presumption. 'How gross of you,' she'd say, 'specially when I'd no idea you'd been asked.'

She was longing to see the boys. Hear their news. Dreaded facing Bill. What would they say to each other? And what about the neighbours? How much had he told them?

'We can go to Betty's for Boxing day,' he said over the phone.

'Must I?' she said.

'Thought you might like everything as usual, Jess.'

He had not asked if or when she was returning to the States. It seemed that they were all playing this silly game of 'let's make believe everything is normal'. Bill, Lilian, and her. Well she'd finally got the threesome she'd imagined all those years ago. Pity it had come too late to avoid the conservatism of middle-age. Too old to enjoy even the sexual imagination of the mind, let alone the tantalizing thought of an extra partner in the bedroom. One should make the most of the courage of youth. Only then can one abandon one's self to fantasies without the guilt of thinking there must be something better to do with one's time.

Chapter Fourteen

It seemed important to be with Lilian at Thanksgiving, bitter-sweet as it was. 'I have much to be thankful for,' Jessica said somewhat sentimentally.

'I guess you mean me,' Lilian smirked.

'If you can call being corruptively taken advantage of when my head was elsewhere, well then, yes, I guess I do mean you.'

'You've enjoyed every minute of it.'

Jessica smiled, and held her tightly until Lilian shouted she couldn't breathe. They did a lot of holding those last weeks. They made plans for Jessica's return in the new year. 'I could take you to New York. Even New England,' Lilian said. 'But you would never come back west with me again. I'd have to leave you there. Just so you could see the fall.'

'Why do I miss it so? Why is it my favourite season?'

'It feeds the melancholy in us all. You especially. That dark side you go on about. Always longing for.'

'Less and less these days. Though I still wonder if the general apathy in my home country will turn me inside out again and desperate for misery as usual.'

'Don't let it.'

It was all so simple for her. The only thing Lilian seemed to ever fear was the loss of their love, and even then Jessica doubted if she'd stay down for long, so passionate was she about living. 'You'll enter heaven like a volcano,' she said to her on one occasion. 'You'll be so angry about giving up life.'

They were invited to a costume party on 31 October. 'Don't make me go,' Jessica pleaded. 'I loathed fancy dress when I was a child, and it humiliates me even more at my age. What is this obsession with Hallowe'en you all have over here?'

'We'll just put our hats on and go as two dykes living in the valley,' Lilian said.

'Charming.'

'Every other couple will be Laurel and Hardy. Same every year. But it beats sitting at home in the dark pretending we're not in when the neighbours' kids start trick 'n' treating.'

They went to their party. None of their friends understood why they were spending Christmas apart, and in a rash moment she asked Lilian if she'd given any thought about joining her in Sussex for the holiday. When the idea was voiced, halfway out of her mouth, she knew it was too ridiculous for words, and Lilian roared with laughter at her innocence and said, 'Maybe we'd better leave that notion well alone for at least a few more years.'

The atmosphere round the dining table in Sussex would have been thicker than the cranberry jelly and twice as sticky. 'Why must we all be so fashionable and friendly?' Lilian said. 'Can you imagine the heads turning at midnight mass in that village church of yours?'

'It would never cross anyone's mind. What was really going on, I mean.'

'Don't you believe it. The English are far less prudent than they pretend. You're obsessed with sex. At least the talk of it. You just don't do it that often. Except your government, of course. And as far as I can tell, they seem to be mainly into dressing-up. Funny lot, you British.'

'It's no good making rude remarks about our island mentality and things like that. I don't have an ounce of patriotism in me. Birth is an accident of location,' Jessica retorted. 'I'll live anywhere, but I'd prefer the leaves to fall at the right time!'

Thanksgiving came and went quickly. The Americans didn't linger over their holidays. One day, and that was it. Jessica wished the English Christmas could be the same instead of the total shutdown of the entire country and the long, tense hours filled with relatives with whom you had nothing in common, except perhaps a past you'd prefer to forget. She'd bought the presents. The ticket was arranged and sat next to her passport on the dresser in the bedroom. Lilian had thrown a scarf over them both after they'd been there for a day. 'It reminds me everytime we go to bed or face the day,' she said. 'I need no reminding. I'm counting the days, the minutes, the seconds.'

It wasn't said to promote guilt. That was never Lilian's intention. Needless to say, it did the trick. Jessica hated the thought of making her miserable and was more and more torn as the day of departure got closer. Too late to change her mind. Too late to believe she could go on hiding for ever with all those loose ends waiting to be tied. Lilian took the week off work prior to the holiday. They made the house festive. 'Christmas can be early this year.' They stayed close.

Norma had changed her mind about waiting for her and had left the first week in November. 'I don't want Thanksgiving this year,' she said. 'It would seem like the height of hypocrisy after all that's been going on.'

'I'll call you when I get home,' Jessica said. 'And how's Chuck taking it?'

'He thinks I won't come back.'

'Will you?'

'What's over there for me?'

'Sanity.'

'It's not that attractive combined with poverty.'

The feeling was strong that Chuck Sarrison would be exonerated for any part he might or might not have played in the charges of procuring. It looked as if nobody was going to be able to prove anything. Whether the hookers were under-age or not was scarcely mentioned. 'Maybe they're wait- ing for the movie rights,' Jessica said. Lilian had laughed and mentioned something about it being time a certain English so-called lady got out of the city of sin for a while, because she was beginning to sound like a producer.

'At least it's kept him in at nights,' Norma said. 'We sleep in separate beds these days, but we watch TV together. It's the most normal our marriage has been, I guess. He's suddenly quite terrified he'll lose me.'

Chuck actually phoned Jessica the day before Thanksgiving just to ask how she and Lilian were, and how soon would she be seeing Norma when she got back to England? 'Tell her I miss her,' he said.

Jessica almost felt sorry for him. But not enough to ask if he'd be alone for the holiday.

Her first Thanksgiving. There were ten for dinner on the day, all of them crammed into the tiny house in the valley. 'The turkey's as big as the kitchen,' grumbled Lilian. Jessica had insisted on cooking, and as usual regretted it halfway through the morning and began to count the hours before clearing up and bedtime. The invitations had been given one drunken night in a restaurant about two weeks prior to the date. Lilian made the stuffing for the bird, and she moaned all the previous evening while they prepared and got in each other's way, and drank martinis, and swore 'that this was the first and last time we'd ever be this crazy, and why hadn't we gone to a hotel like she usually did?' It was fun really. And they were both drinking mainly to stop thinking about Jessica's imminent departure.

They served champagne and smoked salmon, and even toasted marshmallows around the completely unnecessary fire that Lilian had insisted on lighting for the occasion. They all went into the garden when it got late and lit a few fireworks. Everyone had brought presents to either see Jessica on her way home, or as early Christmas gifts.

'I'll be back in the new year,' she kept saying. 'Look after Lilian for me. I have to go back for a while. My passport tells me I should have been out a few months ago. I'll be arrested any moment for illegal entry.' It was a good enough reason to explain her departure. It stopped the questions.

'Like the pilgrims, I've come through,' she smiled over the liqueurs and coffee, refusing a piece of pumpkin pie baked and brought by a friend. 'Forgive me, I love America, but I've always hated pumpkin!'

'You are so full of schmaltz,' Lilian said.

And then at one in the morning everyone went home and she and Lilian went to bed. 'We'll clear up in the morning,' she murmured, and fell asleep so fast she scarcely remembered saying goodnight.

Thanksgiving was over.

* * *

Then it was time to go. She had a last manicure. She went once more to the hairdressers. There was a need to look physically changed when meeting Betty's well-intentioned scrutiny. Jessica wanted 'America's done her good!' to follow her out of every Laura Ashley living room. After years of pity she would have liked to provoke hard-earned envy. She wanted to look as if she'd found the good life, the secret. Whatever that was. Then she could sort them all out, and hurry back to Lilian. That was the plan.

She left on a Saturday afternoon. Lilian took her to the airport and they sat in the bar outside passport control until the last moment.

Jessica wanted to say 'I don't want to go,' but Lilian read her mind, and said quickly, 'Before you even draw breath don't even think what you're thinking. This trip is necessary. You'll be coming home for good if you come back.'

'*When* I come back. *When* I come back. There's no question of it.'

'All right, babe. I'll believe you.'

But she didn't, of course. In the same way she had never been able to persuade Jessica that guilt was a sterile emotion, so she herself had never been convinced in the safety of their union. It hadn't spoilt it, or even lessened the intensity. It was simply tinged with an ambiguous sadness that would never be put into words. And as they kissed and Jessica walked away that late afternoon it was how things stood between them. 'We all have our own demons to conquer,' Lilian said. 'No-one else can do it for you.'

So at last she was going home. To God only knew what, and with not even an idea how the new Mrs Wooldridge would fit into that old life, even for a couple of months. Home to the old and familiar home. To England. To Sussex. Looking forward all at once to the smell of winter in the air. Then the frost, and the lighting of fires in the evening, smoke from chimneys dotted through hillsides, continuous talk of the weather and when and if it would snow. And if it did, feeding the birds, dry bread thrown out hoping Butch wouldn't see it first and fill his greedy labrador stomach.

Halfway across the Atlantic she began to feel the joy of anticipation. She remembered the countryside she loved so much, the reality of decay and renewal and death that touched everything around the old house, but somehow never entered the spirit of Los Angeles. Not simply the quiet, although she'd thought of that often over the last year, struggling at times of tiredness to blot out the screech of car alarms and police sirens that was part of their life, even in the valley. 'One day,' Lilian said time and time again, 'one day, it'll be New England. It'll remind you of home.'

And maybe Connecticut would have kept her soul alight well into old age, but could she ever risk staying away for ever from the world she'd grown in? How did they bear it? Those tedious colonials that berated their new and conquered lands while praising everything they'd left behind, but seldom daring to make the journey back, afraid that time would have played his usual trick and changed their old habitats out of all recognition. So they hung on to the past, the images in their head keeping them disgruntled but safer in alien lands.

She would be the lucky one. She would be the one with a foot in either camp. She had it all worked out. She'd fought hard for the courage in her soul. All but lost her best friend to the values of the spoilt of Beverly Hills. Had not been around to ease the pain for her eldest son. Had become detached. Had grown apart. Had become selfish. She could only deal with all that at home, in England, where emotions were so linked with the seasons for her. She acknowledged her need for the long dark nights of an English winter. For a while she wanted the grey skies and the persistent damp to get into her bones and help her with the nesting of Stephen's pain. Constant sunshine seemed to blunt the edges of reality, and for a while there that had seemed right. But this way was better. A dose of winter rain and cold so that she could appreciate the spring, and the growth that accompanied it. She needed to care. For others as well as herself.

Other years, when March came, she had sewn her seeds ready for her English garden and waited somewhat stressfully to see how many would brave the daylight despite the vagaries of the unpredictable climate.

'Here, in Southern California,' Lilian had once said, 'even geraniums spring from the ground without any real effort from me.' Jessica stared out of the plane window and smiled at the memory of her lover's dirt-smudged face and hands when they'd both tackled the garden one Sunday. A strong and unfamiliar desire for order in their lives had overcome them both for once and driven them out of bed and into the heat of the day instead of the usual weekend trip to the movie theatre along with the rest of the population.

'Every goddamn thing is easy here,' Jessica had grumbled. 'That's the problem, you see. There's nothing to actually struggle for, nothing to panic about.'

'So invent it. Everyone else does. That's what makes the therapists rich.'

Jessica had laughed then, but now she realized it was one of the small things that was driving her relentlessly home, even for a brief respite. She had actually begun to find the ease of life almost too stressful. Something else beckoned. A hunger inside her. Time to go home and feed the melancholy that was endemic in her nature. Seemed she had to wallow for a while so as to see things clearly again. The rose-coloured spectacles could be laid aside on the table by the quilt-covered double bed she shared with Lilian.

Jessica remained awake for the long journey

home. By the time the plane started its descent into Gatwick her eyes were red and stinging with tiredness. And she'd wanted so much to look her best. Still, that evening she could rest. Bill would light a fire and she would make the tea. Butch would turn his body round and round with excitement as he greeted her, and then, with his usual total lack of memory, fall asleep on the hearth as if she'd never been away, only waking with a yelp every time a hot cinder flew out of the grate and singed his fur. He never learnt. The cat would stare at her with the gaze of an uninterested stranger, then turn her back and put her tail in the air to show her disdain.

She could see Lilian's face, Lilian's smile, as she'd watched her disappear through passport control. Jessica wanted to hang on to the image of her standing in the airport bar in one of those silly hats, a glass of wine dangerously near her restless hands, speechless for perhaps the first time. She wondered, as she stared at the grey and wet mist hanging over greater London, if Lilian had felt betrayed by her decision to go back. Did she suspect, despite Jessica's protestations, that she would not come back? Did she know that almost as soon as she stepped off the plane and felt the November chill of London that she might never need Lilian's sunshine again?

She walked from the plane stupefied with tiredness. She wanted the walk to the baggage claim to be longer. She needed still more time before she met Bill. There were no words in her head, nothing to help her through the meeting ahead. Another world waited beyond the barrier. She would see Bill's face again, and she remembered the look in his eyes when he'd heard for the first time about Lilian. What would the goodbyes do to him this time? To him, and all of them.

'Oh Lilian,' she thought, 'I'm so afraid now you're not here. And there I was believing I'd done it all myself. I never dreamed I'd be afraid again.'

She could almost hear Lilian's reply in her ear. 'Honeymoon's over, babe. Reality's back. You'll deal with it. You've tasted the sweet so you won't discard it again. *Your* life. Go for it. You can do anything. No-one else has a say.'

She waited for her three suitcases. So much to bring home. So much to leave behind. One luggage trolley, one bag of duty free, one journey through 'nothing to declare'. A sea of British faces, the smell that was so different from the aroma of vanilla that was reminiscent of American airports, that special smoky, foggy smell that could only mean England. The chill of the air made her shiver and lifted the tiredness as her body braced itself for the familiar cold wind. Her eyes searched for Bill at the barrier. She wondered if he was excited or nervous. Where would he expect her to sleep tonight? Would he use the sofa in the study to sleep on as the boys were home to greet her? Should she offer? How strange and difficult it would be to sleep apart amongst all the memories of their old house. And could they smile with all the usual familiarity as their eyes met, or would the embarrassment be untenable between them?

And then she saw him. Them. All of them. Bill and her boys. Her knees could scarcely support her, shaking with weariness, emotion, fear and suddenly, joyful anticipation. Stephen, standing quietly by the side of his father, towering over him in lankiness, biting his bottom lip, hands in his pockets, the only outward signs of his anxiety. Charlie, seeing her first, grinning, settled as usual into that familiar stance of the confident, legs apart, hands loose by his side. Sam, eyes darting, chewing gum in mouth, one hand on his head as if in haste or harassment, wishing maybe he could be elsewhere. And then Bill found her. He smiled. Warm, safe. The way he'd always smiled. He'd had a haircut too recently to make it look as if it belonged, and Jessica smiled back. He raised one hand in her direction, took one step, then stopped. Tentative. Then, touched from nowhere with a bravery she couldn't have explained, Jessica's legs started to behave themselves and she stood tall and walked confidently towards her family, for-getting for the moment the difficulties that lay ahead, knowing only that there would always be this part of her that would always belong, never change.

So the tidying of her life began. That Sunday was not as difficult as any of them had imagined. Bill had made lunch. An English Sunday lunch, provoking memories that no longer tore at her heart. Almost like building new ones, she thought. The boys joked, and told her stories of their lives as if she'd never been away, let alone *stayed* away to begin a love affair so strange it was hard for them to ever begin to understand. Bill produced the roast beef and potatoes with all the nervousness of a talent newly learnt. The boys loaded the dishwasher and they all insisted she retired to the living room for coffee, as if she were an honoured guest. They enquired about the flight, of course, but all other questions hung in the air, mostly between Bill and herself. Their sons were going back to town that evening so there would be time to sit and talk. The two of them.

Butch had greeted her with all the fervour he always had, at exactly the same level he used to after a trip to the supermarket, then sank, as she had predicted, in front of the fire.

Before the boys got restless and left she asked Stephen about Linda. 'Is it still hard to talk about it?' she said.

'To her?'

'Yes.' He looked into the fire and Jessica watched his face. They were sitting alone in the living room at the time, Bill and the others busy in other parts of the house, keeping away purposely to let them talk. It seemed that only she could even begin to understand the sadness that had so abruptly and surprisingly swept through her son's young life. The winter night had closed in on them as they sat there. Butch shuddered and yelped in his sleep. Stephen turned his head and watched him in his dreams, then smiled. 'He's always done that,' he said. His face towards his mother then, the smile still there, but the eyes so hurt it was hard not to reach out to him, forgetting he was a man at last, and she must wait for him. 'I'm glad you're home, Mum. I've missed you. I'm sorry I didn't phone more often.'

'You had your own life to live. Your own problems.' There was silence for a while. She said, 'Thank you for taking such good care of your dad.'

'I wanted to.'

'Have you forgiven me?'

He looked away then. Her timing was bad. He wasn't ready for questions or even answers about what was going on in her own life.

He said, 'I was being childish. It's hard to understand. I'm not Sam. Or even Charlie.'

'I know, darling.'

'I didn't actually blame you, Mum. And then before I could get it all sorted out in my mind all the business started with Linda.' His eyes suddenly filled with tears and he lowered his face to hide them from her. Even if she'd not seen, she would have guessed. Stephen had never had the Englishman's hang-up about crying, and she loved him for it. He'd been on a journey this last year that she could never share with him, or even fully understand. One that had left him older and wiser, particularly about himself.

His face still turned away, he said at last, 'I still phone Linda. I've been so cruel to her. She won't even come to the phone. I wanted her to be as unhappy as me. Is that dreadful of me?'

'Whatever made you think she wasn't already unhappy? Did you believe that the decision she came to had been easy for her?'

'I don't know.'

'There'll never be a year when she doesn't remember and count the age the child would have been. There'll never be a time in her life when she won't wonder if she made the wrong decision. Not if she's the kind of girl your father assures me she is.'

'She is.'

She wanted to tell him then. About being eighteen, and pregnant, and afraid to tell her own father, knowing he'd never deal with it, having no mother to hold her hand, and the boy in question back in the army after a weekend pass when he'd met this girl at a party called Jess who'd enjoyed sex as much as him, and in a moment of wilfulness had dragged him into a stranger's bedroom and had her way with him. With dire consequences. Nothing about abortion in those days. No choice. Just one. Back street in the poor part of Kensington, a soap opera on the television in the other room, a douche of God knows what, a handing over of what was it? Only thirty pounds if her memory was accurate, as if she could ever forget, and then being sent home to live out the nightmare of the miscarriage with Norma in attendance. And then the years of remembering, the years of regret when her irrational longing for more and more children possessed her.

But she kept silent, her timing for once impeccable. She put one arm out, round his shoulder, and pulled him towards her, his need for her, like a baby's, showed in his trembling. His clinging comforting making her see how much they would always need her, how sorrowful all their lives would be without her there. Different if she'd died. Then they could have mourned. But to have left them with such abandonment? What had she been thinking of? What madness had overtaken her? She hugged him closer.

'Keep on calling her, darling. Don't give up. One day she'll talk to you. That's a promise. I can scarcely begin to tell you how much she's needed you. I know that without even meeting her.'

She would never tell him how angry she'd been with this unknown girl at first. She thought, 'Let me just be here when they need me most and not lead their life for them.'

Their sons went home, back to their friends, their apartments, their lives. And then the house was quiet again. At last she felt the peace of that certain stillness that overtakes a home when visitors leave, and only the people who belong remain. It would always be the boys' home, it was just no longer where they lived. It belonged now to her and Bill. It was a nest. A refuge. What was left were the memories tapped deep into the walls of every room, making them warm. Making them safe.

'Do you want a nightcap?' Bill asked. 'You must be exhausted.'

She smiled up at him from her seat on a sofa still ripe with the old familiar smell of dog hair. Not even Ruth had managed to erase all the smells of home. Jessica liked that. The cat had begun to forgive her, after ignoring her all day, and was sitting by this time on her lap, purring as always and clawing at her jeans.

'I'd love one,' Jessica said. It would have been nice to curl up and sleep by that time, but she saw from Bill's smile that he was pleased with her reply. She sat up straighter, determined to stay awake until she keeled over.

'You can have the bedroom,' he said, his back to her as he prepared the drinks. 'I've been sleeping in one of the spares for months now. Is that all right?' He turned and handed her the glass. Their eyes met.

'Thank you,' she said. There was no need for anything else right then. It had always been hard to underestimate her husband. He never failed to come up trumps.

She called Lilian two days after she arrived, catching her early in the morning before she went to work. 'Is everything OK?' Lilian's voice was sleepy.

'It's fine. The boys are well. So's Bill.'

Jessica imagined her sitting up in their bed in the valley, under the quilt, still smelling of both their perfumes. Lilian said nothing for a moment, struggling to get her senses in tune at the beginning of her day.

'What's wrong?' Jessica said.

'Nothing, babe. It's just good to hear your voice. You sound so English suddenly.'

'Haven't I always?'

'I never noticed before.'

'Are you taking care of yourself?' It was the only thing Jessica could think of saying, worrying suddenly at Lilian's lack of concern whenever she had to cope with her asthma attacks.

'What else? I have to keep healthy to withstand the arseholes I meet in my business!'

Jessica laughed, relieved, 'You sound all right anyway.'

'I made my will,' Lilian said.

'Whatever for?' It was such a practical thing for her to do.

'Listening to this programme on the radio. Those of us in gay relationships, especially with aliens, need to put requests down on paper. Makes it easier if anything happens. Hate to leave you with nothing to remind you of me.'

'What makes you kid yourself you'll go first?'

'Whoever it is up there is going to realize soon

that I've had it good for longer than my fair share.'

Jessica smiled to herself.

Lilian said, 'I've left you all my paintings. I realized as soon as I started they're actually all I've got.'

'Oh, Lilian. Oh, my love.'

'Don't you dare go flaky on me on the telephone. Anyway. I'm glad you're fine, that everyone's fine. I'm going to Jeremy's for Christmas day. He and Harold always have a houseful, and always play charades. You know how you would have hated that.'

'I love Jeremy and Harold, it's the charades I hate.'

Butch got a longer walk that day after the phonecall. It was one of the joys of being back, walking again with the dog. 'Just walking again is good,' she said to Bill. 'Without driving somewhere first where you *can* walk, that is.' The chill in the air heralded in December and blew memories of the Hollywood sunshine out of her mind. Only a week before she'd mowed the lawn and sat in the garden to drink her morning coffee. Now she made her way through the mud in the woods above the house and yelled at Butch as he rolled in deer dung. She could see her breath as she panted to the top of the hill and stood still to take in the view. The downs stretched into the distance, the mist drifting and catching the tips of the hills. Through the high grass she spied the gentle loping of a deer, and as the creature caught the scent of a human, it began to run, swift through the long growth, head held high, frightened eyes staring ahead, bounding towards the solitude and safety of the wooded area. Jessica watched silently, hardly daring to breathe, caught by the beauty of the moment, aware of the disruption the morning walk with Butch had caused in this oasis of nature. Up and down, disappearing and appearing, then the deer was gone, swallowed by the evergreens and tall bare branches of the oaks. Even Butch had vanished, chasing some unsuspecting rabbit that he still had not learnt he would never catch. So much silence. How gentle England felt after Los Angeles. Peace in Jessica's heart. Coupled with the new strength she'd found after all these years. She began to cry because she was home.

'Butch! Come on old thing, time for home!' Tears brushed aside as the cold air left them damp on her cheek. A need for the warmth of the Aga turned her spirit towards the walk back. Butch came immediately, scrabbling with enormous excitement through the undergrowth, abandoning his futile hunting with as much joy as he'd begun. 'Let's go home, boy,' she said. 'Dad'll be home soon. I may even cook supper.' He jumped at her as if he understood the word 'supper'.

She would make no decisions until after Christmas. Being awash with sentimentality was a bad time to jump to conclusions.

★   ★   ★

Bill would never understand how he managed to avoid the subject of his wife's other life for those few weeks before Christmas. His instinct to leave her alone was right, although far from easy. He went to work each day, leaving Jessica with the animals, and the solitude of the house except when Ruth came in to clean. He asked nothing of her. Merely for her to adjust. Ruth virtually ran the house. Strangely enough, there was little tension between them. Neither was there passion. But then, he had expected nothing else. It wasn't the time to tell her how much he'd missed her. How his life was pointless without her. That when she'd left for America, in his tiredness with her depression, he had enjoyed the time on his own, had only wanted the old Jessica back, the one he'd married all those years ago. He had been close to believing he could manage without the woman she'd become. Like her own father had with her mother, he'd started to believe her dependence on him was all they had. But to his horror, and eventual joy, he had come to know that his passion, his need for her, was still breathing. That if she ever came back he would tell her. That it was Jessica he wanted. In his life. In his bed. And in his heart. Whatever that was, whatever she had become, sad or smiling, nice or nasty, whatever the years had marked her with. In any form, she was the girl, woman, lover and friend he'd married. So he waited. Patience often came hand-in-hand with understanding, and Bill had nothing more to lose than what for the last few months he'd believed he'd lost anyway.

Norma phoned at the end of the first week. Chuck was missing her, and her mother was giving her a bad time as usual, this time about leaving her husband in Los Angeles for Christmas. 'And that's coupled with complaining about me never coming home these days! There's no pleasing the woman. I'd begun to forget why I left in the first place.'

'Did you tell her about Chuck?'

'Good God, no! Have you ever met a daughter that could tell her mother something like that?'

Jessica wondered, if her mother had lived, whether she could have told her about herself and Lilian, about her daughter's new life. It was doubtful she would have understood. Her mother believed what so many of that generation believed, a wife stayed with her husband despite any unhappiness. It was a woman's duty. There it ended.

'God knows how I'll get through Christmas,' Norma moaned. 'All my relations are descending on us. I never even saw half of them when I lived here.'

Jessica laughed. 'Does this mean you'll be going back to California after all?'

'What else is there? I know my mother's not well, but Jesus Christ, can you really see me living out the next few years in Surbiton?'

'I guess not. When will you tell Chuck the good news?'

'I'm going to make him sweat until Christmas day, then I'll give it to him as a present.'

'Good for you!'

'He's talking something about us both going to – God I can't believe I'm saying this – "a sex therapist". If I come back, that is. He wants the marriage to really work, he says.'

Jessica roared with laughter. The thought of Norma ever having the need of help with sex was almost unseemly.

'I'll see you after the holiday,' Norma said before she hung up. 'Maybe we could travel back together.'

Jessica was non-committal.

The boys came down each weekend. No girls accompanied them. It crossed her mind that they might have been afraid the subject of her life in America would come up. After all, how does one deal with the fact of a mother who has 'come out of the closet'? She felt rather sorry for them all.

She visited Betty one afternoon for tea, and one Sunday evening after the boys had left, she and Bill went next door for drinks. She was, surprisingly, rather delighted to see them. She wondered if her memories of her neighbours had been stained badly by her own depression at the time. 'So lovely to have you back,' Betty whispered as she was helping Jessica off with her coat. 'It's been quite dull around here without you.' Everyone she'd met since her return had been so obviously delighted at seeing her she began to wonder if the person she'd thought she'd become over the last few years was not how others had perceived her. Maybe, after all, she was in fact a much nicer person than she'd come to believe. Even fun, as Betty had inferred. It was strange, but strengthening.

It became very clear to Jessica in those first few weeks just how devastated Bill had been at her betrayal. He'd lost an enormous amount of weight, and his alcohol intake had gone up by leaps and bounds. In the main, she slept well most nights, but if she did wake in the early hours she would hear him wandering downstairs. It was still too soon for her to find the courage to go down-stairs and talk to him.

The boys had planned to arrive at the house on Christmas Eve, and she and Bill would wait to put the tree up until then. As a family they would go to midnight mass in the village church, then have hot chocolate and brandy round the living room fire before retiring to bed. It was the same almost every year and, now she was back, the thought didn't dismay her as much as she would have believed. The run-up to Christmas was spent sorting out the decorations and untangling the Christmas lights, keeping her seasonal irritation at bay with sherry and mince pies.

'English Christmases are so excessive,' she said one day to Lilian on the phone. 'Every year it's to be dreaded.' It was just a small untruth. She was enjoying herself utterly, and it made her feel so disloyal. It had been so easy to slide back into the swing of their family Christmas, the only thing to remind her of Los Angeles was the fact she remained cheerful in the mornings, that special gift she'd found in America, how to find the joy of greeting each new day. If she had managed to get out of bed and join Bill for breakfast it might have heartened him somewhat to see the change in her. As it was, he wondered how she faced that moment and then spent the hours while he went to the bank. He was suspicious of her good cheer since she'd arrived, wondering if she was counting the days before she could leave, and how often she phoned Lilian.

What Bill couldn't have known was that Jessica was beginning to understand all that her husband had hoped for, and all that she'd failed to give him and herself.

Then it was the twenty-fourth and Bill was home all day from work. 'It's a long time since we put the tree up together,' he said.

'Is it really?'

He smiled at her. He looked more relaxed than she'd seen him since she'd arrived. She did remember of course. All the last few years she'd sat either in glum misery on Christmas Eve, hardly daring to mention her longing for the boys to be babies again – 'which would make more sense of all this performance once a year' – or else drinking too much and being more of a hindrance than a help. But this year was different. Bill had bought an Indian take-away and they opened a bottle of claret. The tree lights worked straightaway when he stretched them out along the carpet, which was the first miracle of the season, and then Sam and Charlie walked in laden with presents just as the local church choir arrived to sing early evening carols. 'They don't get any better, do they?' Jessica said as the choristers were sent on their way with the usual mince pie, and one glass of sherry to the elderly man who'd been singing in a different key to everyone else during 'In the bleak mid-winter'. Which was a shame because it was Jessica's favourite.

At six-thirty, when everyone had eaten their share of tandoori and curry and started on the second bottle of wine, she said, 'Shall we start putting the rest of the tinsel on that damn thing before any more pine needles drop?'

'Shouldn't we wait for Stephen?' Charlie had started on the walnuts and she could already see the broken shells flying in all directions in his haste with the nut crackers.

'He's probably caught in traffic,' said Bill. He began to try and pick the stray nuts from the carpet and Jessica laid a restraining hand on his arm. He jumped back at her touch, but she held tight to his arm. He sat then and put one hand tentatively on her shoulder.

Sam was being boisterous with the dog and getting him over-excited. 'Butch has always known when it was Christmas,' Jessica said.

'You mean his stomach has. Remember when he found the boxes of chocolate we'd been given under the tree, and ate the lot while we were at church?' Charlie said.

'And his first Christmas,' Sam smiled, 'that time he pulled the tree down and devoured the fairy off the top! Mum cried and said we'd had that fairy since Stephen was a baby and she'd never forgive him.'

'Then she punished him the next day by refusing to let him finish off the stuffing from lunch!' said Bill.

They all began to laugh, at Jessica's silliness, and Butch's greed, and all the memories that would always belong to each one of them. She said loudly, 'It was good I refused him the stuffing. It always makes him fart anyway!'

And then Stephen was there, opening the back door and just appearing in their midst while they were all shouting with mirth, and topping it all by saying, 'Mum's stuffing makes everyone fart.'

And then behind, holding on to his hand, was Linda. Jessica knew it was her immediately, and got to her feet. They all did, and went over to kiss her, shake her hand, hug her, and Jessica saw in her son's eyes that he was happy again, and that she could relinquish him to this blond and gentle girl with the knowledge he would be in as safe hands as anyone could be once they'd learned the pain of growing up.

And that was when she knew. Knew she would stay. Knew she couldn't grow old away from them. That her life involved them as hers did theirs, and always would. It was too late to close all the doors. Some bridges just weren't for burning. She could change, had to, but the past remains, and even in changing she must live with it, not throw it out in her passion for the new.

The tree up, the kitchen strewn with wine glasses, presents under the tree, she sat for a time alone with her husband while the boys spread themselves round the house, taking it over like they always did, loud with their favourite music, and pungent with the smell of sneakers.

'She seems lovely,' Jessica said of Linda. She and Bill were drinking coffee before going to church. 'I'm glad he brought her. I'm glad he knew he could without asking permission.'

'He brought her for you,' he said. 'You gave him the courage. Remember what you used to say when they were little? "Home is the oil poured on troubled waters".' And then he added, 'You were a good mother.'

'I was, wasn't I?'

They were quiet for a moment, looking into the fire. 'Have you been OK?' she asked.

He shrugged. 'It's different.'

'Thanks for the lack of pressure. It was clever of you.'

'There was no hidden agenda, Jessie. I'm glad you came home, even if it's just for Christmas.'

'I was dreading it. I just knew it was time. Stephen needed me after all. I tried to kid myself, but it doesn't work.'

'And Lilian? Did she mind?'

'Yes. I think so. She guessed I'd feel like this when I got here.'

He looked carefully at her. 'Like what?'

'I thought I could only stay cured in California, and with Lilian. Now I'm beginning to see that they were just the doctors, and the recuperation. Something pulls me back. Memories, ties too strong, I don't know. Maybe just duty. Mum would be proud,' She laughed. 'I'm just not sure I can stay away for ever, after all. I can't turn my back. I should have been here for Stephen. Not to interfere, just to be here. Like you were. Like you always are.'

He sat quite still and was silent for a long time. Upstairs someone had put on a Nat King Cole record, and Sam and Charlie shouted in derision. 'Must be Linda's choice,' Jessica said. They smiled at each other.

'Are you saying you want to come home?' he said.

'I think so. I think I have to. I'm as surprised as you must be. But tonight, with the boys here, seeing Stephen safe again, how can I be anywhere else? It won't be the same. You know it can't be. But ultimately I miss it. The boys, you, everything that has always made me tick. I just don't want a prison again. And there will be times I'll need solitude. And I'll have to go away, and maybe you'll find that hard to understand. There are still things that'll swamp me here, and I know I'm going to have to hang on with everything I can muster to get me through some days. And I think there'll be times I might regret the choice I'm now making. But it's in my blood, being needed. In America it's only what *I* want. What *I* can get. I'm afraid I might bore me after a while. Even now, when I'm just beginning to like myself.' She looked hard at him. 'I've given you so much shit. I'll have to take it step by step. I want a more selfish life in many respects. But I think I'll live and die in England after all, even if it does infuriate me most of the time.'

'With me?' he said. 'Will you live here with me? Is that what you want?'

'Will you take me back?'

'Do you doubt it?'

She reached across and took his hand. In his easy capitulation and forgiveness there was more love and dignity than any false pride he might have shown. She admired his quick and faultless honesty.

'And Lilian?' he said quietly, not taking his eyes from her. 'What will you tell her?'

'I believe she knows. That she guessed from the very beginning. I'll write to her.' The thought was painful.

She leaned towards him and took his face gently in her two hands. 'Why did all this happen? Was

I so desperate for change that I could go ahead and hurt so many people I care about?'

'I only know I need you more than I realized,' Bill said. 'And I always believed it was me who was the strong one.'

They kissed tentatively, held on to each other, put aside for that moment the thought of the hurdles before them, Bill stunned with a feeling of hope he'd believed would never happen. And then the boys and Linda came back, and Jessica saw their quick and knowing glances at the faces of their parents, saw them smile at each other, and then the tree lights went out and they all began to laugh.

'Nothing changes really,' Bill grinned. 'Every year! Without fail. And always on Christmas Eve!'

Epilogue

She wrote to Lilian the day after Christmas.

My dearest girl,
   Will you be able to forgive me, I wonder?
Except you knew me better than I knew myself.
I believed with all my heart I would find
nothing here to make me stay. Do I even need
to tell you it was my decision and mine alone?
Bill is as surprised as me. I will miss you. I
always will. You have been, still are, the very
best part of me. The thing is, you see, I can't
turn my back. The need for me here is more
than I deserve. And much much more than I
realized. Don't say that, I hear you saying, you
deserve what you believe you're worth. What
am I trying to say? You showed me the way to
live, even with all the things that I believed were
killing me. You taught me to enjoy each
moment, even the bad ones, and because I was
so busy enjoying the misery of them, the bad
ones went past without me noticing them for
what they were. I will leave space in my life for
myself now. By living with you in so much love,
I've learned to live alone. It was that part of me

I needed to make my selfish old self complete and
that you handed over to me without question.
Thank you, my darling. Look after yourself.
Please stay in touch.
  Yours always,
  J

Lilian never read that letter. The day it was posted, two days after Christmas, those dreary days when everyone waits for New Year and dreams about getting back to work, Jeremy called Jessica at home. They were sitting having tea. Just herself and Bill. Sam had fled back to London for a party, and the other three, Linda, Stephen and Charlie had taken Butch for a walk. 'Let them go on their own,' she'd hissed to Charlie. 'Don't you know when you're not wanted?'

'I feel like being irritating. Steve's got so moony-eyed he's asking for it.' He'd grinned and chased after the others. Jessica could hear them groaning as he caught up with them, and Butch barking in agitated delight at the thought of all those strong young arms throwing sticks for him to retrieve.

'Butch much prefers it when the boys are here,' she said. 'I feel quite jealous.'

'Of Butch or the boys?' Bill smiled.

'Butch, of course. I'm quite looking forward to the boys going. Although it has been a great Christmas.'

When the telephone rang she was in the kitchen

filling the teapot with hot water. 'I'll get it,' she yelled to Bill, who'd just turned on the TV to watch one of his favourite movies.

It was Jeremy. 'Happy Christmas,' she said. 'What a surprise.' It was hard to keep the trepidation out of her voice. Either Harold had taken a turn for the worse, or Lilian was ill. The letter to her was still winging its way across the Atlantic. That other world intruded into her life suddenly.

Jeremy said, 'Jessica forgive me, I have some dreadful news. Are you with someone?'

And she knew.

'Is it Lilian?' she whispered. She sat down on the stool she'd pulled up by the phone.

'I'm so sorry, Jessica. We came home late last night, this morning really, about two-thirty, and Lilian's lights were still on, the TV still loud. Carole had left a message on our machine, several in fact, that Lilian hadn't turned up for dinner and she couldn't get through on the telephone. Would we please go and have a look? See if she was all right.'

'Go on.' Dear sweet Jesus, she thought, let me be wrong. I swear I'll never hurt another living soul, but please let me be wrong.

'It must have been an asthma attack,' Jeremy said. 'She'd tried to get help. The phone was off the hook. The police have been. We had to call them to break in. We found your number. Carole's still here. D'you want to talk to her?'

It was as if someone had turned her upside

down and emptied her of feelings. She remembered talking to Carole. She would make all the arrangements. Would she, Jessica, come back for the funeral? She didn't know what was said, who said it, or how she eventually put the telephone down and told Bill what had happened.

So Lilian had died alone. Worked up about something probably, something silly or badly executed on the television. That was always guaranteed to set her off. Jessica could see her, ranting and raving round that living room, asking Jessica why she watched such crap, why did they make it, and 'Was there ever going to be any hope for this godless Pacific paradise?'

Jessica couldn't even remember crying. The family, her family, put her to bed. She remembered later lying in the bedroom with the table light on and looking round at the pale blue walls thinking, 'I must get some primary colours in this house. Lilian would hate all these pastels.' Silly, irrelevant thoughts, unworthy of the way they'd felt for each other, for the passion she'd brought back to Jessica's life, brief as her presence had been. But if she hadn't dwelt on trivia the pain would have been too much to bear. There'd be time and space to think of Lilian, and when it had all sunk in, then she could let go. Then she'd allow herself to recall the art gallery, and the sanctuary, and the silly hats, and all the colours of the rainbow she'd put so firmly in Jessica's life. They would live with her in security for ever.

*   *   *

The very next day, Bill picked up the late posted cards that had arrived only that morning and he handed Jessica an airmail letter that was lying on the bottom of the pile. It was from Lilian. Posted only a few days before she died. It was a week before Jessica could face reading it. After the funeral, to which she hadn't gone. Not for Jessica the sight of that box heading to the incinerator. Not Lilian. She would remain bright in the memory without the ritual. 'Don't cry over me when I go,' she'd said once, 'just stick me in the trash. It's only an old body. My soul'll be out of that real quick. I intend to get to heaven before the old guy in hell gets wind of my passing!'

Most of all, Jessica was glad she never got her letter. That she'd died pretending to believe her lover would return. Jessica had asked Lilian once why she thought America, with all its noise and peculiarities had charmed her own very English spirit and what was it about that somewhat abrasive country Jessica had found so captivating and springlike? What did it have that convinced a person like her that it was a viable possibility to hold her head up high again without fear or anxiety of getting it knocked off her shoulders?

Lilian had no answer at the time. But in her last letter she did.

I believe the basic emotion, feeling, whatever you want to call it, but the one that makes this country tick is hope. When that goes we get the violence. Hope is what built this country. There's a kind of cynicism in Europe that I believe will be the death of you all. You enjoy it so much. Maybe too much went wrong in the Fifties after the war. You tried to emulate us, but you'd been around for too many centuries already to make that work. Maybe it was all just mismanaged. And by the wrong people. I don't know. We're still children here. We still believe the possibilities are endless. Even the most radical of us thinks like that deep down. It's in our culture. Christ, it's in our genes. We don't always admit it, but it keeps us all ticking along. And believing in hope makes us begin to try and comprehend eternity.

Seems to me, babe, after the kids had gone, when there was no more nesting for you to drown yourself in, you believed there was no hope of anything else to care for. But why should the purpose in your life spring from other people? Maybe it's just in yourself. Just that. We can't do anything to make the big injustices go away. We can only have a damn good go at erasing the small ones we encounter as each day comes and goes. That's the triumph of life. It's enough.

California was your romance. It was where

you took that stiff old British corset off. We all
need that from time to time.

Look after yourself, and enjoy. My love to you
always, Lilian

It was typical of Lilian to have made things easy for her, by dying before she'd read the 'goodbye' letter. Long after, Jessica said as much to Bill, on the day when the paintings she'd been willed arrived in England and Jessica cried in her husband's arms the way she had wanted to since Christmas. And it was as if Lilian was with them, and the triangle in Jessica's heart was complete at last.

'Do you mind that I loved you both,' she sobbed. 'It was such a different kind of love. So near myself. Like loving myself. As if she taught me to love you better.'

And Bill said nothing, just went on holding her as she was holding Lilian's favourite painting. As if, by dying, she'd placed herself in both their hearts for ever.

THE END

ADDICTED
by Jill Gascoine

'He stood, solitary, by the window, staring out at the well-groomed garden, feeling the luxury of the large, light, gentle house all round him. There was something about it, a forgotten experience of order from his childhood that he found dangerously seductive. It was a family home, basking in complacency . . . just asking for destruction.'

It was the morning after Rosemary's fiftieth birthday party when she first met Ben Morrison. Rosemary was smart, successful, self-possessed and self-contained. She had her own TV show, a house she loved, and enough money to live as she wished. Men didn't really play a great part in her life-style.

Ben Morrison was thirty-three, an actor, a huge, dark bear of a man, half Spanish, half English. He was relaxed, attractive, casual and had once had a brief affair with Rosemary's daughter. On the face of it, he and Rosemary had absolutely nothing in common.

So when he erupted into Rosemary's life, smashing her tranquillity with an untamed, passionate greed, she was unprepared for her destruction. Gradually he eroded everything about her, personality, pride, sanity.

It took a full year for Rosemary to fight back, to be cured of Ben Morrison and his addictive, all-consuming sexual possession. It was a year she would never forget.

'Gascoine has written a page-turner which involves a glamorous heroine and lots of sex . . . without abandoning either sense or observation. The book has humour and a certain astuteness as well as narrative drive'
Sunday Times

'Sexy and poignant'
Today

0 552 14231 X

DADDY'S GIRL
by Janet Inglis

'A story of tremendous power'
Literary Review

Olivia, almost fifteen, feels like a piece of unwanted baggage left over from her parents' broken marriage. Daddy is about to marry one of his former students, who is young enough to be his daughter; Mummy's men friends sometimes stay the night. Her parents have turned into strangers, and neither of them seems to have room for her any more. She feels a burden to everyone she loves.

Then Nick enters her life: Nick, her mother's lover, an amoral, street-wise photographer with an insolent, assessing gaze. Nick violates the sanctuary of Olivia's home by moving in with her mother, and before long he has violated Olivia as well, causing her to become hopelessly addicted to him as he teaches her the meaning of desire. At last she comes to a shocking solution that will change forever her life and the lives of those who have denied her love.

'In this arresting first novel Janet Inglis's writing is wonderfully, brutally and perceptively honest, and poses questions that need answering'
Maureen Owen, *Daily Mail*

'Janet Inglis writes extremely well, with speakable dialogue and imaginable descriptions . . . I believed it was all happening, and very much wished it wasn't'
Jessica Mann, *Sunday Telegraph*

'Few contemporary novels have dealth so thoroughly with the destructive power of sex'
Vogue

0 552 14207 7

A SELECTED LIST OF FINE NOVELS
AVAILABLE FROM CORGI BOOKS

THE PRICES SHOWN BELOW WERE CORRECT AT THE TIME OF GOING TO
PRESS. HOWEVER TRANSWORLD PUBLISHERS RESERVE THE RIGHT TO
SHOW NEW RETAIL PRICES ON COVERS WHICH MAY DIFFER FROM THOSE
PREVIOUSLY ADVERTISED IN THE TEXT OR ELSEWHERE.

13984	X	**RACERS**	Sally Armstrong	£4.99
13992	0	**LIGHT ME THE MOON**	Angela Arney	£4.99
13648	4	**CASTING**	Jane Barry	£3.99
12850	3	**TOO MUCH TOO SOON**	Jacqueline Briskin	£5.99
14103	8	**RIDERS**	Jilly Cooper	£6.99
13895	9	**THE MAN WHO MADE HUSBANDS JEALOUS**		
			Jilly Cooper	£5.99
13644	1	**PANDORA'S BOX**	Elizabeth Gage	£5.99
13964	5	**TABOO**	Elizabeth Gage	£4.99
14231	X	**ADDICTED**	Jill Gascoine	£4.99
13872	X	**LEGACY OF LOVE**	Caroline Harvey	£4.99
13917	3	**A SECOND LEGACY**	Caroline Harvey	£4.99
14284	0	**DROWNING IN HONEY**	Kate Hatfield	£4.99
14220	4	**CAPEL BELLS**	Joan Hessayon	£4.99
14207	7	**DADDY'S GIRL**	Janet Inglis	£5.99
14262	X	**MARIANA**	Susanna Kearsley	£4.99
13709	X	**HERE FOR THE SEASON**	Tania Kindersley	£4.99
14045	7	**THE SUGAR PAVILION**	Rosalind Laker	£5.99
14331	6	**THE SECRET YEARS**	Judith Lennox	£4.99
13737	5	**EMERALD**	Elisabeth Luard	£5.99
13910	6	**BLUEBIRDS**	Margaret Mayhew	£4.99
13972	6	**LARA'S CHILD**	Alexander Mollin	£5.99
13904	1	**VOICES OF SUMMER**	Diane Pearson	£4.99
10375	6	**CSARDAS**	Diane Pearson	£5.99
13987	4	**ZADRUGA**	Margaret Pemberton	£4.99
14123	2	**THE LONDONERS**	Margaret Pemberton	£4.99
14298	0	**THE LADY OF KYNACHAN**		
			James Irvine Robertson	£5.99
14162	3	**SWEETER THAN WINE**	Susan Sallis	£4.99
14318	9	**WATER UNDER THE BRIDGE**	Susan Sallis	£4.99
13526	7	**VANISHED**	Danielle Steel	£4.99
13747	2	**ACCIDENT**	Danielle Steel	£5.99